A TAILOR

A Valadfar story

BY D S M TILLER

A Doodle Rat Publication

There are so many people to thank for helping me complete this story, everyone who is part of TAUP, everyone from Aesica who have spent months listening to my ideas for it. Gwen for the editing and a very special thanks to Jo Dickinson for the many hours spent walking around the cold streets with me while planning this story and to Alice Dickinson for her part in the final stages of bringing this work to print.

A Tailor's Son
A story from the world of Valadfar
By Damien Tiller

ISBN: 978-0-9573986-2-7 Paperback

Prologue: **Dear Diary**

Valadfar is a world full of heroes. Magic wielding mages, demonic dark lords, brave knights and brutal barbarians; but we mustn't forget the everyday man on the street. People like the bakers that wake up long before dawn to tend the ovens and make the bread, candlestick makers covered in wax and the tailor. Yes, the humble tailor, master of stitch and twine. But what would happen to this most humble of craftsman, this most gentle of man, if the world crossed his path with a darkness to rival even that of the demon Rinwid. That is what this story will tell. The year has moved on since the time of the Dragon Lords return to Neeska, and the Brilanka calendar now sits on the page of 128ab, the month of Wastelar, the first month of winter. Sitting in the dark alone and frightened Harold wrote upon the darkened candle lit parchment. If he was to be asked, he could not be as precise as to tell you the time, for he did not know it. All he knew was that it was late. The last bells heard from the tower of the newly constructed cathedral before the rain drowned out the reverberations of the bells had sounded midnight.

Midnight had come to be known to the people of Neeskmouth as the witching hour. At first, it had been called this from the rumours of shadows, living darkness which supposedly hid demons from the end of the Dragons return. But when these stories faded the title of the witching hour remained in the common tongue. The phrase had gained weight as the city stopped its celebrations of freedom and fell into depravity. Its population boomed above what could be supported by the current infrastructure. It forced those at the bottom of the barrel to do whatever they could to put food in their bellies and clothes on their backs. Now the witching hour was the time of muggers, pinch-pricks, and even the constables themselves, who were supposedly charged as protectors from the previous but were just as, if not more so, corrupt. It all made going out after sunset a living nightmare. Although numerous, it was not for any of those reasons that Harold's quill shook in his hand. The weather did little to help to settle his skin from its vibrations, his flesh seemed to attempt to crawl away from his body with outstretched hairs, and although that might make an onlooker think it was the cold that caused him to shake so, it was not that. At least not purely, he had a fear in his belly so powerful that his heart raced like the hooves of a post masters horse at full gallop. The night sky was thick with smoke, a small curse that the end of the war with the Poles had brought. The golden age that descended onto the city, as the treaties were signed, had brought with it an industrial growth that spread with the speed of a forest fire and with any fire comes smoke. The choking clouds poured from the newly built factories by the harbour and flowed inland on a strong westerly wind that blew from the sea. This almost nightly occurrence cast the moon to be hidden behind a deep blanket of smog so the only light outside was from the newly installed Dwarfen gas lamps. They struggled that night to stay alight, the downpour the gods had seen fit to tarnish the sky with threatened to dowse them. The rain clouds swirled as they moved across the sky. There was barely a break in them letting through starlight as the wind, so vicious in its path, pushed the rain hard and bullied it to fall more severe on Harold's shutters. With each creak and slam of the aged windows, Harold's heart missed a beat, for you see he couldn't help but wonder what would happen if the creature came looking for him. Even with the strong oak, brought in from the newly grown forest at the edges of the Scorched Lands, pressed tightly in the doorframe there was a draft creeping in. The breeze as it crept in under the frame and rattled around the room made Harold's fire dance and flicker. The shadows it casts across all four walls seemed intent to taunt him, adding to his panic-ridden state. The rhythmic gloom turned a hat rack into a shadowy assassin and back again with each pass of light. With each flash under the door Harold was forced to stop breathing and listen, just to make sure that he couldn't hear footsteps outside. This goes some way to show the pure terror he felt as he sat alone. He worried that the thing would come for him, so much so that even the lack of footsteps worried him. What if it was someone intentionally making no noise outside the door? The paranoia drove him mad and that was why he felt the need to record the passing of the last few days. He had unwillingly become the antagonist for a grim fairytale, one that as the day grew to a close he could not seem to escape.

Harold was the only surviving son of James Spinks, a tailor of East Street. East Street was nestled close to the canals north of the markets in the mid section of the city of Neeskmouth. Harold was not even the head tailor and was of little importance to the history of Valadfar for the most part, few people would recognise him as they passed him in the street. He worked out in the back room most of the time, doing repairs on the richer folks' clothing, and if he was honest with himself, he liked it that way. Harold was a loner of sorts. His job did mean he had to interact with people occasionally but he did his best to keep his contacts with others at a minimum. He enjoyed a quiet life in his own solitude avoiding the bustle of the city. Neeskmouth had been growing rapidly since the second war with the Dragon Lords, factories and God only knows what else had been springing up along the Copse Hill road. The industrialisation of the city marked a time of change that meant little family owned tailors like Harold's fathers would soon be outdated. He had worked for his father all his life with few stories to tell that didn't involve a pricked thumb or a missed stitch, until that accursed night. The night of the explosion at the local tavern, it was that fire which started it all. His eyes were so sore that he could see how reddened and bloodshot they were even in the deep blue reflection of the ink well he dabbed his quill into. Yet he refused to close them and continued to write on the parchment that lay on the desk in front of him. Harold was no hero from a story, he was not the brave warrior or bard that filled the tales of the many libraries in Valadfar he was a normal man. For him, writing was the only thing keeping him sane. He felt terrified and alone. The true reason he scribbled so madly onto the pages was to keep his demons at bay, he knew that it may be his last night on Valadfar but what choice did he have but to continue. If he was to fail his notes might be the one thing to save the city. Now, before you grow too weary of these ramblings, let me take you back to the night that it started. To the last time Harold was just a tailor's son.

Chapter 1: The *Queens Tavern*

The night that would change Harold's life forever started fairly normally. It was a fortnight before that wintery evening he spent in darkness writing his notes. The date was Nymon the 16th of Thresh, a harsh autumn and one that hinted to an even harsher winter just around the corner with an icy breeze that kept the rats off the street. It was the worst anyone had seen since the poor harvests of 99ab that had almost plunged the city into total recession. The winter had come around early yet again this year, and with the ban on imported food from Gologan due to the damnable potato famine, everyone was feeling the pinch. The price of food was the highest it had been in centuries and meant that most people had taken on a second job just to make the ends meet. Harold was no different. His family did have some inheritance so they were not as poverty stricken as most, but would still be classed as one of the poor souls the city came to know as 'unfortunates'. The worst-off worked the streets and docks around them barely scratching together enough to survive while the nobles continued to live off the rich pickings of their broken backs and scarred knuckles. Harold's father was very tight with the purse strings and had lived through the war that almost brought Neeskmouth to its knees during the first century. He had learned not to spend a single copper coin where it was not needed, a trait that had been passed on to his thrifty son. Harold had just finished working at the little tailor shop on East Street in order to make more coins that would no doubt hibernate in his father's moth filled wallet. His father had taken on an order from one of the local factories, two hundred aprons to be finished by the end of the next month. Harold had argued with his father that they couldn't finish the order in time; he had tried to convince his father that one of the sweatshops that were filled with clanking machines, which the Dwarfs had brought to the city in trade, would have been more suited to handle it. Harold was ignored as always, and his father took the work. Harold was not sure if he did it for the money or if he feared giving work to the machines that drove the industrial revolution forward would speed up the inevitable end of their little family business. Whatever his reasons in his blind hope he had taken the massive order to be just a challenge, and as usual wanted to face it head on. He knew Harold would do everything he could to make sure they succeeded. It was this need to please that had made Harold stay late working on the aprons that day. He should have left the shop a few hours earlier but they had already been running behind on the day's work and his father had rushed home sick with signs of influenza. This had delayed them even further on an almost impossible order. Harold had to admit that he was worried for his father's health. The man was in his fifties and was starting to show just how old he had become, he had begun to weaken. Over the past year, Harold had seen the huge mountain-like man that was his father shrink. The flu was a killer and in his aged state Harold was worried about him carrying such an ailment. Harold did not have time to linger on his worries for long, no sooner had the last stitch been pulled tight he left the shop for the night. With the door bolted behind him, Harold was off to the Queens for his second job.

The Queens was a little Drow run tavern down by the docks. Harold had started working there once or twice a week in the evenings to help maintain the cost of the family estate; it was a way to make up for the short fall in earnings coming from the tailors. That particular night Harold was running late, but he knew that no one would notice. They never did as long as Harold was there before the kegs ran dry. The money was good for the hours he worked and for the menial tasks that he was required to do, like lugging empty kegs of ale from the cellar onto a wagon, or unloading full ones that just arrived and tapping them ready to keep the foul smelling grog flowing. The money was much more than the work was worth, but the reason it paid so well was the hush money to avert his eyes from things going on there. The Drow had always had strong ties to the White Flag pirates and the Queens was a real den of iniquity. Gambling, fights, prostitution and other unmentionable acts that should never be carried out by decent Neeskmouthain men and women, were the stock and trade for the little back alley boozer. The tavern was favoured by the worst Neeskmouth had to offer. Still, Harold was left alone to do his job and he was the kind of person to go unnoticed so he did not let himself worry about what went on inside its walls. His only worry was the amount of liquor that used to go in and out of the place. Harold was a tailor, so he was not used to heavy lifting, but thankfully, he did take on a little of his father's shape and was bulky. Not overly muscular like some of the bruisers that he saw fall in and out of the Queens of an evening but he was not a reed pole. All the same, the full kegs almost tore his arms from his body and with the number they had going in and out of the place you would have thought half the harbour had gills.

Harold walked the quietening streets alone on his way to the tavern not eager for the weight of the kegs that awaited him. His body had begun to yearn for sleep although the sun was only just setting. He had walked this same path many times before and knew each loose cobble, each rise and fall and slope that cluttered his path. For just that moment, Harold could relax. He did not need to think as he passed the high and preposterously tall buildings all around him that helped to block out the hustle and bustle of sound. As usual as Harold walked along the canals and he was daydreaming. It was a good pastime for him which he had carried and used most of his life. The trait had started back at school when Harold was just a boy and had caused a fair few chalk rubs to be thrown at him by his teacher, old Macgregor, not to mention the cane once or twice. Harold had hated Macgregor. He was from the Western Reaches somewhere and seemed to detest all children. He was the headmaster of the school and he ran the place more like a prison, often taking some of the more poorly behaved children and locking them away in his room for hours at a time. Those he took would always come out crying followed by a red-faced Macgregor. Harold had been lucky enough to never go into his room. Macgregor was a Pole, not an Iron Giant as his people were known in times of peace, but a cold blooded warrior, a giant-like barbarian race of men named after their Polearm weapons, and there were rumours that he had slaughtered children during the war. Harold never found out whether it was true or not and he did not wish to know. Harold was a coward at heart and did his best to just block out the memories of his school days. As he grew, his cowardliness continued into his adulthood. The city scared him, although his family lived on the edges of the more lower class parts of the city, he had been sheltered from the worst it had to offer. Now as a man working for the Drow, he had seen a lot he had never wished to. So to avoid spending too much time surrounded by the horrors poverty could bring Harold had learned to daydream.

The dreams Harold had walking down the Harbour Path were the same ones he had as a child. They had always been about the coast. His mother and father had taken him to the Port Lust when he was young and the sights and smells of the sea stayed with him all his life. Harold remembered staying in his grandmother's little cottage and how the gulls had flown overhead, they were a beautiful white, not the dirty black grey of the pigeons that painted the rooftops around Neeskmouth. Harold swore to himself that one day he would go back there, but the house was ruined. It had decayed with years of isolation. His father had always been too busy to travel down and maintain it and his mother was unable to manage the Neeskmouth home, let alone a far away holiday cottage that was rarely visited. The painted walls of the seaside retreat had begun to flake and the once pure green grass of the expansive lawn was now little more than a jungle of weeds. However, in his daydream, it was still as perfect as when Harold was a boy. Small and full of character, it had some small birds nesting in the thatch roof – swallows Harold seemed to remember they were. They used to dart back and forth through the air chasing the butterflies as he sat on the cliff top watching them. Every morning Harold used to travel down the stairs that lead from the garden straight down to the shore and spent the day at the beach pestering rock pools and chasing clouds, then at night they had slept with the sound of the ocean as it brushed the rocks, stealing pebbles as it went. The little windows had wrought iron bars in the shape of a perfect cross. The shutters themselves were engraved with flowers. Harold felt happy and safe there, both as a child and now in his dreams as an adult. Harold found a fossil of some long dead creature at the base of those pure white cliffs and still had it to this day, sitting above the fireplace. For him, it is a last memento of his childhood, a memory of innocence that seems so rare in a city full of beggars and thieves.

Still daydreaming Harold came down from the bridge that crossed one of the waterways on the Harbour Path. The sound of the waves in his dream married off well to the very real sound of a ship's bells that rang out from within the haze of smog. The changes to the harbour had brought in a lot of work and made money for those that already had it, those that did not suffered even more, working longer hours in hot, smoke-filled, and cramped factories that were run by oppressive managers who had little care for those they worked to death. The thick clouds these factories produced seemed to grow denser with each passing year and now covered most of the city. They mixed like an unhealthy stew with the smell of the canals. On some days, it was so thick that it seemed almost pliable. The buildings around this area of Neeskmouth had already begun to take on some of its blackness and were quickly losing what little charm they had to start with. They were overcrowded with multiple families being squeezed into each one of the hovels like wharf rats. Many of the households also had nowhere to graze their animals so kept them inside with them sleeping with the slurry and straw in the same space they cooked. It was a breeding ground for fleas and rats and sickness often plagued the poor. With the promise of yet more gold to be made from the secrets the Dwarfs were finally sharing from the Kingdom of Goldhorn drove the greed of the rich. It meant there would be need for more people to come to the city to work within the factories and it only promised to get worse for those already below the bread line. The sun was falling over the horizon as Harold's daydream was broken by a husky and desperate voice close to his left ear.

"*Looking for a good time? You look clean enough so I'll do it for half pence, what d'yer say?*" The young woman leaning against a nearby wall asked him as she staggered out of the shadows looking like a scarecrow. She instantly made Harold feel ill at ease. She sported two blackened eyes, no doubt from an unhappy client the night before or from her pimp or, worse, her husband. Her ginger-red hair was pulled tightly into a ponytail and was thick with grease. The few hairs that escaped the grasp of the ribbon clung to her forehead as if glued in place. She gave Harold a smile full of remorse and the smell of cheap bourbon hit him. Harold watched unsure if he should risk aiding the poor girl as she almost lost her grip on the wall she had taken to holding. She had been drinking, maybe to keep out the cold or to block the thoughts of what she would have to do for her meal that night. Harold could not say for sure which. It was a world he didn't understand, he skimmed along its edges and in his naivety he even went as far as blaming the poor girl for letting her life end up this way. Because of his sheltered upbringing he did not understand. He could guess that having to work the streets could not be an easy task, but he didn't know that for some single women it was the only life they had ever known being driven to the trade as children by their own parents.

Taking a closer look at her Harold noticed that she was young and not one of the leathery skinned old hags that he normally saw at that time of day. It was a horrible thought but Harold knew that some of the girls working the streets were as young as twelve or thirteen years of age. It sickened him to his core to think that this poor girl might actually be that young. He could tell she was nervous by the way she clasped her hands together, all the while fiddling with the pocket of her blouse which hung loosely from her young body. She did not seem to carry the same hard-edged attitude as other bangtails that Harold had seen throughout this area of the city, but if she was as young as he thought then maybe she had not long been on the streets. That made the whole situation worse for Harold. It upset him to think that this little girl still had a heart; it was easier to think of prostitutes as soulless beings plying a trade. Harold had no love for whores or their work. He didn't understand why they didn't leave the city and go tend to the farms or head off to one of the southern cities away from the reach of the Poles or Drow and start again, but Harold thought for a moment about what would make such a young girl turn to a craft like this and his disdain for his employer at the Queens flashed through his mind once more.

Whatever the young girls' story, O'Brien would have had a part to play in it. Harold's anger was due to the fact that O'Brien was no doubt her pimp. He imagined her story. Her mother died in labour as was common and her father, a drunkard like most men from the wooden built part of the city had most likely abused her. She had finally collected enough courage to run away, just for O'Brien to find the poor little girl begging on the street somewhere, no doubt asking for nothing more than a scrap of bread. O'Brien would have spoken to her in his charming Drow accent and offered her to come back to the Queens for a meal. He would have given her a bed for the night, no doubt treated her really well, all the while getting her drunk on ale without ever a mention of its cost. Then when dawn came, he would have demanded payment for the ale, threatened her, and finally when she couldn't pay, he put her out to work, the bastard. The workhouse would have been better for the poor girl, although Harold did admit only barely. His heart sank at the thought and as if she sensed the sorrow in his eyes the girl looked away. She brushed her front down, loosening the rags to reveal more of her young bosom. Small freckles dotted her chest that mirrored those around her nose and cheeks. Harold could imagine from her small trim jaw that she would have been attractive but for the swelling on her face. One eye was almost closed and yellowing from the bruising.

The story in his mind continued. O'Brien put the girl out to work but she was not bringing in enough money so he taught her what happens to those that did not deliver what O'Brien wanted. He beat her up a little, not enough that she would be permanently useless to him, but no one cared if a prostitute has a few bruises and before the blood on her nose had even had time to dry he'd sent her back out on the streets to stand in front of Harold. It was then Harold noticed the filth on her, so much dirt on her clothes that maybe calling them clothes was too much of an honour. They were more like rags that had once been a cheap cotton dress but all shape had fallen from it so that it hung loosely over her small shoulders. One sleeve of her blouse was torn and Harold wondered if that had been an overzealous customer. Harold looked at this unfortunate girl in such sadness. She approached him with the same statement as before in her brittle tone as his glance met hers.

"Alright, quarter pence, what do you say?"

Listening past the cold she carried and the slur from the alcohol, Harold could hear in her voice that although young she was likely to be a little older than he first thought. It was hard to tell under all the dirt. No matter her age, she was desperate and that was for sure. If Harold had thought of it at the time, he would have wondered why she hadn't moved towards the ships with the rest of the whores who wanted easy coin, but Harold guessed she had some reason to avoid sailors. It saddened him that there were so many nightwalkers along the docks. The place was littered with them, all hoping to make an easy penny from the sailors coming in from their long voyages. There were plenty of nameless young women or old hags for them to satisfy their urges with while they visited the shore. Most of the poor women received a black eye or a blooded nose from their swift visit lovers. As much as Harold hated the sensual crafts, he hated the men that abused such desperate women even more. It pleased him that fate would have the last laugh as the cowardly bastards had no idea what they would carry back with them onto their ships. They would have a rash, and a vile one at that, but it served them right no doubt as the scurvy took them and sent them mad. Harold thought for a moment as he stood there awkwardly. He did not want the services the young woman offered but he felt obligated to do something to ease her pain or be as bad as those that caused it.

"*How much do you need to earn for a room tonight?*" Harold asked, feeling around for the loose change in his pocket. He didn't have much to give as most of what they earned went straight to his father and the little Harold had, well, he had reasons not to want to be carrying it on him after sunset in that part of town.

"*I only need a half penny more. I will do whatever you want and I'm clean too. No warts or anything.*" She replied trying to sound provocative but being clueless as to how to achieve it in her drunken state. That might have been enough for some of the potbellied pond-scum that had somehow managed to get a handful of coins to bed her but Harold had no interest in anything but getting her off the street and to work before the kegs ran dry and O'Brien turned his anger towards him.

"*Anything I want? You promise that?*" Harold asked her as he pulled the lint out of the handful of small coins he'd found at the bottom of his pocket. It was his whole earnings for the day but Harold knew he would still have food waiting for him when he got home, more than could be said for the redhead.

"*Yes, for sure, mister no matter how weird, less it's magic. No magic.*" The young girl said, eagerly snatching the small handful of coins from him. *"Cor-blimey, there's got to be almost two pence here. What weird stuff you after?"* She said and suddenly her face changed. It seemed darkness had seeped into some people's hearts ever since the demon broke through the spirit realm into the waking world. There had been bodies found that seemed to have been bled dry and rumours of cults spreading that worshiped the evil presence in the crater outside the city. There had been talk of working girls going missing. It was clear she was worried just what Harold would expect for such a payout.

"I want you to get home, get off the street. A young girl like you shouldn't be working like this." Harold said with a smile. Suddenly his attention was diverted as a coach rattled by passing between him and what he would loosely call a woman, almost knocking them both over. Harold took his chance to trot on quickly leaving her behind. The near collision had startled him and it took him a few minutes to notice the leaf that had entangled itself in his cropped brown hair. As Harold removed it he began to daydream again. He had needed the money really, but not as much as the girl probably did and it was worth it for the thought that for just one night she could sleep peacefully, just as peacefully as Harold had in the bed at grandmother's cottage.

The Queens was already in full cheer when Harold arrived. The proprietor, O'Brien, could be heard singing some old folksong, the patrons inside clapping and jeering him on. There was no doubt in Harold's mind that O'Brien was half-cut already, usually finishing off a whole bottle of whisky before the sun fell behind the horizon. Harold wondered if it was from the money of poor innocents like the little girl he had passed, or was it on the backs of tortured souls that he had build his criminal empire. Harold thought to himself that at least he had helped save her from the vile sweaty job for at least one night. As he relished on his good deed for the day Harold looked straight up above the towering buildings and into the sky. As much as he hated what had been happening to Neeskmouth in the last few years, he did have to give the city its due. The sleeping beast that was Neeskmouth with its disgusting polluted breath had created such a spectacle. The last golden rays as they fought their way through the thick smog above the city were a secret beauty only known to those of them the nation classed as unfortunate, providing they didn't breathe in too deeply. The nobles locked themselves away safely in their homes while the poor still worked or begged for coins from those barely any better off. It was as if the Gods made the little beauty just for them, a silver line to an otherwise blackened cloud. It was a shame that the sound of a drunkard vomiting in the street spoiled it for Harold that night.

Harold's eyes grew accustomed to the coming darkness as he drew his vision back down to the streets. He didn't know why but his gaze fell on the buildings as if it was the first time he'd seen them. They were not huge stone towers like those estates at the noble end of town. No, these were not the rich four or five storeys high masses of brickwork. They did not overhang with polished windows and sculptures that had been painted in the dried excrement of the flying rats that littered the skies. Instead they were a mix of wood and clay, simple hovels made for purpose over beauty. The buildings were all so square and unwelcoming, coated in blackened ash and moss from the ever wet air. They still managed to both impress and impose on Harold even after all these years. Most of the city was built in the same style, crushed together with no space between the buildings. The overhanging balconies blocking out what little of the sky could be seen behind the smoke. The city was growing so quickly that there was no space for houses and it would not be many more years before stone giants took their place instead, if construction kept going at the pace it had since the war ended. With the prosperity that the golden age had brought, people came from miles around to work in the factories that were sprouting up like weeds. The city hummed with the sound of machines and the hammers of stonemasons building places for the cheap labour to live. It made a man feel like each street was a secluded island with only one or two spots within the city where they could see the sky clearly, and that was why with the light bouncing off the clouds and the moon starting to climb ever higher in the sky, Harold savoured the moment.

The Queens tavern was a real contrast to the buildings around it and was one of the last of its kind. Harold did not know its history fully but it was one of the oldest buildings in the city and had survived the fire that had swept through the harbour when the Poles first invaded. It was one of the last reminders of the days before the city was occupied by the Iron Giants. At one time, not so many years ago, the stone buildings ended at the Market Crescent, aside from the statues at Celebration square, but now they pushed further north and only the most common parts of the city were still made in the old way, with clay and beam. It had been both a blessing and a curse for Lord William Boatswain when he opened trade with the Dwarfs of the Goldhorn Mountains. The city prospered and grew, giving birth and helping fund the Brilanka monks' march into Neeska. They had been called in to aid in the battle against the shadow demons of Briers Hill. Their first Cathedral had started to be constructed with this newly found wealth just south of Celebration Square. Close by a massive wall that stood five men high was built running around the natural Neeskmouth ridge from the west and south of the city, to save it from ever falling to barbarians again. The city folk felt safe and blessed but not everything had been so wonderful. With so much money flowing into the city and so quickly, the sudden boom of new technologies released from within the secretive Dwarfen halls, trouble was guaranteed. The machines themselves rivalled even the magic of mages and lead to corruption, the likes Neeskmouth had never seen. It was not only pirates now that threatened the harbours. With their wealth from bringing in these Dwarfen masterpieces the Brilanka monks funded a crusade that saw mages outlawed and in 118ab William, one of the saviours from the return of the dragons at the turn of the century, was voted out of office in place of the current lord, Malcolm Benedict. Malcolm Benedict was a mad man, obsessed with stamping his religion across the city and getting more and more Dwarfen machines. How the Queens tavern had survived all that and not been forcibly torn down in the developments, was a mystery. On the other hand, maybe it was not. After all, it had been in the O'Brien family for almost seven generations. The upper classes of the city were so corrupt that the O'Brien's no doubt held a lot of sway with them and that had kept the place as it was. There were even rumours of their coercion reaching as far back as the monarchy of the dethroned Handson's. The Queens was a small thatched building, not as pretty as Harold's beachside home but it did have its own charm, if you looked under the blackening of age through the thick clouds of smog.

The side street was emptying and only a few people headed along it making their way home. Harold watched them from the shadows wondering what stories their tired and worn-out faces hid. As always they seemed oblivious to his presence as they busily scuttled home like disturbed woodlice from under a dampened log. As Harold untied the barrels from the horse and cart he prepared to move them into the tavern; the drunkard who had ruined the sky painting earlier, staggered off out of sight and Harold was alone once again. It was strange how it always happened. The city had a twilight period where the beggars vanished to go off to sleep wherever it was they went, the shops all closed and the streets emptied. Given another half an hour the streets would be bustling again with a different type of Neeskmouthain, but for now those families that could afford food ate and those that could not still sat around the dinner tables. Once the meals were finished, the tidal pulse of Neeskmouth would change; the street gangs would come out, the prostitutes would move away from the docks and into the markets, the children would vanish, and the lantern man would light the city up which seemed to signal the seedy underbelly of Neeskmouth to awaken.

The wagon of ale was waiting unattended by the opened cellar hatch. Very few places could afford to leave things unattended nowadays, but no one in this part of the city would steal from O'Brien. Half the whores in the district worked for him, and most of the men he called friends were more than a little disreputable. The few constables that had been issued to this area of the city got more of their pay from O'Brien than they did anywhere else. When William had first brought back a city guard he had made the city safer than it had ever been, but after he left the castle the budget for the safety of the common man was sent upstream and didn't make it past the last noble brick. If you wanted anything O'Brien could get it for you and if you wanted anyone disposed of, then he could do that as well and the guards knew that. For the small pittance they were paid they turned a blind eye to anyone whose allegiance lay with the O'Brien family. It was rumoured O'Brien had connections to the pirates on the White Isle, and even as far as Portse on Gologan, another one of the Drow pirate coves that dotted the furthest reaches of the map.

The smell of spirits almost choked him as Harold approached the trapdoor leading into the tavern's cellar. Harold rolled the first keg in front of him with relative ease making the most of the silence before the city re-awoke. The sun had gone down and Harold was tempted to light a match to see if he could shed some light down into the depths. His hand was already sliding within his white sleeveless jacket for his tin, but common sense took hold just in time. The fumes, that were strong enough above the hatch to get a sailor pissed, would ignite, and Harold did not fancy burning to death that night. He admitted that he could really have used the lie down but he would rather have done it above ground than below, and anyway, Harold had never been a fan of worms. Pressing his sleeve against his face Harold had to wonder if one of the barrels must have fallen from the racks and smashed. It if had been a full keg, like the smell suggested, then half the rats in the catacombs would be waking up with a hangover, if the eye watering smell was anything to go by.

Harold gazed into the darkness trying to see what had happened down there and reached gingerly for the rope. The last thing

Harold wanted to do was lower down onto broken fragments of keg, so he hesitated. They could not afford two sick people in the family and Harold had his good shoes on. They were red leather and decently made – a favour from a local cobbler in return for a repair to his daughter's wedding dress the last year. Harold swung himself back giving up on seeing anything by leaning over the dark hole, once up onto the cold cobblestones of the street he laid the keg on the ground. He still used his arm to cover his face as Harold tried to peer over the edge again. It was no good. He would have to get down there and clear up the debris before being able to lower the fresh keg in. Harold couldn't afford to lose any more money after giving everything he had to that working girl. He doubted very much O'Brien would accept it was a mistake if he broke the barrel by lowering down without clearing the way first. As Harold had reached for the rope a second time, he thought, just for a moment, that he'd seen something move down there in the darkness. Harold took it to be nothing more than a large rat, which was another one of the many plagues that littered the docks. It did occur to him that the shadow had seemed too big for a rodent but then, what else would it have likely been.

As Harold started to lower himself down he couldn't help but notice that, although he might not be an expert on spirits, the smell down there was so potent that it had to be more than just one drum that had split. The cellar was dark and Harold didn't fancy staying in it longer than needed. He took only a few moments to look around and it was obvious that whatever had broken must have been cleared up. There was no broken debris on the floor at all, only an ankle deep puddle of liquid. Harold could not see any splintered wood or signs that one of the kegs, barrels, or any other container had leaked. It almost seemed like every keg had been emptied on purpose. Harold thought about mentioning it to O'Brien once he'd loaded the new kegs in. If someone was emptying alcohol into the cellar on purpose then O'Brien should look into it. Harold pulled himself back onto the street, glad of the fresher air. As he begun to tie the rope around the barrel and slowly ushered it towards the opening, a sudden small flash from below lit a figure in silhouette. Harold could see clearly that it had not been a rat that he'd heard down below but it was in fact someone watching him. Harold had barely enough time to realise that whoever it was had just lit a match before a wall of heat forced him to turn his back to the cellar door barely giving him time to scamper out. Another much brighter flash shot into the air sweeping him clean off his feet as the fumes caught ablaze.

Time froze, and for what seemed to him like a lifetime, Harold sailed through the air in the explosion before he came crashing down into the centre of the street, barely missing the cart that held the rest of his workload. The horses fled in fear of the sudden noise, sending loose barrels rolling towards the river's edge. Dazed and confused, his breath stolen from his lungs, all Harold could do was lay there and watch as the flames danced their very own Drow jig to O'Brien's song. The fire did not dwindle in the slightest as it spread, the blaze feeding on the fuels inside. The whisky, rum, and ales gave it speed as it riddled the aged woodwork of the walls. Flames leapt out of the small hatch with burning fingers that searched for a way to escape. As one of these long red fingers wrapped around the barrel that Harold had held in his arms only moments before, it shot into the air before exploding and showering down burning timbers setting the roof ablaze. Within seconds, the song inside the Queens stopped and screams echoed out. Harold could see from his resting place in the now frozen street that the flames had made it to the door before the first person could escape. Smoke poured out from the doorframe like rivers carving their way through the sky. The inside of the tavern echoed with the explosions as more kegs, barrels and bottles joined the massacre from the ground floor. The explosions so loud caused Harold's hearing to vanish, replaced with a continuous whistle. Cries faded as smoke pushed its way out of the second-storey window. The music had gone, the singers dead yet the flames danced on. His head was sore and pounding from his flight and Harold could feel himself begin to lose consciousness. Harold raised his hand shakily to his bleeding forehead where some of the debris must have hit him. His body shook and Harold felt cold even through all the heat. Shock filled every pore in his body, a coppery taste of blood in his throat, and he was sure he could feel death calling to him. The horror that was unravelling in front of him became little more than a dream as his eyes lost focus and whitened. The sound of the sea and the sight of brilliant sandy beaches filled his mind. Falling in between the dream and the living nightmare, Harold swore just before his head fell back against the cobbles, that he had seen a man crawl from the flaming hatch in the street. His clothing still smouldered and his flesh was bright red like a lobster, yet Harold heard no yells of pain. He turned and gazed at him, this stranger's flesh blistered and raw, hung from him like a decaying corpse. The zombie like vision, something out of a nightmare, took to running off away from the blaze leaving Harold to his fate.

Interlude: Small eyes often see more

The flames had barely missed him as Dante had darted into the hole just below the bucket that had been left at the eastern corner of the cellar for weeks. The little hairs that had once been on his tail were singed in the heat and the smell of burnt hair followed him down into the cold dampness of the crack that ran between the brickwork all the way to the sewers. Dante had crawled up through the same crack just a week before, on the hopes of finding something tasty to eat, and thought he'd struck gold with all the fine meats and bread and cheese that had been left out once the tall ones left the pub at night. He had got used to the odd interruption as one of the Drow came down to carry up a keg back into the bar. For the most part they didn't notice him as long as he stayed still but if they did, they'd just throw something at him, but Dante just darted under the shelves and vanished until they were gone. It was still safer than on the streets with the rat catchers and there was no sign of a cat to be found within the Queens. Dante had planned to grow old and fat there. Maybe start a family of his own, but as the smoke made its way down behind him as he escaped, it was clear that was not going to happen. Dante was a renegade rodent; in so much that he had jumped ship away from his flee ridden relations in search of a better life on dry land. Life on the boardwalk by the ships hadn't been easy and the local black rat population had chased him further into the city and into the path of the rat catchers. It had been that human that had taken away his safe haven beneath the Queens. Something had smelt different about the one that had set the fire. All humans smelt dirty, a mix between souring milk and lustful regret, but the one that started the fire smelt like soiled meat. He smelt more like the corpses some of the less refined rodents chose to feast upon in the darkest alleyways of the harbour. There was the way he moved to. Dante has seen the bipeds walking funny if they smelled of the spirits but that one didn't smell like he'd consumed any, and yet he still moved like his actions were laboured. Some of the sailors on the Cassandra had moved in a similar way after consuming a keg of dark black rum brought in from the Green Stone Isles, Dante's homeland. Even when the tall and presumably walking dead, humanoid had almost stood on Dante, he hadn't seemed to notice him. Dante had never known a creature with two legs not try to kick him or scream when they saw him. It was strange really why they seemed so scared of Dante. He was around the size of their feet, and wanted nothing more than a quiet life somewhere warm with enough food to feed his fluff covered belly, but for some reason all humans hated him. That was aside from the fire-starter; he was different, he oblivious as if in a dream. So strong too; he hadn't needed a hammer to break the kegs like the rest of the humans that came into the cellar. He'd done it with his hands. Dante had barely managed to avoid getting wet as he clambered up onto the loose cobblestone slab next to the bucket he'd made his escape near. The weird smelling one let the alcohol poor out over the floor while he just stood there motionlessly, staring off straight ahead like he was entranced. Dante had seen the patrons upstairs do the same from time to time, the odd tankard being spilt onto the floor but that normally sparked off a brawl, and he couldn't understand what the human was doing down here in his home. Dante would remember that one's smell. He was more dangerous than the rest. Dante didn't know why but his nose just told him to stick clear of that one. He would do his best to avoid ever coming across his smell as he made his way back to the harbour in the hopes his ship was back docked with his kin at the wharf. The pickings aboard the Cassandra weren't as nice as the Queens, but at least it was safe. The ship's old tom cat was as likely to catch a rat as he was to take a bath. The fire was the final straw that sent Dante heading home.

Chapter 2: Reverend Paul Augustus

Time is a funny old thing. Even with all the magic that swirled around Valadfar like freshly splashed milk into a mug of black coffee, there had been very few mages that had ever managed to travel through time. This was a shame, for had Harold known earlier his part, and those of others in the acts that were to come, he could have stopped so many deaths. Hindsight is a wonderful thing. Harold, just as many others, had passed Saint Anne's chapel so many times in his life. His father's tailors had used to deliver repaired frocks there for the priest occasionally. It was also the place his parents married shortly after its construction was complete in 112ab. It held some happy memories for his family, but Harold knew little else that had gone on there, as few who were not part of the inner Sacellum did and his family, although religious, were far from devout. The massive stone and brick churches were a new thing for the city; they had started sprouting up a few years after the war when the Brilanka monks first came to Neeskmouth. It seemed they were integral for the Sacellum religion and their priests to spread the belief through the city. In the years after Malcolm Benedict took the seat as governor of the city, the old religions were all but banished. With the old teachings fading in book burning, Harold's mother and father remarried under the eyes of the great creator, the god of the Sacellum religion, in fear that they would not be allowed into the holy city of gold when they died, if they did not. It was fear mongering like that which had allowed the Brilanka monks to take over almost every position of power within the city in less than two decades. It gave them access to more of the city's funds than any other guild. With their riches they built massive structures to impose their beliefs even further. Saint Anne's was by far the biggest and had taken twenty one years to complete. A blink of the eye compared to what it would have taken before the Dwarfen machines with their steam driven belts had been released from the mountains. It had been built in stages, first as a small stone church, and wings and floors had been added as the flock that congregated grew. It now stood taller than any other building in the city aside from the castle, which once belonged to the royalty of Neeskmouth and now served as the governmental halls. It was said that the foundations for Saint Anne's had been dug so deep that they broke into the catacombs and the hidden labyrinth that ran below the city. The plot of earth it sat on was almost as spacious as Handson Castle and showed the true power in the city had shifted from the once powerful royal line of the Handson's to that of the Brilanka monks.

The fear of the demons that the battle with the dragons had brought into the world fuelled the religions growth. It was this fear, and this need of the presence of something greater than the standing army to face them, which led to the humble beginnings of Saint Anne's to turn into the stone gargantuan it was today. This fear also pushed many of the priests past the boundaries of normal men. They had begun to be seen as demigods themselves and people begun to follow their word as gospel, despite the fact that behind the mask of their religion they were merely normal men and women, and some with just as dark a secret as any dockyard thug. It was one such secret that lead to the fire at the Queens that had changed Harold's life for good.

It was already dark before Reverend Paul Augustus made it home from Saint Anne's. The walk from Common Road south of Celebration Square was too long for his liking and made all the worse by the chill to the air. The cold got into his bones and set off his damnable arthritis. That, mixed with the fact he had to battle past the masses of people that cluttered the streets, put Paul into a foul mood. His knee ached but he refused to show his weakness and struggled on without the aid of a cane. They were for old and feeble men and Paul refused to be either. He thought that the leeches he kept at home would help, but at that time he still needed to do more experiments to make them safe first. He was not a man of science but was doing the best he could to learn the secrets they held. Paul slipped off his collar as he turned the corner from Common Road into Monks Walk. The newly paved and constructed Monks Walk had been built with small basic accommodation to house the rapid influx of monks and priests from the order that Paul was part of. His home marked the very eastern edge of Neeskmouth, and few travelled the path that curled back in to join the city again by the canals. He turned into the last dark alley before he reached his front door. It was a place where he could finally relax. Although the small white collar had been keeping Paul's neck warm in the cold breeze, he hated people pestering him with 'Father' this and 'Father' that. He was always glad when he was almost home where he could remove it. The grace and majesty of the church would captivate most but Paul Augustus had grown bored of its beauty some time ago and now he had started to find distain in himself while he wore the marks of his office. If anyone had asked, he could have pinpointed the moment his faith had left him. It was during his trip through the Eastern Empire. He had been a missionary, trying to pass the word of the saviour to the uneducated of the human provinces, but shortly after arriving in the Green Stone Isles, his zeal for God had left him. The memories of the place flooded over Paul, engulfing him in a past he wished he could forget. Leaning against the wall of his house Paul Augustus faltered. He forced his mind to focus, and physically shook the graphic memories from his head. He continued onwards.

'*God damn it.*' He muttered under his breath with a wheeze. His stomach churned over almost forcing him to arch forward. Biting down hard, he swallowed the feeling deep within until it fell into the pit of his stomach. The images faded from his mind but not completely – they never left him completely. No man could forget the imagery of the sacrifices. How could the word of Sacellum be true if the freedom of man could lead to such vile and violent acts? The whole teaching of the Brilanka monks was to prevent the debortuary of the demon world spilling into Valadfar but if men could do such horrible things without the sway of dark magic, then what meaning had his life had? Breathing heavily, Paul gazed around the poorly lit alley hoping no one had heard his outburst. A faint smile slid across his lips when he found he was alone, just how he liked it. Since returning to Neeskmouth, a year ago, he had grown to love being alone. With no one around to pester him, he could give up the act, stop playing the part of the priest, and finally relax. His clammy hands still shaking, white at the knuckle, Paul hunted through his black clothing for the familiar coolness of the copper keys that worked the lock.

The house he stood outside was an absolute contrast to the grandeur of Saint Anne's. There was no grand dome above the doorway, no tower reaching to the very heavens. The windows did not show-off the colours so rich and vivid that they never left the mind. There was not one idol to his God illuminating the dark alley. Instead it was a simply built multi-storey hovel. It was the home supplied by the church for Paul. It was hidden away behind the huge stone giants that blocked out the skyline in an alley littered with filth of every kind. Paul had chosen to have the dull scent of the smog, darkness and cobbles over the solitude of the Brilanka Isle, because here he could continue his work unquestioned. There might have been dead animals cluttering the gutters, and rats the size of small dogs, scurrying around, yet, this was his favourite place to be. Paul did not own the whole house but merely one room inside. The others were full of dissidents and drug addicts.

As Neeskmouth had grown and prospered the common man had found he had more money to spend, more gold to flash in taverns, and spend on herbs imported into the city. This had started a plague that even the wise lord William had not been prepared for and scores of people had started toppling into decay at the wooden edges of the city. It gave the Brilanka monks more sway as they through false modesty gave a home to those that could not home themselves. The main door slid open on rusted hinges. It was made of rotten wood, and the corridor behind it was filled with damp. It was more than a little cold and unwelcoming. Inside doors lined every few feet of wall space. It was a hostel for the poor and smelled of old stew. It was not much of an improvement from the smog filled air outside, but it was what Paul called home. The sound of shouting echoed from some far off room. No doubt another couple arguing, thought Paul. He heard a thud and then the quiet murmur of a woman crying.

It seemed the glory days of Neeskmouth were coming to a close. The brutality of the Iron Giants becoming more prominent as the native Neeskmouthains numbers dwindled. Paul sealed the outside world away with the click of the latch and made his way to his own room. Once inside, Reverend Paul Augustus closed and bolted the door. One could never be too careful. He slid the second latch into place. There was a thud on the wall behind him as the drunken husband stormed out into the corridor before crashing against the wall. Paul sighed as he dropped his keys onto a small and beaten table close to his front door and reached for the matches he always kept there. They had been sold to him by a match-girl from one of the flats upstairs. She was an orphan now. Her father had been one of the unlucky souls who had to guard the crater out by Briers Hill. In one of the uncommon appearances of the shadow demons his life had been taken. The mother who had been unable to maintain the rent on the family home had moved into the building shortly after. The very next winter she had fallen sick with the flu and succumbed to the bitter cold. Paul did what he could for the girl, bringing her food from the church donations and buying her matches whenever he had the coin to spare. Although Paul had seen and done things that would curse a man to an eternity in hell, he was a good man and he had a good heart, before he was changed by the coming darkness, desperation can lead even the most righteous down the wrong paths.

With a sharp flick against the uneven brickwork, the match illuminated the one small room that Paul called home. Paul savoured the warmth the match gave off in his hands before limping forward. Cupping the small flame as he went, he passed the mess of books and manuscripts that littered the floor. They had cobwebs coating them and small black pellets that Paul guessed were rat droppings. He had no idea how long ago it was he had tidied the room, but then it didn't matter as no one came to visit him anymore, he had made sure of that. Stepping over a torn copy of chorus songs, Paul looked for the darker shadow in the centre of the dull room, one he knew to be his table. On it was the remaining stub of a candle. He couldn't be bothered travelling to the market to get a new one, not now, not while he still had work to do. People may find out what he was working on and he couldn't have that. Paul's weakened mind was riddled with echoes of paranoia. He skulked across the lonely room and married the match to the wick. The glow from the candle was reborn, pushing back the remaining darkness.

His room was pressed so tightly against the surrounding buildings there were no windows. All four of the walls were solid brick. The room was bare apart from a bookshelf against one wall that was jammed from edge to edge with religious books. It was clear from the cobwebs they had not moved from their resting places for some time. Paul knew all the sermons within them off by heart, such lies and hypocrisy, he now thought, but at one time he had lived for them. Alone in his room was not a time to dwell on such things though, for he still had much work to do. A final glance towards the door and Paul pulled back the only chair and sat at his dining table. The candle in front of him flickered gently in a draft that crept in from under the door. The moving light caught the ridges of grime and showed up the many ring marks in the table's top, each from the hot tea Paul enjoyed so much. It was one of the few pleasures left in his life since the darkness came. The pattern of rings almost made a decorative top of an otherwise plain piece of furniture. Paul had stolen it from the monastery before he moved. Stretched from one corner of the room until it almost touched the table at which Paul sat, was his bed. Unmade from the night before, the blanket huddled in the corner as if scared of the intrusion. Paul had made sure it sat close to the fire to keep out the cold and stop his damn knee from locking during the night, although it had been many weeks since he dared light it.

The fire brought back the nightmares. In his dreams, he could hear the screams of the tanned skinned person from the beautiful Green Stone Isles. Paul had seen a child ripped limb from limb in a sacrifice while he stayed there. Paul wiped a bead of sweat from the end of his hooked nose. Those ingrates had such strong magic but their mystics turned the wisdom to such barbaric acts. None of these acts had made it into the report that he passed to the bishop. As far as the church was concerned, the mission had been a success. The village had renounced their false gods and taken on the word of Sacellum.

Without fear of interruption, Paul Augustus pulled open a large leather bound book that had not moved from the table in some weeks. Inside were the notes on his research and documents from the mission. The pages were yellowed with age and the ink had smudged from a hand rapidly scribbling words with a blunting quill. On the first page, a creature taunted him. It was a detailed drawing of a leech. Around it were notes scribbled with arrows pointing to different parts of the creature's anatomy. The bloodstains on the page were a memento of the dissections Paul had carried out on the creature in The Dark Gulf. Paul hovered above the page for a while, taking in the detailed description of the creature and trying hard to see what he had been missing in his research. After all, he had seen many leeches in Brilanka having being born in the country and lived there until his thirtieth birthday, he couldn't have not. As a boy, he had found a few stuck to his leg from swimming in the stagnant pool behind his house, and every time he had been to a doctor's he had seen them in jars around the consulting room. It seemed leeches were used to cure almost any ailment since magic was banned. However, it was not until the mission to The Dark Gulf, the sea around the Tropical bounding and the Greenstone Isles, that Paul saw creatures as large as this. The holy crusade of the new century was what the bishop had nicknamed it.

A sudden flutter from the candle's flame caused Paul to regain his focus and he continued scanning through the pages. His notes described his time in The Dark Gulf, the villagers he had stayed with and their way of life. Paul missed the village so much and found himself almost daily wondering why he had returned to Neeska. The only reason he had come back was to complete his research but that was almost finished. The last test subject had been so close to a success that soon he could return to the village in Chhottaa-Ghar. Paul longed for the solitude and peace of the isle. It was so remote that most of the people who lived there had never before seen a white man, and mostly he longed for his mistresses he had left behind.

When Paul had first arrived in Chhottaa-Ghar, miles of thick jungle surrounded the village so that it felt separate from the rest of the world. The villagers did not fear him as he had expected them to, but with hindsight and knowing the secrets they held within the place, why would they? No, instead of fearing him, they treated him with a kind of mild neglect. That which you would show a stray dog found starving in your street. A few children came and gave Paul scraps of food then stood around staring as he wolfed them down. It took weeks before they started to respond to his so-called teachings, but Paul watched them from his isolated pew and during this time, he started to study them. As he began to understand their customs he had noticed an air of fear over the whole village which confused him. It was something he could not see nor understand, and although his stay was only supposed to be for a few months, it quickly became a year. This was unauthorised by the church of course, but he could not leave the people.

He became more and more accepted and soon moved into a hut with a bereaved woman. During his time talking to the women, Paul learned that they all seemed to be scared of their devil God. They did not share the same beliefs as the rest of the Green Stone Isles. Their teachings mentioned nothing of the Titans but instead fixated on the changed ones, which had been a shock to the bishop in Paul's final report. During the twelve months Paul had stayed in the village, he had tried hard to learn the secrets of their religion, more obsessed with that than preaching the word of the Brilanka Bible. It was only after his first night laying with his landlady that she told him that the Abrus herb, which each villager hung around their necks, was a ward from their god. She had also given him a small cluster of the herb to keep with him as the villagers believed this herb would protect them or grant them some power over the bestial creature they worshipped. Paul continued to flick through the book until one word caught his eye from the page. It was a reference to the villagers' idol. The false god he was to rid them of, the Rakta Ishvara as the locals called it. Paul had learned enough of their language to get by during his time there and had learned that the bestial god's name roughly translated to 'blood god'. The memories of the day he finally gained access to the temple flashed through his mind and he dropped the book to the table with a thud. Paul cradled his head in his arms, the sickness returning to his body once more. Paul had seen the bodies that littered the temple and had watched the child torn in two and then fed upon. So scared where the people of this being that they celebrated as it devoured the child knowing it would bring them another period of peace.

"*What have I done?*" Paul whispered to the shadows of his cold and tiny room as he remembered back, but the shade did not answer his question. Paul Augustus gave in to his anguish and wept.

Chapter 3: Unknown Questions

A rather well dressed gentleman used to come into Spinks and Sons to have his suits altered in size. He worked for The Times, a newspaper press that had opened up a few months before the fire at the Queens. The single ply broadsheet newspaper had started to replace heralds in the streets, the once proud profession fading into nothingness. With pennies the Times could get children to sell the one or two sheet long parchments at half the cost it used to cost to pay educated men to proclaim the news and the pages could be transferred from person to person allowing the news to travel at twice the speed it used to travel around the city. The Scorched Lands being slowly cultivated back into a lush forest by a selection of Elves from the Alienage had allowed the price of wood and thus paper to fall allowing this new industry to enter the city and boom. It was the reason for the noble's regular visits to Spinks and Sons; he was growing fat on the fine foods his booming business allowed. This well dressed noble had told Harold that it was estimated that some three thousand Iron Giants were living in Neeskmouth since the end of the war. They had all settled when the Dragons had been beaten back and William had taken the throne. The noble had a long moan about the subject and Harold remembered thinking to himself at the time that most of them lived close by in the wooden parts of the city and not near the stone houses of the noble district so what did it matter to the posh reporter with his creamed hair and manicured hands? The Iron Giants worked in the sweatshops and factories or as pinch pricks for O'Brien.

When the war was first won everyone expected the Iron Giants to stake claim to the noble parts of the city, and to start with they had, but they were not cut out for it and it didn't take long for the more cunning Neeskmouthains to out-trade them or wangle their way back to the head of the pile. After twenty-eight years, all but a handful of Iron Giants that came to the city now made up a large part of the lower classes. The only people lower down on the social ladder were the poor mages that suffered at the hand of Baron Malcolm Benedict, and below them in the criminal underclass were the Drow. The city truly began to slide into depravity when Lord William had lost the vote and was removed from office in 118ab. His successor had cancelled most of the rejuvenation projects that William had started and it was the reason many parts of the city lay unfinished. Not only had Malcolm Benedict left the city unfinished he had brought back the purge of mages. With magic outlawed and any mages who admitted to the gift being imprisoned in the Tower there was little or no chance to make use of the limited medical resources the city had to offer. Even less if you did not have the wealth of the noble district to back you. The gentleman from the Times had gone on to protest against the work that a Drow pastor had been carrying out as he tried to establish a hospital for poor and sick that could not afford private fashions. His answer was to send them back across the oceans where they belonged if they could not afford to look after themselves why should they rely on the charity of the city and those, like him that had worked to make money? During the many months he visited the small family tailors, he complained to Harold more and more about this idea as its backers grew and a plot had been picked to begin building it. Harold didn't realise it as he slumbered but when he awoke he would be more than thankful that this spoilt swine did not get his way and the hospital found backers from across the sea and had since been built on Duck Street. The streets' original name had been replaced to reflect the new occupants and the strange apparatus the doctors often wore. The porcelain masks which covered their faces and came off at an angle looking like a duckbills to protect them from sickness and so called bad air. Harold hadn't really held an opinion either way as during the many times he heard the Times reporter complaining, but he may not have survived the explosion at the Queens tavern if it had not been built.

Harold awoke to the loud pounding sound of rain against glass, matched only by the drumming inside his own skull. It was another cold and damp Thresh night. Harold had no idea how many hours he had been out cold. He could remember the fire at the Queens, the heat and whiteness, then the beach. Amongst the confusion stood out the memory of the burning man. He had seemed so real, but as horrid as a nightmare at the same time. It took some minutes for Harold's mind to clear fully and the random confusion of his thoughts to align with the waking world. The journey from the explosion to his hospital room was a blank but even with his sore head Harold could still remember the image of that man crawling from the flames. Harold knew the man's face from the papers, a bonus of The Times man's visits. He always brought a free paper and Harold often read them. Harold tried so hard to remember the article from which he'd recognised the sketched face. He had always had a great memory for faces but could never remember the name that went with them. Perhaps he was a criminal that had done something horrible or he might have worked with the O'Brien's. No, thought Harold, that was not it. Suddenly his mind sparked and it came to him like a racehorse across the line. He was the man found dead in Common Road. Harold remembered reading the article on how the man had died. It was a mugging, and a vicious one at that. There was no way that it could have been him. After all, dead people do not generally get up and become arsonists, yet Harold was so sure. He put it down to a concussion and moved on from the haze ridden day dreams waiting for the rest of his senses to awaken.

Laying there with his thoughts, Harold could hear the rain outside falling heavily. His vision was still impaired and the darkness did not help matters. He tried to push himself up the hard pillow his head rested on without luck. Harold could feel himself being beaten in his efforts to sit up. He was unable to gather his bearings with the pain agonising every part of him it felt like he had bruised everything from his hair to his toes. The weight of his own body pushing him back onto the mattress, Harold felt defeated. He slid his hands up his body and reached for his forehead, as his arms slipped out from under the blanket that was laid over him. The cold instantly bit at his fingers and goose bumps dotted his arms. Harold felt blood on his face and needed to find out how badly he was hurt. His fingers quivered as they found cloth wrapped around his skull. It was a bandage, coarse and softened only by the fact it was damp with his blood. Harold tried hard to understand what was going on but needed to stop the beating behind his eyes to do it. He had a headache worse than ever before in his life, and with a trade of long hours sitting in the dark trying to thread needles, he'd had a few. It made sense that Harold was in a hospital but the question became which one? He had heard some horrific stories from clients that had lost loved ones to the hospitals.

When the mages went and the last of their potions vanished from the market stalls. Butchers or nobles with a macabre mind took to setting up small surgeries close to the dark streets of the harbours. Most of them had no clue to the biology of the human body and the healing arts they practised were little more than experiments. Mistakes in surgery, people catching infections from the filth and open wounds, as well as the medical practices themselves, killed more than they cured. Harold knew he was safer battling his wounds at home rather than letting some knife-happy surgeon at him with rusty implements. At that moment Harold wished to the creator that the apron had taken just a few more minutes to stitch together the previous night. If it had, none of this would have happened. Harold would have arrived at the Queens after the fire started. This small thought began an avalanche of questions in his mind. Harold had to get some answers and soon, before his head imploded under the pressure of his own thoughts. He had stayed unmoving for long enough. It felt like days but Harold knew it had only been minutes, the constant thud behind his eyes keeping time like a pendulum on a grandfather clock. Harold pushed himself up onto his elbows, not giving in to the pain this time Harold continued until his back rested against the brickwork behind him, grunting with the effort he allowed himself an imaginary pat on the back. The room felt warm to him but his breath crystallised in the air and Harold knew that it was the pain that warmed his blood from the inside blocking out the chill. It felt like his insides were an oven, but Harold could see the signs of cold on his arms. He was suffering from a sort of fever from the agony and could only pray it wasn't an infection from the dirty sheets.

A light shone in the hallway outside and Harold could just make out the silhouette of another door close by. If that was another ward then this was not some small practice but could be only one of a few places. As the darkness lost its power over his vision Harold began to see in monochrome the room around him. He could tell there were other beds in the large room and along the walls. Harold could just make out an assortment of jars, no doubt containing leeches or body parts in formaldehyde. A small table sat next to his bed and Harold could see a jumble of shiny tools on it that looked more like something a carpenter would use than a doctor. The sheet that covered him was dirty so Harold dropped it to the floor, relieved to see he still had all his limbs when it fell from him. He was surprised that there were no candles or gas lamps in the room, the only logical reason Harold could think of was that he was the only patient in the room and he had been out cold so there had been little point lighting the room for his benefit. That did make him wonder if the doctors had actually planned for him to wake up or had they just left him here until a dead collector came around.

At that moment something flickered causing a brief shadow to darken the light outside in the corridor, it cast a deep phantom that engulfed the whole ward in blackness. His heart leapt to his throat and Harold hoped that it was just the wind blowing out a candle. Harold thought of calling out but his throat was so dry that not even a squeak escaped. He really needed a drink but the taste of smoke and the awful smell of the spilt spirits still haunted him. The shadow receded but Harold could hear footsteps clapping against the flagstones outside in the corridor. The disturbance to whatever source of light that dimly lit the walls around him had not been the wind as Harold had hoped.

Someone was coming this way. The light grew brighter as the candle of the intruder to his thoughts grew ever closer and Harold got a better look around the shoddy ward.

A wardrobe was open at one end below a barred window and inside it hung six pure white nurses' uniforms, including their silly hats worn to keep their hair from falling into open wounds. The beds around him were empty and some had the sidebars up, turning them into odd-looking cots. The floor was surprisingly clean and partnered well to a bucket and mop that looked to have had a lot of use. They hid in the corner next to two peeling, white tables, similar to the one next to his bed. Being able to see in colour in the light was pointless. Other than the whites in the room, the only other colour around him seemed to be gray. The floor was a gray, the walls were plastered gray and the only hint of colour was a limp plant sitting isolated at the other end of the ward and the odd stain on another of the beds that Harold didn't want to think about. Harold glanced to his right and took a better look into the tools the surgeon had placed next to him. They were not, as Harold first thought, just tossed on the table but were displayed rather neatly. It was their strange shapes and jagged edges that gave them a cluttered look in the dark. The tools themselves had fine ivory handles. The fact that each one seemed to end in a point or blade, and a large wooden hammer around the size of his fist sat next to them, meant Harold didn't want to stay long enough to see them being used. His attention left the macabre tools as the footsteps stopped outside the room. The door slid open and Harold prayed it was someone coming to tell him he was fine and would be going home soon. As the door opened a self-assured man strutted in and made straight for Harold's bed.

The visitor was full of confidence. The only other people Harold had seen that cocky were the constables. As he got closer, Harold began to make out the blue of his uniform, confirming his suspicions that it was indeed the law and Harold wondered what a constable would want with him. His uniform was impressive. It had huge brass buckles all along its front and buttons that, with a little imagination, could have been bronze ashtrays. It was neat, pressed, and still dry. His visitor must have arrived by coach otherwise he would be sopping wet from the rain which Harold could hear was still clashing against the window. The officer wore a full top hat that nestled against his huge bushy sideburns which he removed and tucked under his arm as he drew close to Harold's bed, but not before Harold noticed the bronzed marking embossed in it. It showed him to be a city guard.

Harold thought that you could bet your day's takings that the constable was corrupt and no doubt on O'Brien's pay; they all were.

"*Good, you're awake. I had half expected to have to sit around and entertain the nurses.*" The officer jested. "*My name is Inspector Francis Fraser, and I'd like to ask you a few questions, my lad.*" He said to Harold in a voice that was deep and dry showing an accent foreign to the city. There were too many hints of southern Neeska blood chiselled into every syllable for him to be able to hide his lineage, but strangely he still tried. As much as he attempted to mask his accent, his bright orange hair, which grew down through the slug-like sideburns into a full beard, gave his true heritage away. The inspector was from southern blood, no doubt from Stratholme and Harold guessed he hid it to allow himself to progress in force. Most people in the city were still holding a grudge against the kingdom of Stratholme because they did not send aid during the Dragon's Blight, it did not matter to most that they were being ravaged by a plague that threatened the very existence of the city at the time. A rounded fat face and a reddened nose showed signs of heavy drinking and it was not until he sat down on the end of his bed that Harold noticed the band the officer wore around his wrist marking him as a high-ranking commander. Francis was stocky and from the scarred knuckles, Harold knew that he was a man that got the answers he wanted. Harold did wonder at the time if he was the type of man who joined the guard force for the good of the city, or if he was just another crook that had joined to abuse the laws for his own benefit. The inspector coughed abruptly, and it was only then Harold realised he had not replied for some time. Harold guessed the concussion made his daydreaming habit even worse. He had been fortunate to have the tendency, as had Harold not been daydreaming at the Queens, he might have been quicker loading that barrel down, and have actually been in the cellar when it went up in flames. His heart sank as Harold realised that at some point the O'Brien's boys would also be in to see him. O'Brien no doubt had died in the fire and they would be out for the blood of whoever started it. Harold was probably the only witness still breathing. That must be why the inspector was with him but once he left the hospital Harold would be at their mercy, all he could hope was that he was discharged before O'Brien's gang found out where he was being treated.

"*Let us get a few things straight shall we?*" The inspector continued ignoring Harold's lack of reply. "*William Boatswain might have let the guards go soft, but he isn't in power anymore. So how about you give me your name and you get to leave here with only the bruises you came in with?*" Francis said, hinting at his allegiance to Malcolm Benedict. The city had been torn in two ever since William was superseded in government. Harold truly believed that if the people of Neeskmouth did not so strongly fear another long and drawn out war, like the one at the turn of the century, then the tension between the religious and the common man would have lead to bloodshed. Those loyal to the extremist Sacellum Malcolm and those who, like Harold, wanted William back in power.

"Sorry. My name is Harry Spinks, son of James Spinks, tailor of East Street." Harold replied having no idea why he automatically introduced his father's name. He guessed it was to show that he came from a good family and was not the type to go setting fires.

"Not a Pole is you then, boy?" Francis asked unexpectedly. Harold waited for a second to see if it was some kind of inside joke, but his face remained unchanged behind the walrus moustache.

"No, sir" Harold answered. The question annoyed him. The Poles had been the name given to the army of the Iron Giants when they invaded the city. They only carried that name during times of war and they now worked hard for what they had, though you could see in Francis' eyes that he did not think they deserved it. Harold's annoyance was ignored by the inspector as he continued to scribble into his notebook as he spoke.

"You saw the fire at the Queens Tavern earlier tonight. In fact there are reports that you were seen to be loading things into the tavern where the fire started, would you like to give me your account of what happened, or shall I just get the cuffs on you now?" Francis spat out in a mouthful, seemingly without the need to breathe. He obviously thought Harold had done it and was praying Harold was of Iron Giant descendent as it would have been so much easier for him to pass the blame onto him, without any questions from his superiors if Harold was. The law was so corrupt that if you were of any race but Brilankan – home of the monks and the current ruling leader - decent laws, such as a fair trial, did not apply, and they could have him in the cells by morning, such was the fear of the demons.

"Well, I know you're not deaf and dumb so answer me, boy." Francis said with spittle forming on his lip. Harold could see the anger growing inside the inspector. He tried to remember the fire, but the details caused him to shake again. The fear had left his mind for a while but it seems it had not left his body, his fingers trembled and Harold could feel his mouth dry even more, if that was possible.

"Where am I?" Harold croaked, ignoring the question for now. Harold had a few of his own he needed answering first and felt he could get away with pushing the inspectors temper a little more.

"You're in Saint Bartholomew, the Drow hospital just off Duck Street if you have to know. Though, if you don't give me an answer to my damn question now, you'll be out of here and off to a rat infested cell before you can call your bloody mother to wipe your snotty nose lad." Francis said and the angrier he got the more the almost musical tone of his southern voice came through.

"I was loading the kegs into the cellar as always, when I smelt spirits-" Harold replied carefully.

"Well, I should hope you bloody would or there'd be little point putting the kegs in there?" The inspector interrupted and Harold supposed he had a point. The kegs did always smell of alcohol but never as strong as that night. *"Get to the bit where you set the fire."* Frances said seemingly growing bored of listening already. Harold didn't answer straight away because his attention was snapped elsewhere as, in the distance beyond the ward; he could hear a Drow accent. It was faint but could just be heard over the whistling wind. That was all he needed. Harold had the law trying to slap him in irons and O'Brien's gang on their way to gut him. As much as Harold wanted the inspector gone, he knew he had to keep him there. Inspector Fraser's humour was less painful than what would happen to him if O'Brien's gang even suspected Harold had started the fire.

"Ok, you really want to know what I saw. I'll tell you then." Harold said still barely able to believe it himself. *"The place stunk of spirits, More'n normal. As I was about to lower myself down to check for a broken drum or something then I saw someone inside the cellar light a match."* Harold said trying hard to fight through the fog inside his head and focus on the memories of that night. It sounded mad to him even as Harold said it. Someone had burnt themselves for no other reason than to torch the tavern and then crawled out of the fire and ran away. Harold guessed it could have been a mage that had somehow protected themselves from the flames, but then why use the match when they could have cast a spell from a safe distance away? It didn't make any sense. Harold doubted anyone else saw the man either as he had darted off in the panic. Harold was the obvious suspect so he had to tell the whole story in the hope that Francis would believe him. *"I was tossed into the street by the blast. It was then I saw him crawl out from the wreckage. I recognised the person from a newspaper article. The guy was supposed to have been killed about two weeks ago, but it was definitely him."* Harold said and instantly felt stupid. There was no way it could be him. Harold didn't know much about magic, but even necromancers would have had trouble controlling the dead the way Harold saw the burning man run, but it was definitely the man he

had read about. The more Harold thought about it the more he was sure.

"So, let him get this cock and bull right. You want me to believe you did not start the fire. It was started by a dead man? He came back to life somehow and set fire to this pub. Then, and let him be totally sure of this, he crawled out from the burning building in which twenty people died and ran off down the street?" Francis said and Harold noticed the inspector had stopped taking notes.

"Yes, that's about it." Harold said lamely. He had seen it happen and it seemed like madness even to him, so how could he expect anyone else to believe him? Francis was waiting for more from him but Harold had nothing to give. The awkward silence went on for what seemed like eternity before the door to the ward opened, swinging on its hinges, until it bounced off the wall with a thud that caused one of the nurse's hats to fall to the floor. In walked two dark skinned Drow, both of them short and in almost matching brown overcoats that reached down to their knees. They wore similar red shoes to Harold's own, though not as nicely cut. An odd thing to notice, but even in his weakened state Harold noticed the single beading stitches which showed their shoes were cheaply made, Harold guessed it was the tailor in him. Even in the dark Harold noticed the pair's features. They both had curly dark hair that bounced as they walked and squashed noses no doubt from countless drunken brawls. A glint in their eyes showed they owned the room. The one on the right had a limp, and Harold noticed his hands were shaking slightly, a sign of the scurvy no doubt caught from one of their own pinch pricks. Something told him that as small as these men were, they could handle themselves. Harold knew by their faces they were O'Brien's boys, in every sense of the word. They were not just a couple of his gang but his two sons. Harold had seen them at the Queens before. They eyed the guard inspector at the end of his bed and his breath froze as Harold saw one of them reach into his chest pocket.

"Please god not a crossbow." Harold remembered whispering to himself. If they had even the slightest likeness to their father's personality then they were dealing with a couple of psychopaths. They were twins that O'Brien had fathered with one of his girls back when he first took over from his father. It was almost like a lineage for the O'Brien's as every one of them for as far back as the first ship docked in the city had ended up having a child with the first girl he signed up to work for the family. Harold was thankful to see that it was not a weapon that came out from the recesses of the brown-shagged jacket. Instead it was a wedge of pound notes tied together with string. It was

more money than his tailors would earn in a month. The one holding the money chucked it at Inspector Fraser before speaking.

"*There is a mother-hen there, copper top, why don't you go buy yourself a drink or a brass tart and forget you seen us?*" O'Brien's son said, his Drow accent strong even though they had probably never even seen Lashkar Gah, their homeland. Inspector Fraser scooped up the money, before turning to Harold. He was on their payroll that was all Harold needed.

"*I'll be back to talk to you later boy.*" He said. "*Don't hurt him too badly, lads. I need to take him in alive.*" Francis said as he pushed his hat back on his head and shooting Harold a smile.

"*Slimy bastard.*" Harold had wanted to say but he was far too scared to. It was no wonder no one had any respect for city guards with so many of them being on the payroll of the criminal families. The door clicked closed as the inspector left without another word. It was just the two O'Brien boys and Harold. As the two goons took a final glance into the corridor to make sure they would not be interrupted, Harold closed his eyes asking himself again why he had not been late earlier that night.

Chapter 4: Restless Dreams

Paul Augustus's dreams were plagued by the secrets he held. He lay in bed with the fireplace out regardless of the cold. The darkness that hung like a smothering blanket over the room comforted him and helped to block everything out. Even over the cold's waking grasp the urge to block out the waking world won over and he sought out absolute black. The rain stopped for a short time as the clouds moved on and with the sky clear the temperature was falling fast. There would be snow by morning, not that Paul could see any of this from his windowless room. He tossed and turned below the sheepskin blanket. He knew his knee would lock and that he would suffer the agony that came with arthritis if he didn't keep warm, but the shadows were the only thing that kept the dreams at bay, so it was worth the pain. He had to hurry up and finish his tests. The experiments he had been carrying out on prostitutes had been going well, that was until that bloody Drow swine O'Brien had got involved. Paul fell asleep thinking on the Drow's involvement. Exhaustion finally won but his mind continued on its trail of thought back through the last few weeks. His eyes shut and the back of his eyelids made the perfect screen to show his dreams.

It had all seemed so simple when Paul had set out. The catacombs under Saint Anne's chapel had been empty for so long, the church was using it for storage. The rumours of them being haunted had been spread by Paul himself and meant the altar boys would never go down into the gloom. Capturing a pigeon from the street and letting it loose down there had been pure genius on his part, with the fluttering and crashing around it made sure the rumours had some substance. Once he was sure that no one would go down there it became the perfect place for him to work. The damp and cold of the underground tombs kept his failed experiments fresh and stopped them smelling too much of rot. The conditions, if not a little icy, were otherwise perfect for the leeches he had brought back from the east. Once the makeshift laboratory was set up the priest became, by his own admittance, a mad scientist.

At the start he had tried using the leeches on animals that he had gathered from the streets. If anyone had noticed Paul as he walked into the church at night with a stray animal he would just tell them that it was the creator's work. He relished in the foolishness of the average degenerate on the street. Because they feared the demons coming so much they could have caught him flogging a child and if he said it was the creator's work, they would probably have joined in. He had tried attaching the leeches at the neck of the animal as he seen the mystics in the Dark Gulf do, but they drained the animals of blood too quickly. The process had killed them off before the parasite could cross into the animal. Paul was unsure of just what happened to make the changes take place, but whatever it was, it did not have time to take effect on such small creatures. After a number of failed experiments Paul found that one corner of the catacombs had turned into a pet cemetery. If anyone had braved coming down there then it would lead to too many questions. He found getting rid of the dead dogs easy. All he had to do was sneak them out into the gutter outside when there was a heavy rain. The citizens of Neeskmouth were so used to seeing rotting animals in the gutters after a strong downpour that no one would question a few more. If anything, it brought more prosperity to the area with an increase of rodents for the rat catchers to claim.

The first tests on humans had proved a little more difficult though, as the corpses were harder to get rid of when experiments went wrong. Things improved when Paul found a loose slab on one of the sarcophagi. A couple of urchins from the street helped him open and clean it in return for a free forgiveness. This made the perfect place to drop the bodies as they would slide into the miles of hidden labyrinth below the city. This allowed Paul to progress at speed in his research. The frustration of what Paul had missed had almost driven him mad. It had taken five girls' lives before he found the secrets in his notes that the herbs which hung around the neck of the town's people, weakened the transition of the Rakta Ishvara, the blood god. These herbs poisoned the leech and killed them off before they could drain their victim fully. Not, however, before the toxin had entered the body and the change had started. Paul knew it was a toxin of some kind as only minutes after the leech fell from the neck of his subject, the veins in the area blackened and eventually the blackness seemed to spread to the eyes, at which point the subject generally died. It was on the night he had become impatient and taken two girls at once that things started to go wrong. He became greedy. The anticipation of mastering his technique forced him to make the mistake. Both girls had come willingly with his pound notes pressed tightly in their blouse, their young skin exposed down to the neck and the corsets working their magic, Basque styled they flowed down over the girls pale bosom. Their dresses looked to be made of cotton and had a decorative frill at the edge. The two girls were from somewhere in Lashkar Gar and chirped back and forth to each other in a language Paul did not understand. Their hair was messy and hung down in greased mats to their shoulders but they showed no sign of disease and that was enough for the experiments. Paul Augustus was no longer a celibate priest, he had forgone that teaching of Sacellum during his time in the Green Stone Isles and when he entered the catacombs he was already hard with excitement. As he led them down into the darkness, his hands caressed the poor girls. He tried to reach into their clothes with his lecherously old and wrinkled hands groped them as they walked. The two girls, although used to this sort of sordid ordeal, were made uncomfortable by the urgency of his need. They seemed to relax slightly in the dull light, after all it was cleaner than some of the places they had been forced to work a man, and at least they could relax in the knowledge a priest was unlikely to hit them. Paul was sure they noticed this was not in character for a priest, but for what he paid them, they did not seem to care. Paul had planned to just restrain the girls and attach the leeches, but seeing them in the dim candlelight had made his mind wander from his work. His God had stopped listening so long ago, who would notice or judge him if he were to sin? Therefore he did. He bedded both in the dank setting, deep under the streets where the girls were used to working. They both swarmed over the priest hoping to earn his favour for future visits for the wealth he offered. They touched him frantically, doing their best to please him. The pleasure was great but his mind never left the real reason they were there. As he grew close to climax, the faces of all the girls he had killed flashed across his mind but they did not halt his violent thrusts and hard grasps, his nails and teeth drawing blood. His orgasm came quickly, but not quick enough for the girls he soiled. Once it had passed, Paul rolled off the top of the young girl that had become his favourite. She was still panting below him as she wiped blood from the teeth marks on her bosom. His own breath was short but he had to move fast before they grew too eager to leave. The second girl, who had not come off quite as badly, was already getting dressed. Paul knew he would have to get her first. He reached for the tongs on the side table and pulled open the water filled jar. He reached down inside it and pulled out the large black mass that shook itself out of a coil. The size of the leech still amazed him, its full length around a foot long. The dressed prostitute turned to look at Paul and went to scream as she saw him come at her with tongs outstretched. It was too late as Paul grabbed her around the mouth. He may have been old but he was not yet completely feeble. He pushed the leech against her neck and it attached itself instantly. Her struggling stopped quickly as the pain paralysed her. The priest went back to the table and delved into the jar again clutching another leech in his tongs.

As he turned, he noticed that the girl on the floor had moved quicker than he had expected. She had run for the door in tears leaving her friend behind. Being nude, as shameful as it was, was not the be all and end all for the prostitute. After a life of servicing men, she had grown used to her bareness. Paul took a step towards the door with his anger rising in him but it was cold down there and he could not give chase. His arthritis-ridden knee ached and he knew it would lock if he tried. As he looked down he could see the assault on the first woman had left her lying, eyes closed, on the floor. The leech's toxin was already sedating its prey. Paul reached for the table once more and let a scattering of dry leaves fall onto the girl's body. It would stop her dying, he hoped. He looked back at the now open doorway into the main church. Paul thought about following the girl but decided that it did not matter that one girl had escaped, his experiments were too important and the guard would not believe her anyway. It did mean he would have to work quickly to remove the bodies however. Such an inconvenience to his work but that was the benefit of doing his experiments from the chapel as it allowed for plenty of graves to use.

  The images of the bodies in his dream made Paul struggle in bed, battling with the quilt. He wondered in a brief moment of clear mindedness when he had lost himself to this shadow, but at that moment his dream flickered onwards. Hours of real time passed in moments. It was during morning confession while Paul was alone in the booth that they had come to him. The slut that had escaped had been one of that Drow mob's whores.

  "Morning Vicar." A Drow's accent rasped through the carved wooden grill in Pauls dream. Paul went to flee the confession room realising his mistake instantly, but a strong arm was holding the door firm from outside. It was much stronger than his was. *"Please sit down Vicar. My friend seems to be blocking the door and will be until they've had a little chat."* The same voice said. Defeated, Paul reluctantly sat down. The shutter slid open and Paul could see the shadow of a man sitting in the next room through the grill. The stranger continued to speak, his Drow accent prominent. *"A little birdie tells us that you got a little over excited with some of our girls last night. Muriel is still stuck at the Queens and O'Brien is not all too happy that she cannot go to work. Ruby-May is still missing. What do you suppose happened to her?"* The Drow asked in a blatantly patronizing voice from inside the dream. To Paul it felt real. He actually felt like he had slipped back in time and was no longer in his freezing bed but trapped again in fear inside the confession box. That damnable hussy, thought Paul, she should have died too. *"Also-"* The voice continued. *"We seem*

to have misplaced quite a few other girls recently, and we happen to wonder if that is to do with you Vicar? Now, Mr O'Brien is not too worried about the girls themselves. They are just stock and trade and another boat will be over soon enough no doubt, and he would not, after all, hurt a man of the cloth. It is just the money side of things. You see we need that back. So, you stay in your little box there and forget we ever came here and we'll just collect what is owed from the church, right?" Ernest had said and the anger boiled inside Paul, he would make these pigs pay. At that moment Paul started to wake and he faded from the dream world to thought. He reached for the parchments from the floor by his bed and as he had taken to doing scribbled down the events from his dream.

His experiments may have failed but the body he had used from the morgue seemed to have worked. The banker had been stabbed in a side alley and left to die. The guard had put his picture in the papers in the hope they could find the killer, but Paul could not care less if they did or not. The body had taken on the toxin perfectly. Everything had been a success. The man was even controllable for a short time, his own mind as dead as his body was. Paul was so sure of this at the time, but he would soon see he was wrong. Whatever it was that the leech transferred and used to bring William back from the dead had taken over and William went rogue. Paul had sent him to get revenge on the O'Brien's for leaving the church in such a state and he had burnt the Queens down as ordered, but then he had disappeared. His blood hunger would start growing soon, one of the downsides to the so-called cure that becoming a Rakta Ishvara promised. He knew that the victim would have to start feeding. Paul had to cure the hunger before he used it on himself, he didn't want to go around killing people. He just didn't want to die, but had to find a way to get the leech to attach correctly in the colder climate first before he could worry about that anyway. He wanted the toxin to cure his own suffering, stop the pains and weakness his age had begun to bring. He had learnt in the Dark Gulf that the temple held the infected one who had lived for millennia. Pauls experiment, this so called William the banker, would be the same, his strength would be unparallel to anything anyone had seen before in Neeska and he would be brutal and deranged. He had to feed off fresh blood often to satisfy his cravings. The people of Chhottaa-Ghar had taught Paul that the leeches offered long life and strength for a price, but it was against their laws to use them and the Rakta would kill anyone who tried.

The gods, as they called them, were very territorial and wars had plagued the Green Stone Isles for centauries even as the Titans walked Valadfar. It was for this reason the village had hidden in the jungle away from the rest of the world. A sudden thought crossed his waking mind. The image of the Rakta Ishvara ripping a living child apart burned like smiths' fire in his frontal lobe. The sound of the demon god's screams as it fed on the child echoed through Paul's mind. The image was so vivid that it shook him to his core. His pores leaked a cold sweat. Morning had arrived and with it the burden Paul carried.

Chapter 5: Welcome Back William

As Harold lay in hospital he knew little of the bloodsucking William except seeing him blow up the pub, but their paths would cross more than once in the days that would follow. The second time Harold would come across the recently deceased body of William, started the moment the flames claimed their last victim at the Queens. William had fled the scene of arson leaving Harold unconscious on the floor and he had headed for the sewers. The fire had burnt away the herbs that Paul had placed around his neck and had allowed the parasite to extend its tendrils up into William's brain. He had been a mindless zombie similar to those raised by necromancers but with the herb gone the Rakta Ishvara had been free from Paul's control. It spread quickly and its first instinct was to flee to safety. William had raised a sewer grate not far from the burning building. He was driven by the urge to supply the parasite with the moisture it needed to survive.

The sound of water running overhead had become familiar to William in the days that passed. The darkness of the sewers was no longer a problem for him as it would have been had he still been alive, his eyes seemed keener. Now, much like the vicar who brought him back from the grave, gloom was comforting to him. The only source of light was a series of small dust flecked rays that fell in through small slits high above in the city street. It was so dark that even a cat with their shining eyes would have had trouble seeing but William could see every crack in the slime-coated wall of the sewers under Neeskmouth. The sewers were a new construction to the city and many broke off into people's cellars or led to unfinished tunnels that had been abandoned after the funding was withdrawn for the 'frivolous expense' as Malcolm Benedict had called it. This almost total abandonment of the tunnels had given William the perfect place to hide. In the days that followed the fire William had rarely left the sewers and spent most of his time in the dark. It had given him time to think and control the urges. He felt strange in his own body, so much of his mind felt as if it was missing. Memories and emotions had gone and in their place was another consciousness, one whose hunger seemed to be getting worse. William had to keep himself there in the filth that the rest of Neeskmouth ignored so that he could fight what was inside him. The strength the parasite had given him made it impossible for anyone or anything to stop him, not even the fire in the cellar had killed him. The parasite inside had begun to heal him before the flames even blistered the skin. By the time he hid away with the rodents, his wounds had vanished.

He had wanted to go to his family to tell them what happened and that he was still alive somehow, wanting more than anything to hold his baby in his arms once more, but he dared not. William knew he was only a passenger in his body now. Something in him had changed and it was unsafe to go to them. His mind was fighting the control of the creature inside him but he could feel he was already losing. William's teeth dripped red with the life fluid of one of his fellow residents, as they pressed deeper sinking into the soft and quickly cooling body. The rat's head hung limply between his jaws like the prey of the great jungle lion.

In the silence, William watched as a raindrop slid down a stalactite and fell to the floor with a splash. It sickened him that he was feasting on rats, but the hunger in him never ended. It was worse at night, William sat and dropped the rat's carcass to the floor where it bounced off the stone and fell from the upper steps motionlessly into the small brown stream below. It floated along with the putrid waste of the living city as it slowly sunk into the filth, the rats struggle for life faded as its corpse disappeared into the darkness towards the canals. Satisfied for now, William rested back against the wall but he knew it would not last for long.

A lot of Williams' memories had been taken when he passed into the spirit realm, but he could remember his family. He could remember the smell of his newborns head. He could also remember the fear as the mugger beat him to death. William hated that he had died and left his family but he wished he had stayed dead. It had been dark and peaceful, so very restful. Then without welcome or invite, the intrusion came into his body. This soul had come like blinding light and confused matters, the Rakta Ishvara becoming one with him. It had begun as a faint whisper, the words of a priest strongest in his mind. Something had kept the Rakta Ishvara at bay, its demand little more than a whisper but eventually the priest's words had fallen away like a discarded item of clothing in the void that remained. His mind now echoed of a past that William had never lived. The being inside his soul seemed to have a voice of its own, but not one that William could understand. It took over at times and then faded again and left William confused and alone in the dank sewers. The smell down there was terrible, choking William's senses. His thoughts flickered back to the world of filth that surrounded him. He could not risk going to the surface as there were too many people to feed on and he knew the hunger would return. He could already feel it ebbing just below his consciousness.

Beneath whatever he was becoming he was still human, at least for now. Deep inside, he still felt guilt for the fire at the Queens. He had heard the screams and seen the death, but he had not been in control of his actions, he was not fully in control now but Paul had worked him like a puppet. The thing inside him taking over had a voice and personality of its own, one that seemed pure evil and filled with hatred, but at least he seemed able to fight it.

It was ever since the sting of the herbs had fallen away. William's body had changed so much since he had come back from whatever death was. He had been an averagely built man before. Nothing special but when he came around as he was wrenched from the spirit realm he found his body had grown stronger, each muscle pushing hard against the skin, growing with renewed purpose like the barbarian chiefs of old. His chest heaved and contorted as it forced outwards with the growth of this new parasite, a hardened shell replacing his broken ribs. There had been a change to his throat as well, his tongue splitting, his pipes opening and twisting and his teeth growing and sharpening to look more like the mouth of a wild cat than a man. With his newfound strength and speed came more than just one burden, the hunger and company within his own mind was not the only thing to plague William. He had pains in his chest that came fast and were suddenly very painful.

Even though he had never read the research Paul had carried out, and couldn't even point to where the Green Stone Isles were on a map before his death, William now knew where this pain came from. The knowledge came from the memories from a past he had never lived. It came from the parasite. They were becoming one. The knowledge that had been crammed into his skull like a complete collection of encyclopaedias explained why it was that his chest hurt so much. It was the being inside him, weaving its way into him more each day. His own heart had stopped beating long ago and where it had been something new lived. The pulsating parasite moved stale blood around his body, it lived in a hard shell and its tendrils ran through the body like roots through soil. It was keeping William alive but at the forsaking of others. It needed fresh blood to keep its host body alive. The memories that appeared in his mind were the shared hive mind of the parasitic Rakta Ishvara.

A light from a sewer worker came into the tunnel drawing William from his thoughts. William could hear the man's heart beating and the fainter sound of a canary before they even entered the same tunnel as he called home. They had come to fix the bulwark of dead rats that William's hunger must have caused. The piles of decaying corpses had blocked the tunnel and had forced rainwater and sewerage to breach into the wine cellar of a noble. It did not matter to William what the reason was that a person had come into his domain, for now it was time to feed. Within seconds and without a sound, the sewer worker's lantern fell into the water. There was a spray of feathers and the clanking of the empty cage as the bird escaped in the commotion. A red colour mixed with the others floating in a place no one would see.

Interlude 2: Dante's visit

The journey through the sewers below Neeskmouth had been largely uneventful for Dante as he made his way back towards the harbour and hopefully the Cassandra if it hadn't already set sail. The flagship Cassandra had many a tale to tell of its own. It had started life as a cargo ship for the Dean family before it was commandeered by William as the prize of Neeskmouth when he took office at the end of the Pole invasion. The irony that the ship Dante so desperately sought had once belonged to the Dean estate was missed by Dante as he sat watching the young girl and old woman who were talking at the other end of the damp corridor he now hid in. Dante had left the Queens and made his way through one sludge lined path after another in the darkness below the city before the smell had hit him like many a thrown shoe. It was the stench of death. Hundreds of his kind had come to their end close by. There was something in the dark feeding on them and even with his rodent sized brain Dante could see it was a safe bet it was that same walking corpse that had evicted him in a bath of flame from his easy pickings at the tavern. Dante had already sworn to himself he would never cross paths with that twisted soul again and so he had doubled back, headed away from the harbour and started to make his way up to the city streets. He knew once he was up there he'd have to avoid the stray dogs, cats and rat catchers and just about any human with a shoe or shovel that took a dislike to anything with four legs a tail and a taste for cheese. But something deep inside him said it was safer than facing the shadows of the sewers with death waiting just around the corner. Shuffling up between two rotten floorboards Dante had found himself in a small, and just as putridly damp, corridor as the sewers below. He was somewhere along what the humans called Monks Walk. It was there with his nose just peeking out from the shadows that Dante watched and listened.

"So you just move in then lady?" The young match girl Rose said to the old woman who had been struggling in with a bag thrown over her hunched shoulders.

"Lady, I'm no lady my girl. Call me Granny most people do, but yes dear sadly I have moved in." Granny said as she tried to smile through a mess of gums that lined her thin wrinkled mouth. The irony that Dante missed was that the old woman standing in front of him had once been housekeeper to the Dean Estate. That was back before the war. She had fallen on bad times when both the men of the Dean estate were killed and lady Dean remarried a noble from Stratholme and moved to

the south. At one time Granny would have had just as much authority to clamber aboard the Cassandra as Dante, but much like him she wandered aimlessly within the city.

"Be nice to 'aver a Granny, don't know where mine are. The old priest used to be like a Granddad to me but he's been weird lately and he's starting to scare me, don't seem right no more that-one." Rose said with the usual carefree chirp she carried. She'd lost both her parents and lived alone, scraping by on what she could get for a few matches peddled to those with the coin to spare, or from the gutters. She was not averse to eating half eaten apples from the edge of the street if it meant filling her belly that night but she never seemed to lose the thin smile that coated her lips.

"There's a lot not right within this city now young miss. Help me up to my room with this bag will you girl and we'll see about getting you something to eat in return." Granny said. It had been a long time since she had looked after children and she'd never had any of her own. The late Darcy Dean had been the closest she had ever got to having them and she felt she had failed him. She'd been the one to pack his bag and send him off after that stupid Dragons Heart but how was she to know he'd end up dead and buried in the Scorched Lands. Maybe this young girl was her chance to repent. She could look after her with what little she had managed to hide away before leaving the Dean estate. Dante watched as the two shuffled up the corridor. Once they were out of sight he twitched his nose and pulled his backside out from between the wood with a bit of effort, it seemed that time gorging at the Queens had made him fat. He'd have to be extra careful not to bump into any flea ridden cats in the rain filled streets or he'd be an extra plump meal for them. He made for the door with a squeak happy he was still 'just' slim enough so slide under it.

Chapter 6: Ernest and Neill

While William skulked around in the sewers ending the lives of rodents and sludge shufflers alike, Harold was still counting his breaths at Saint Bartholomew as morning came to Nywek the 9th. After the inspector had gone Harold did not think he would survive the night. These were no gentle rogues that had come to visit him, they had no honour among thieves and even less for those they figured to be marks. They were not honour bound pirates of the White Flag era, they were common thugs. Harold knew they would shed no remorse for his death. He shut his eyes as soon as the inspector left and sunk back down onto the paper-thin mattress. Through the sound of the wind outside Harold could hear the mismatched clatter of the bow legged thug clambering towards him. Harold could sense the other thug, the one who had passed Inspector Fraser the money, had not moved. He stayed back towards the door.

Before Harold could wonder why, a sudden sharp point at his neck caused his eyes to snap open. Harold was staring into the deep green eyes of his attacker. He could feel the cold of metal pressed against his neck, not hard enough to cut his skin but enough that he dare not swallow. Harold was scared half to death instantly and feared for his life. If he had been a brave man maybe he could have fought them off, leapt from his hospital bed and somehow made his way past them. He could have escaped into the cold city streets where he could have stolen a horse and ridden to safety, just like a hero from one of the great stories he'd read during one of the cold winter evenings in his armchair. But he was just a tailor's son and could barely hold himself up on his elbows after his injuries let alone take out two of O'Brien's own blood. If the stories of O'Brien boys were to be believed, and Harold had no reason not to believe them, then they were a pair of right evil bastards. With the city torn in two more than ever before between the haves and the have not's, the criminals' numbers had flourished but sitting at their head was O'Brien. There had to be a reason for it.

"Don't worry. I'm not going to kiss you." The goon closest to him whispered with a laugh. Harold could smell the halitosis on his breath, obviously a lifelong friend. Harold felt a sudden warm sensation drip down onto his bare chest and realised the point of the knife had pricked his skin. It was no more than a scratch but the blood that trickled from it confirmed Neill's threat. With the slightest wrong move on Harold's part or at the will of this man, Harold would become another dissection dummy for the surgeons to play with. Harold bit

down hard and clenched his teeth together. The urge to swallow grew, as did the pain, but Harold dare not risk swallowing.

"So, Harry is it not?" The thug by the door asked. "It would seem you were at the Queens when it went up. We have a few questions for you. You see; the relic that was our old man died in the fire. But I'm guessing you realise that, or there would be no need for my brother there to be getting so close to you." He said nodding towards his brother with an almost worried smile. "Now you're lucky in some ways, my-old man was passed-it and it's about time that I got to take over the running of the business. Still, someone's got to bleed for his death. What kind of son would I be if I let it go without retaliation? So you might want to answer quickly if I was you. My-brother can get a little excited." The words confirmed Harold's suspicion that even Ernest was unsure of his brothers' sanity. "Now, how is it that your scrawny little self managed to climb out of there alive, when my own kin went up in smoke?" The room fell silent as the statement hung like death in the air. Harold could not answer with all the pressure on his neck. The slightest movement would sink the cold edge of the blade deeper into his flesh. He had this sickening feeling that they were going to kill him. A sudden flicker of shadow before Harold's eyes and the Drow heavy had pulled the weapon from his throat. Harold waited for a second or two to see if he was dying. When there was no sharp pain across his throat he realised he had not been sliced open and instead he remained in the living hell that surrounded him. The knife's new resting place did not give the impression of being any better for him. Neills's face was so close to Harold's cheek that he could feel every foul breath that Neill took. Harold would have turned his face away from him if the knife was not now touching his upper eyelid. With the shakes Neill had from the scurvy Harold could see the point wobble back and forth like the pendulum of a grandfather clock.

"Now, you will be telling me what you saw or you won't be seeing much of anything, you get my meaning? Pop's always brought us up to believe an eye for an eye." Neill joked. The knife slid back with a sway of his hand and Harold took his chance to blink. His eyes refocused and settled on Neill's companion, Ernest, who was pacing back and forth by the door like one of the governors guards outside the Handson Castle. As if he knew that Harold's gaze had fallen on him Ernest stopped and looked towards Harold. Harold could see he was uncomfortable and it surprised him to realise that he did not like what Neill was doing any more than Harold did. He guessed that is why he had not taken over from his father before now, he lacked the killer spirit. A stupid man may have thought this meant he was safe but Harold knew he was not. Just because Ernest did not want him dead did not mean the short goblin of a man next to him would not as soon as kill him than waste his time with questions. It was then that Harold felt the expectance of Neill by his side and Harold mustered up an answer.

"William." Harold damn near shouted the name, his voice trembling with a mix of fear, anger and just plain fatigue. The random outburst seemed to confuse matters but what else could he say. He dare not say William's last name, as scared and confused as Harold was he was clever enough to realise that telling the over-eager Neill that it was a dead man whom had killed his father was suicide. Harold thanked the gods for the moment of genius that struck him. *"Some drunk in the street called out his name just as the cellar went up."* Harold lied. The lie slid out easily and Harold just hoped they would not notice. *"I don't know any more than that honestly. Your father paid me well and I needed the work. I would not have had anything to do with this."* Harold added hoping his time serving the family would give him the benefit of the doubt at the very least.

"Sounds like old Cavanaugh to me. The swine's sobering up back at Brandies." Ernest called out from his doorway patrol.

"Don't be going too far though Harry. I wouldn't want to have to go visit your father if you've been telling us porkpies. Say, he still own that place up on East Street?" Neill asked sounding disappointed that no one had been killed. The question was followed by another stench ridden and deep-throated snigger. The anger peaked in Harold and he wanted to attack the swine, to stop him before he got to his family. Harold had never really had a fight before but he couldn't just stand there, or rather lay there, while the brute threatened his sick father. Harold started to slide up on his elbows ready to, well - do something. He wasn't really sure what he had planned but Neills's fist came down and across fast, striking the side of his face with a blow like thunder. Before he could do anything Harold felt the world shake as he sunk back into the sheets.

"You leave them alone." Harold demanded but he knew his warning was worthless and so did Neill. He let out another chuckle from between his toothless grin.

"You got spirit and that's for sure. No wonder the old man gave you the job as barrel slugger. You'd just better hope you got sense not to have lied to us." Neill said to Harold and his stomach churned like so many sour curds. Neill turned to address his companion and joked. *"Let us leave her ladyship here alone. She could most definitely use her beauty sleep."* He said and paused. *"He's still a damn sight better looking than your ma."* Neill added with a belly laugh.

"That's your mother too you half wit." Ernest said with a sigh. It was clear who the brain in their partnership was. Neill slid the knife

into his jacket as if nothing had happened and made for the door. Harold could hear the two of them bickering playfully as they left the ward. Harold had been lucky for now, but he had to get to his father and warn him. The blow to the head had left him shaking and darkness soon swept over him once more. It seemed his body was not ready to deal with the stress it had been put through in his dreams the cottage called to him once more.

Chapter 7: Father

While Harold's concussed brain went on another a trip down memory lane that would last all of three days, William's story continued. Later they would blame it on trapped underground gas but Harold always knew it was William. He had killed those four sewer workers and it was before the last corpse had even cooled that William decided to seek out Paul Augustus and find a cure for his hunger. He was still conscious of what he had done even with the evil growing inside him. Unlike the demons that were rumoured to be stalking the night without any remorse, William was still human enough to feel the guilt for what the presence inside him made him do. It was on the evening of the 17th Thresh that William left his sewer home and headed for a confrontation with Reverend Paul Augustus. It would be the last time he was truly himself before the Rakta Ishvara devoured the last of his humanity.

William listened under the roadway grate while he waited for the crowds to pass by. It was still raining heavily which meant the streets would soon be empty as even the pinch pricks did not stay out in weather this bad. A whistle in the distance and the clatter of horseshoes marked the departure of the guard officer William had seen entering the hospital earlier that very evening and more than once in the last few days. He'd over heard the officers' name called out by the driver of the black guard cart. Francis Fraser had come back to see Harold a few times while he rested, unaware of the world around him. But thankfully for Harold, as William watched he was unaware who it was Frances had been coming to see. If he had then William would have had to kill him. The Rakta Ishvara would have made sure of it. It could not risk anyone knowing it was within the city before it was strong enough to rule it. A final glance through the slits into Duck Street and William pushed the grate open and its rusted hinges creaked with the effort, the grate had only been down a few years but the small budget put into manning the sewers had made for shoddy crafts and the poorly set iron had rusted almost solid in the wet winter. William felt the new strength inside him grow further as his arms strained under the force of the reluctant grate. The creature within William's chest beat and squirmed sending a pulse of stale blackened blood into William's muscles and with a sudden snap, the aged metal broke free, landing some yards away from its housing. William climbed up into the rain-sodden air enjoying the fresh, if not somewhat fierce wind.

It was only a short walk to Common Road and the streets were empty apart from an old tomcat chasing down its dinner, but the fat rat gave it the slip sliding under a crack in the nearby masonry. William had to fight the urge to join the hunt the sensation drawing him like a drug, but he had plans for that evening. It would be at Saint Anne's chapel that William would wait for the priest he remembered from his rebirth. William's legs began to move with vigour he had never had while alive. Having spent most hours sitting behind a desk he'd grown feeble and sluggish while he had been alive, but now he ran faster than an athlete from one of the Solar games. The rainwater splashed up from the puddles and pounded against his face. He ran faster than any horse he had ever seen and in that moment William felt alive. He made it to Saint Anne's chapel unhindered. He knew that the Reverend would not come to the chapel until the morning and he would have to wait. He didn't mind though, Saint Anne's was far more comfortable than the sewers he had been calling home, but the air was too dry even in all the rain for the Rakta Ishvara sitting on his chest like a giant callus. So William would make his way down into the basement below. It was the first place he remembered after the mugging that had killed him. When he had been dragged back from the lifestream as a visitor in his own body, William had awoken in the catacombs. It was there he chose to wait out the night.

William sat skulking in the obscurity, unmoving. He was like a spider waiting for a fly. One of the strangest attributes to his new state was the lack to need sleep. At night, when most people would tire, William felt more energised. The creature inside him despised sunlight, but in the darkness it could grow. The blood god, the Rakta Ishvara, grew in strength as the sun hid from the night. Its barb like tendrils pressed deeper into William's body each night piercing his organs and turning them black as it, slowly, night by night, took over his soul.

William was becoming more powerful than a giant and swifter than the fiercest of wild cats but the price to pay was the total absorption of everything that made him. Eventually the sun rose outside the chapel. It was a perfect and calm day, bitterly cold but beautiful. William's night blessing faded and the weakness of mortality coated him once more. The door above him opened and Paul shuffled in, making his way down the stairs. William waited until the grumbling had passed him by, the soreness in Paul's knee obviously playing him up in the bitter cold made him more vocal than a town crier. In the flick of an eye the shadow skulking in the corner had moved and with it William now crouched at the foot of the stairs. Even with the true strength of the Rakta fading William moved with lightening speed, before the dust he had unsettled had even landed he had blocked Paul's escape. Paul turned slowly his eyes wide with fright. He saw William standing behind him. In a moment of fear and as a kneejerk reaction Paul reached for the table trying desperately to grab the tongs he had left there. They were not sharp and Paul would have preferred the point of a blade between him and his experiment but beggars, or in this case, priests, cannot be choosers. Paul barely blinked but he did not see William's lunge and a sudden and firm grasp upon his collar lifted Paul clean off his feet sending him sailing against the cold stone floor with a painful thud. Lying there helplessly, like so many of his victims, Paul ached all over fearing for his life. Even riddled with fright it was funny to Paul to think that he would come to an end at the hand of the Rakta Ishvara at the very place he had created it.

"William, wait." Paul begged, hoping the controls he had put in place would still work. Paul had no idea how William had broken free, the herbal leafs that the villagers had given him should have worked. It was the only reason the Rakta Ishvara from the Green Stone Isles had not left its temple. It should not have been able to resist them. It was a kind of old magic, a controlling spell of sorts that occurred naturally within the plant. As William bore down on Paul, Paul could see through the rags of scorched clothing that hung from William's muscular form that any trace of the leaf had gone. The fire, he thought, it must have been the fire that destroyed them. Paul felt foolish and old. It was an oversight he should have thought of. The dry leaves would have turned to dust and ash in the heat of the inferno at the Queens. That was why William never returned as he should.

"So, you at least learned my name before you did this to me." William said through a snarl. Inside the hunger was demanding he kill the wretch in front of him and feed. Old blood was still blood to the parasite, but William fought against the urge. He had too many questions to ask first. *"What is happening to me?"* He asked.

"You are alive, I saved you." Paul said his fear subsiding somewhat *"Surely you are thankful for that?"* He added, glad that his test subject was still human inside and that the Rakta Ishvara had not fully taken over. William was not yet like the beast he had seen rip the child apart back in The Dark Gulf, no, he still had humanity and people were easy and weak. Paul hoped he could talk his way out of danger and convince William to put the herbs back around his neck enslaving him again.

"Alive? You call this existence alive? Do you know what I've done?" William asked showing his blood stained body as an example. His clothes had burnt to a crisp during the fire and some fibres remained attached to his fully healed skin much like that of long dead mummified corpses, but instead of blistered and rotting skin. William looked refreshed, almost sculpted, with renewed muscle mass. Paul shook his head buying himself time to admire his creation. The burns had cleared up completely and Paul could see the solid and rock-like structure attached to William's ribcage. It moved and pulsated like the heart of a normal man but looked more like a crustacean clinging onto William's chest. It had grown to the point that it had ripped out of the skin. It looked almost crab-like in structure but with the points of the legs still buried deep beneath the flesh. Paul knew from his experiments that once the parasite had taken such a strong hold onto a host body, it was almost impossible to kill. If the host body were mutilated, then as long as the Rakta could feed on fresh blood, the parts would re-grow. The only way to finish it off was to insert something hard and sharp into the ribcage structure. If the Rakta Ishvara was punctured in that way, it could safely be removed. Paul remembered for a moment the huge golden spikes that had lined the temple in The Dark Gulf, their devil god so sure of its own strength taunted the villagers to try to kill it. Shaking the memories from his mind, Paul flashed back to the urgency of his own situation.

"You mean the fire? They had to pay. They were going to stop what I have achieved here. I am so close to perfecting you." Paul said obviously proud of his work. He tried to push himself up. His fear, almost gone it was being replaced by the anger of his creation's stupidity. That was until William grew infuriated at the snivelling old man in front of him and sent his foot crashing into Paul's chest with the strength of a blacksmith's hammer. He pressed him back onto the bitterly cold floor and then the fear returned as did Paul's silence. William told Paul in gory detail the entirety of what he had done. How he had escaped into the putrid sewers, how he had fed on mice and rats and how his hunger had grown and he had lost control killing no less than five people.

"Stop, just stop please. You don't understand what I'm trying to do." Paul begged like many of his victims before him. He felt a mix of trepidation and self loathing as he begged for his life. Paul could tell by the blackening of William's eyes that he did not have long before the beast would need to feed again, if he really was going to talk his way out of this he had to do it now. *"The Rakta Ishvara – I mean you – it will save us all, it's the cure to so many things. It can stop even death, just as soon as I cure the*

bloodlust and I am so close, so very near." Paul said, offering the cure up like a carrot to a donkey. He didn't know much about the man he had chosen to raise from the grave but he did know he had a family. Paul hedged his bets that William would want to see them again and the curing of his bloodlust would let him do that.

"I don't care what you're trying to do. I want to know how to stop this thing inside him." William snarled. His hands shook as they clenched around the priest's collar. The hunger inside his mind urged him to sink his teeth into the priest's wrinkled neck and taste the sweet bitter nectar within.

"I don't know how to yet, but-" Paul began to grovel as he saw the blackness growing over William's eyes.

"-When?" William interrupted the urge inside screaming louder than a flock of gulls. If he didn't leave the priest soon and get back to the sewers he would end up killing him.

"Soon I will. I just need to do more tests and it will be perfected." Paul hazarded a smile as he tried to play to William's sensitive side, if he still had one. Paul had seen the newspaper article. He knew William was a family man. He had been a good man before he was killed and if enough of that remained then Paul just might get to see another dawn.

"More tests? Is that what I am to you, just a failed experiment?" William was losing control and his words became deep and animal-like he needed answers but would not be able to hold on long enough to get them. A huge grin filled Paul's face and William knew that the man he held in a vice-like grip had long since lost any hold on sanity.

"No, my son, you were his first success. From you I may find the cure. You will be the one to give me life, just as I did you." Paul Augustus said in a revelation that William would never understand. Paul was sick, dying, he had lung cancer. It had spread through his body and would soon kill him, there would be nothing that the doctors could do to cure his pox as they called it, and the magic which may once have saved him was now outlawed. Paul had resigned himself to death before he found out about the Rakta Ishvara. This parasitic vampire could cure him, if only he could stop the beast from taking over. It would repair the damage done and kill the disease. It would make Paul all but immortal. *"If you allow me to use your blood in my tests then we may be able to perfect you."*

"We - when was it that we became a team? I never asked for this." William said backing away from Paul. The urge to feed was sounding off like cannon fire inside his skull. William had to silence it. He dropped his head heavily onto the ornate stone sarcophagus close by,

sending a chip of stone across the catacombs. The hunger was almost blinding now.

"True, but then most do not ask for the blessing they are given. I brought the creature that shares your body with you back from The Dark Gulf. It is because of that that you still breathe. Do you still think about your family that lost you when you were murdered? If we stop your hunger then they can have you back." Paul bargained. He knew it was risky keeping William close by but the opportunity was too great to miss. William was the first successful application of a Rakta Ishvara leech. William suddenly withdrew his face from the stonework and staggered back toward the stairs, something changing within him. The blackness filled his eyes completely as the Rakta Ishvara pumped dead and congealing blood through his pupils.

"No, I will not help you. I've done too much for you already, I've killed for you priest. The creator will judge you for your sins." William spat as he ran up the stairs and through the door of Saint Anne's. He had wanted to kill the priest but knew if there was any hope of ending this nightmare he was now living it would rely on what Paul knew.

"It is a shame that he will have to be culled. The toxin has gone too far. Damn it." Paul cursed to the dankness as he pulled himself onto his aching knee. He breathed a sigh of relief at his solitude and relative safety. He knew he was too weak to kill the Rakta Ishvara in its final metamorphosis, but then an idea came to him. The fire did not finish them all off, so O'Brien's sons may yet prove useful.

Chapter 8: Arms of a Woman

If Harold had looked back over the times to come he would have been both thankful and remorseful that William did not kill the priest Paul on that fateful visit. If he had, then the way the story plays out would have probably been quite different and Harold would be rotting away in jail blamed for the fire at the Queens. A strange thing to wish for but at least Harold would have been safe in jail. If William had spent just a few more minutes in the cold catacombs feeding on the priest then Harold may never have crossed paths with him again and the Rakta Ishvara would have never got to see Harold's face. As fate would have it Francis Fraser, the inspector, had finished spending his bribe money and had come back for Harold on the 18th accompanied by two officers from the special unit. He stood by the door reading his rights while the two other baboons forced Harold to his feet, dressing and cuffing him.

They dressed him in the same smoke-stained and scorched clothes that he had been brought into the hospital with. The off-white woollen trousers felt like ice as they were brutally pulled up and buckled around his waist. Before the sleep left his eyes they led him out of the hospital pushing Harold ahead of them, his arms pulled behind his back in restraint. The two officers loaded him in the back of a closed black cart. The chairs inside resembled two large wooden boxes, one was fixed to either side with a small gap in-between. The two specials sat up front on the riding porch while Inspector Francis Fraser was inside the booth with Harold. He was the only other occupant in the back. They both sat gazing out of the barred windows at Neeskmouth as it rattled past.

Harold had barely been awake a matter of hours before Frances came to collect him and his mind was still fuzzy from the time he had lost. The opening of the market stalls ensured Harold had plenty of witnesses for his lowest moment. Harold assumed he was their prime suspect for the fire as it was blatantly obvious that his story of a dead man burning the pub was not being believed. In the back of the carriage inspector Fraser's eyes turned on him as if he was trying to assess him.

"Something is bugging me, lad. Why did you do it?" He asked, trying to drop the formal edge he carried the first time they met.

"Look, I didn't do it." Harold replied, frustrated. In the silence that followed Harold watched as a young girl that seemed to be being

followed around by an old woman tried peddling matches to some noble in a suede black top hat.

"Right, yes I forgot." Fraser looked at a grubby old notepad that he had filled with illiterate scribbling of the case before finally settling on his notes from their first meeting before continuing. *"It was William Bailey that started the fire. You do know they found him dead over a week ago and buried him at Saint Paul's? I even watched his funeral procession myself. Now tell me, before you went to work the night in question, had you been chased by the dragon, perhaps?"* Frances asked flatly. To start with Harold did not realise what the inspector meant and it took some moments of silence before Harold remembered reading about a new fad in the city called being chased by the dragon. It was a form of opium abuse that had been coming in with the influx of Drow since the end of the war. It had taken its name as it was mainly - at first - ex soldiers that used the drug to try and block out the images of the many men they had witnessed screaming, burning to death, during the last recurrence of dragons.

"I have never used opium." Harold replied seemingly onto deaf ears. It was true. Harold wasn't even that hard of a drinker and stuck only to ale as a way to avoid the foul tasting water that was drawn up from the well close to their home. It was becoming common to try fancy spirits that were being shipped in from across the sea that had the power to blister wood and bleach clothing, but Harold rarely touched the stuff.

"Then how else do you explain a dead man walking into a bar? It sounds like the setup to a bad joke. Then you claim he set fire to it and walked away down the street. Now, I've been in this job for twenty five years and this is the best story I've ever heard." Francis said as he sat looking at Harold expectantly. Harold knew what he had seen even if it did not make sense. He was sure he was right and the more Harold thought of it the more convinced he was that it had been William Bailey. It was not unheard of for mages to dabble in necromancy. It was banned even by the Tower itself and no one would dare openly use magic in the city anymore, but that did not mean that there were not little pockets of resistance to the imposed laws.

"I don't know, perhaps he had a brother. Maybe it wasn't him but it looked like him, maybe it was a renegade mage." Harold refuted, trying to convince himself as much as the inspector.

"Now, that could be the case but-" The inspector was interrupted as the cart hit something in the road jolting it forward. Harold smashed his already sore head against the painted black pine interior and the force of the impact sent Francis flying to his side of the carriage. He

bounced from the wall knocking hard against the floor with a crunching sound that could only be breaking bone.

"What the hell's going on out there?" The inspector bellowed from his slumped position on the floor, his voice sounded forced and his nose was bloodied.

"Someone jumped out in front of the horses. We hit the curb trying to dodge the imbecile." A muffled voice called back. Suddenly, Harold could hear screaming and the sound of running footsteps receding into the distance.

Shortly after, there followed a second smaller judder to the carriage and a commotion which sounded like the two specials grappling with someone outside. Fraser, who was still watching through the hatch, suddenly bent double. His face paling as he covered his mouth. The vomit escaped from around the edges of his fingers as he slammed the door open and fell out into the street. Staring in amazement at the scene before his eyes, Harold saw William ram Fraser against the side of the coach, the attack had come so swiftly Frances hadn't even had time to call out. William bit down hard into the inspector's neck and as he came up, his face coated in blood. William looked straight at Harold. What madness would drive a man to do such a thing? Harold did not have time to consider before he was out of the coach and running. Harold had not gone far before he wanted to look back to see if he was being chased, but he was too scared of what he might see. His fear kept him going over his aches and pains. His vision was blurry from his head wound so he almost didn't see the girl who stood by the side alley. She grabbed him, almost spinning him off his feet as Harold passed her. He froze in front of her and could see she shared his fear. She beckoned him to follow her and they ran together down another side street.

Pale brown walls overhung above their heads. The street had a gully running down its centre and debris seemed to clutter every inch of the road. Washing lines ran between the buildings and the hanging gray linen slapped at them as they ran past. They fled down side streets after side roads and along main roads, dodging past market stalls and barely missing a child playing with their hoop. Kicking the wooden ring from his legs, they finally darted into another alley, Harold felt like his lungs would give out at any moment. Suddenly the girl stopped while she fumbled with some keys. Spinning around Harold gazed up the alleyway back onto the main street where there was still no sign of William, thank God. Feeling a tug on his arm, Harold followed the girl into the house where she quickly slammed the door shut and bolted it behind him. Harold slid down the wall until he sat on the floor, panting.

"*Thank you.*" Harold said instinctively, the girl had helped him, a convict, to escape. After a moment of catching his breath he continued. "*Why did you help me?*" Harold asked sounding ungrateful, but he was more in shock as to why she risked her life after what William did than questioning the ethics behind it.

"*You don't recognise me, do you?*" She asked "*The other night, not far from the docks, you gave me money and told me to head home.*" She said and even without the slurring it came to him. She was the prostitute Harold had seen before in what felt like another lifetime. With the bruising gone, Harold realised she was much older than he'd first thought. She had aged well for a working girl and Harold wondered not for the first time what her story was. She had to be closer to his age but she had kept a youthful gleam to her skin that was not common of the local tarts.

"*I do, but that doesn't explain why you waited for me.*" Harold said in a half-truth. He felt a slight pang of guilt, as Harold knew if the tables had been reversed, he would not have waited for her. After he had given her the money Harold had not even spared a second thought for the young girl or young woman as she had turned out to be. Without the bruising she looked almost sweet and innocent and Harold found himself intrigued by her, almost forgetting the horrors he had just witnessed. He did not believe in love at first sight but he could not deny his heart fluttered and not just through the exhaustion of the escape. He brushed the feeling off under the pretence that she had just saved his life but that did not mean that his heart slowed any as they rested from the run back to her home on the Knoll.

"*I saw you that night, could tell you didn't have bad in those eyes. Whatever the guard had you for was wrong. Anyway, I couldn't just let that mad man get you. I have seen a few things in my time, but never anyone that bloody barking. Let's leave it to the city guards now, eh?*" She said showing strength of character Harold had never imagined her tiny frame could have held. "*I meant to ask you but you ran off so quickly. Why did you give me that money the other night? That was many a coin to cough up without turning a trick for you.*"

"*If I am to be truly honest with you, I thought you were little more than a child.*" Harold answered, too tired to think of an excuse other than the truth. His mind was spinning with what had just happened.

"*Ah, so you just wanted to get a youngling off the street for a night. Well, bless your cottons. Aye, I do look young. Plenty a man that pays more for me just for that reason, they like the little ones you see. Sick bastards the lot of them, but it puts food on my table and shoes on my feet.*" She replied seemingly impressed at Harold's generosity.

"*Thank you for saving me.*" Harold offered by way of changing the subject. He paused before asking. "*What is your name?*" Right there and then she was the only person who either did not think Harold was a murderer or want to kill him and, as one of the many gods as his witness, Harold needed someone to consol himself with and whoever this girl was she had a strength that drew Harold in like a moth to a flame.

"*Muriel Smith, if you must know. But to most people I will be whoever they pay me to be. That is, if they even bother to want a name some men prefer not to even think of us working girls as people, like stray dogs don't give us names. You are an odd one. What do I call you then odd one? What's your name and why were you arrested?*" She asked with a smile.

"*My name is Harold Spinks. The reason I was arrested is they blame me for the fire at the Queens last night. No, it may have even been the night before.*" Harold said realising he had no idea how long he had actually been in the hospital.

"*Try three nights back and you might be closer. So, you do it?*" She asked so bluntly it forced Harold to smile.

"*No.*" That was all that Harold could answer, not wanting to go into the details again. She was one person who did not want him locked up and Harold wanted to keep it that way.

"*Didn't think so, you don't seem the type. It was that other guy right, the one that attacked you? Makes sense that no one goes after the specials like that without reason. I saw it all. There was something not right about him. The cart hit him square on, should have damn near killed him but he just got up and attacked those city guards. You were lucky, you know that?*" The dry huskiness had fallen from her voice without the drink in her belly. Harold knew he was lucky all right. He was getting used to nearly dying and longed for his boring life back where the worst he faced was a pricked thumb, bad back or the odd headache.

"*Yeah, lucky I guess.*" Harold replied.

"*Let's get you cleaned up a bit shall we? Make yourself at home while I get a brew on. Nip of tea and then you can wash some of that blood off before you ruin my rug.*" Muriel said before slipping off into the kitchen. Harold actually shook his head in disbelief. This girl had just watched three men killed and it did not seem to have traumatised her in the slightest, maybe it would sink in later but for now she seemed unaffected by it all. Harold slowly pulled himself up from in front of the door. If William was coming this way then he would have been there by now. It was a strange feeling to be in her home, modest as it was. There was nothing but a few scattered and worn rugs on the otherwise bare floor. A table in its middle with a bed sheet rested over its top serving, Harold suspected, more than one purpose. A small set of shoddily crafted wooden stairs led up from beside the kitchen door and Harold wondered if her bedroom up there was a place of comfort and security, or if she worked from there too. His mind lingered on the thought of her bedroom longer than was proper, confusing even himself. His feelings towards unfortunates had always been the same; one of pity and disgust, but now Harold started to wonder if his opinions were wrong. After all, this girl had saved his life.

Chapter 9: A Late Order

Thankful as Harold was that William did not follow him, he was still too scared to leave Muriel's and she seemed more than content to let him stay. They spent most of the day talking about what had happened. Harold felt he may have been too open with Muriel but even then, in the first few moments of being with her, Harold knew there was something about her that just made him feel at ease. He told her almost everything he knew about what was going on. It was almost like he was unable to hold anything back. Harold wasn't sure if it was just because he was so tired that his mouth was running away with him or if it was because Muriel was pleasing to the eye. Her red hair, washed since the first time Harold saw her, now flowed loosely down over her shoulders. She was petite and slender and for a woman of her trade moved very elegantly. It hinted that Harold's suspicions of a hidden past were more plausible than he had given to first believe.

Maybe it was the escape from custody or William and the horrors Harold had seen, but Harold felt close to Muriel. He wasn't the type who normally made swift bonds of friendship, there are some who meet someone for the first time and swear to be friends forever. Harold couldn't think of anyone he really called a friend but for some reason he could see potential in Muriel that should have taken weeks or even months to develop. A shiver flew through his spine every time she spoke, each time he caught her gaze he turned away worried she would see his intentions hidden behind his eyes. Even after the many long hours that passed and with all the tea Harold had drunk he still had not told Muriel that a dead man was responsible for the fire. He'd been so open with everything even telling her about his job at the tailor's and the Queen's', but couldn't find a way to tell her it was the deceased William who had attacked the carriage. It seemed like madness to him but any doubt Harold had when he first saw him at the Queens had faded during the attack on the guard cart. The man at the scene of his escape was without any doubt the banker Harold had seen in the paper. His wounds had been all but gone, leaving no question in Harold's mind that he must have used magic. He must have some tie to the Tower. Necromancy or some other spell to bring him back from the dead, whatever it was he was dangerous and a stone cold killer.

Once Muriel had changed Harold's bandages with some rags from her own sheets - with an expertise that Harold found surprising - he said his goodbyes. He was scared of William or the guard finding him but he needed to check on his father, to warn him before O'Brien's thugs got to him. There was an uncomfortable moment as Harold left with Muriel standing just inches apart. Harold guessed that because of the way she earned her living, she had no fear of closeness, but the feel of her warmth emanating from her stirred something in Harold he wasn't sure how to deal with. Harold looked down to say goodbye and felt his lip trembling for the touch of hers. He did not give in as he was not sure if she felt the same. He didn't know how she could, they had only met a few hours before, and he felt stupid for feeling the way he did. Maybe her kindness was just a ploy to score more money from him. Harold hoped not, but it would still have been improper to kiss her, they had only just met and Harold was suffering from shock. As Harold left Muriel's home the fresh air outside, bitterly cold as it was, faded the image of her soft lips from his mind and helped him make sense of everything that had happened and allowed him to prioritise.

The walk to his father's was a hard one, his nerves on edge as Harold watched every shadow on the way, worried that it would be either a constable ready to arrest him or William again come to kill him. Harold didn't know why, maybe it was some kind of intuition but he was sure after seemingly escaping William's path of destruction for a second time he would see him again. If Harold avoided either of those fates there was still the chance that the O'Brien's would come to kill him. The odds of him making it home safely were not in his favour as Harold ducked into an alley between Homefield Avenue and East Street. Harold watched, hidden, as two officers chased down an orphan who had pick-pocketed some well dressed man who was still shouting loudly from the other end of the Avenue. It was a welcome distraction from his own mind, for someone who had always loved day dreaming Harold wanted to keep his mind occupied on anything but his thoughts at that moment. Other than watching the orphan give the guard the slip it was an uneventful journey as Harold passed the many shades of white and brown that made up the north end of Neeskmouth's buildings.

It was not until Harold stood outside his father's house, with his hand quaking above the knocker, that he could relax even slightly. Harold knew his parents would either be worried sick about his disappearance, or maddened by the unattended shop. In a twisted way Harold presumed he was trying to find some light heartedness in all the darkness, but it now seemed amusing to him that a few nights ago getting that order ready had seemed so important. Now Harold could not care less about making clothes. He dropped the fish shaped knocker with a gentle clap and waited for an answer. When none came,

Harold felt the panic rise inside him. What if the O'Brien's had arrived before him? His parents may lay dead inside his father's home. Thinking of his parent's death sent a sudden image of the guard inspector at the roadside flashing across his mind. It was followed by a cold numbness that stole his breath, it left him feeling faint. It was the first time Harold had seen someone die. In only a few days, Harold had been present while everyone in the Queens had burnt to death and then he had seen the chunk ripped out of an inspector's neck while two, already dead, specials slumped against the reins. Harold froze outside the door with his stomach churning over as his mind raced. With everything happening so fast Harold had barely had time to think on it, even while talking to Muriel it seemed like a dream. It seemed like it was a nightmare and Harold was going to wake up and find himself slumped in the chair with a reel of thread in his lap and a sore thumb from the long hours of darning that had sent him to sleep. It had taken the cold and returning home to make it real and Harold froze.

Once Harold was able to think clearly, he realised it was unlikely that the O'Brien's had paid a visit. The door was locked shut and it was late, very late. In fact, it was well after two in the morning and his father was probably asleep. His mother would have gone up to bed leaving him sitting by the fire in his slippers. His pipe would have smoked itself out on the arm of the chair and whatever book he had been reading would have fallen to the floor stalling time in that fantasy world. Harold knocked again, a little louder this time, and heard movement from inside. His father came to the door the sleep still evident in his eyes confirmed Harold's suspicions. His father was wearing his red smoking jacket and his thinning hair on his wrinkled head fluffed at one side showing that he had been asleep for at least a few hours. The dents in his face matched the embroidery of the chair his father always sat in perfectly. He looked sicker than when Harold had last seen him, the flu was obviously taking a lot out of him.

"Harry, where have you been?" His father asked his voice weak and laboured. His breathing worried Harold terribly. It was so harsh, like air escaping from one of those new fangled Dwarfen steam engines. Before Harold had time to answer his father looked around the darkened Greenway around them and stepped aside. *"Come in, come in, you'll catch your death of cold out there."* He said as he turned and scuffled along down the hallway and Harold noticed how much older he looked. It seemed like old age had caught up with him in only a few days. Harold followed close behind his father and he could hear the rattle in his father's chest even over the sound of their footsteps. As

Harold followed his father he noted that nothing in his father's home had changed from his last visit. It had, after all, been only a few nights since Harold was last there but to him it felt so much longer. The thin golden and red aged carpet with its decorative ivy still ran the length of the hallway it was handmade in one of the cottage industries that now faltered in the wake of the toxin spewing machines that could produce rugs in their hundreds in a third of the time. The wallpaper, a pattern of little flowers in baskets, shone in blues and pinks across the walls, stained yellow from tobacco smoke. Some of the sheets had begun to peel from their top-most corners but his father was too old and Harold too busy to replace them. Entering the sitting room his father headed straight for his own chair. Similar in design to the wallpaper, it was now yellowed and threadbare. The arms and legs were a dark mahogany and matched the rest of the furniture in the room; two large bookcases filled to the brim and a table between made from wood that had been cut from sacred oak and stained, before the Dragons had been vanquished for the first time, 128 years prior. It showed that their family had been prosperous.

Harold did not know to which side of the battle his linage belonged. He suspected purely by their stature and strength that they had been the invading Iron Giant army that had settled in the city, but his family never spoke of it and Harold was born after the war had ended. It had been common place for some of the Poles to take a second name to try and integrate with the Neeskmouthains. It was then Harold noticed it. The vase on the reading table was empty. To most people that would not have been something of note but his father had kept it filled with fresh flowers every day since his mother and he had married. If it was allowed to sit empty then his father was in much worse health than Harold thought. Harold walked across the sitting room to his chair, a lesser-used copy of his father's, which sat opposite his by the fireplace, itself echoing of the riches that once filled this home.

Although the house was close to the memorial of Execution Fields, the place the late barbarian king Ingaild first displayed his might in executing many of Neeskmouths heroes. It was within the poor parts of the city and thus was built of wood and clay. It was not a shabby house and rather stood as a marking of a new class of men, not nobles and not poor but a working man, men of industry, a class between the two. A middle class and such it showed both sides of life, luxury and necessity, without the aid of servants.

"So, where have you been, Harry? Your mother's been worried sick." His father asked while he fumbled, trying to load his pipe with fresh tobacco. The doctors said the stuff was good for you, but Harold was sure they were wrong. Harold could not see how breathing in a weed was good for the body but his father smoked it regardless of his protests.

"Dad, please believe me-" Harold said, before explaining anything. Harold really needed someone to believe him and, although he had told Muriel about the fire, the visit from O'Brien's hit men and the guard, Harold had left out the fact that it was a dead man who was responsible. Harold needed someone to know, someone who would believe him.

"Believe what?" His father replied, his voice muffled by the long shaft of the ivory head that hung from his lips. It was shaped to resemble a lion and had been in the family for years. Harold had no idea where it came from and only knew what a lion was by its carvings. A trade ship or explorer must have brought it back to Neeskmouth at some time in the past.

"Nymon night when I left the shop, I went to the Queens as normal. It was burnt down." Harold said starting with just the basics.

"I know. It was in the papers. Your mother has already got you burnt to a crisp and buried in an unmarked grave. You know what she's like. You should have got word to us." His father always had a habit of interrupting Harold and it drove him mad at the best of times let alone now, but Harold hid his frustration as he continued trying to tell him what had happened.

"I was taken to hospital." Harold continued before he was interrupted again but didn't get far before a plume of smoke was sent his way as his father carried on talking.

"I guessed that, boy. The bandages give it away. Such terrible stitch-craft on them though. I wonder if we could offer to do them better." He said and it made Harold smile a little inside. Even as sick as his father was he was still looking at ways to increase trade to their family shop.

"Father, if you let me finish without butting in, then you wouldn't need to ask so many questions. Please just let me finish." Harold said, a little out of turn. His father nodded but Harold could see the scowl even through his reddened cheeks. He did not like the fact Harold had become a man and his equal, not just the boy he could take his belt to if Harold spoke out. He had not been an abusive parent, far from it. It is just that he held discipline and respect at the head of all he did and had brought Harold up to do the same.

"The guard came to the hospital. They blame me for the fire." Harold Said.

"Preposterous!" His father exclaimed. *"Harry, I won't have it."* He yelled and Harold knew he was serious as he put the pipe down.

"It's not just the city guard, father. The Drow of the docks, the O'Brien's, they threatened to come here, father." Harold explained, ignoring his outburst. Harold wanted him to believe it wasn't him but he also hoped his father would take his mother and leave the city. Neeskmouth suddenly started to feel very small and unsafe, but Harold should have known how stubborn the old fool would be and it took less than a second for him to show it.

"Let them come, there is still life in this old dog yet." Harold's father said before choking heavily and ramming his sleeve against his mouth. His body convulsed with the effort and when he came back up to look at Harold, his eyes were glazed and watery.

"The guard arrested me, father. I was being taken to the station but, before we got there, the horse and cart was attacked by the same person that set fire to the Queens. He killed the three guard officers escorting me and would have killed me, too, if I had stayed, so I ran." Harold said, hoping he sounded innocent because, despite being in his twenties, Harold still feared his father's wrath, even though he could barely lift his own weight now. His bushy grey and white eyebrows wrinkled, Harold was not sure if it was from confusion, frustration, or maybe just plain surprise. What stunned him more was that he didn't reply, he just sat there looking at Harold. *"Muriel helped me escape."* Harold explained.

"Who's Muriel?" His father said, his breath still short from the coughing fit.

"She's a working girl from the harbour area, father. She saw the fire at the dock and was there when William attacked the guard officers. She grabbed me and helped me escape."

"Sounds like she has something to do with it all, you can't trust those pinch pricks. I take it she was the one to bandage your head again? That explains the cheap work. We best get them off soon, lad. God only knows what diseases she has. You checked your purse since you left there?" He said innocently. The question annoyed Harold but his hand slipped down to his trouser pocket, feeling for his wallet, which was still there. Only a couple of days before, Harold would have shared his father's opinion but the girl had risked her life to save his.

"She's not a thief." Harold said thankful that it was true. *"Anyway, I'm sure she's nothing to do with it. I saw who did it, I even recognised the man."*

"*Then why didn't you tell the guard?*" His father asked. He was unaware how corrupt the city had become. He still thought it was as prosperous as when William Boatswain was still governor after the war; he still thought the city guard did what was just and right. In other words Harold's father was a man who refused to see the downfall of the city he had fought to join.

"*I did, they didn't believe me. The man is dead, Father.*" Harold said bluntly, wishing he had found a better way of saying it, but how many different ways are there of saying you saw a dead man running around as if he were still alive?

"*What the hell do you mean, the man is dead? You said you escaped. Did you see him die? Someone shot him maybe, serve him bloody right. Bet he was one of those immigrants. You mark my words, all those Drow are trouble.*" His father grumbled. He was not very accepting of people. He was almost as bad as the inspector had been, before Harold watched him die.

"*No, Father. I mean he was found dead last week.*" Harold said, knowing it sounded insane. If Harold had been his father, he would have put it down to the head wound. His father's gaze froze and Harold could see he was investigating him, studying his face for any sign of madness, but he knew Harold had never been one to believe in fairy tales. Hell, as a child Harold did not even believe in monsters under the bed.

"*Are you sure, son?*" His father asked, his tone quiet. The last and only time Harold had seen him like this was when their dog had died and he had to tell him when Harold was about five or six.

"*Yes, I am, but then I also know it is not possible.*" That was the honest answer.

"*Sounds like total codswallop, lad, but I believe you. There is more to life than man knows, Harry. When I was a boy, I swear I saw a woman walking down our lawn, all dressed in white she was. She got as far as the stream that used to run towards the cliff and then just vanished. I got one hell of a hiding from my old man when I told him. I promised myself then that if anyone ever came to me with a story too unbelievable to be true, I would give them the benefit of the doubt.*" His father had never told Harold that before. When he was younger, Harold's father was a strong man, in every sense of the word, and Harold guessed sharing ghost stories did not really fit in with who he was. Harold's father flicked the last of his pipe into the fire before laying it on the side of the armchair. "*It's late.*" He said as the sounds of Saint Anne's bell tower echoed across the city. After counting the chimes, he continued. "*Rather it's early, three already we'd better be heading to bed. Take my advice, Harry, and steer clear of the devil's work. I don't want any son of mine getting involved with walking corpses, thank you very much, and I'll have no more talk about it. Once my chest has cleared up a bit, Harold, I will help sort things out with the guard, until then just stay home. I'll get your mother to get Janet's boy to mind the shop for us until this is over."* He said, before struggling to his feet once more and walking out of the room.

Harold sat there for a while longer watching the fire flicker, but he was tired and went up to bed shortly after. Harold had not slept well for days and expected to collapse as soon as he crawled into bed. Harold did not, however, but instead lay there thinking how he had never had the courage to make the final move and actually move out of his childhood home. Harold knew his father wanted him married but housing was expensive and Harold could not afford it alone. The fact was that Harold had never found the right girl. They were either too self-centred or typical of the middle class or below his standing and Harold knew his father would never allow that. Now with his father sick, Harold could not see him leaving any time soon. As if to reinforce the point his father exploded into another choking fit down the hall. He would have to convince him to send for the doctor in the morning, Harold thought to himself, as he drifted off to sleep.

Chapter 10: Daybreak

If Harold had hoped for a return to normality the following day, he was to be disappointed. The morning papers were filled with the news of the dead. The inside pages covered the missing sewer workers. The front page showed the picture of one Mildred Köln, left brutally murdered during the early hours. A young match girl had found her mutilated body outside the butcher's shop where she had been visiting to collect scraps. The inside pages described the story. Mildred was not the only prostitute found dead. Two other working girls were killed in the city by the time the brass font of the printing press had been set. By Duwek night, the Times was getting a new story of more bodies found, ready to hit the streets the following morning, but it was the Midwek papers that horrified Harold. A whole brothel, clients included, was added to the list of those found dead. The broadsheet described how someone had managed to subdue all the occupants and feed on them in a cannibalistic way. The reports included the information that the vicious murders had all taken place after an attack on a guard transit transporting a known arsonist who had subsequently escaped. The guard were asking any witnesses to come forward and Harold knew then that the whole city thought that it was him who was responsible for these horrible and most heinous of crimes. Except, that is, for Muriel and his father.

Harold did not know what really happened to the poor victims William took, but if he had known what William was becoming, then he could have hazarded a guess. William was losing who he was. Hearing Paul talk of his family had sent him into a rage and he had wanted to rip that little balding man limb from limb, but he knew that Paul was his only hope of finding a cure. After the incident with the guard wagon William had skulked around the city streets in his search for somewhere to hide and fight the hunger. Somewhere before he made it back to his hide away, Mildred Köln must have crossed his path and made the mistake of trying to arouse him, hoping to make a last bit of money before heading home to bed. Instead, she ended up satisfying his hunger. William had waited with her cooling body, distraught at what he had done. He was not pure evil, not yet anyway, and he wept for the young girl, knowing he had taken his youngest victim yet. The youthful girl's body lay in the gutter, with what little blood William had not fed on, trickling away. William had been there when the girl had found her and heard her scream. He prowled towards the girl, wanting to feed again. He moved slowly so as not to startle his prey and could hear the girl's heart beating. The sensation excited the beast within his chest but, before William managed to grab his new victim, a crowd had started to gather on the empty streets, the girl's scream obviously rousing those from the houses close by.

William waited while he watched the sketch artist from the Times setting up for the moment to be captured. The child, promising such a sweet feast, was worth waiting for, but William was left disappointed. The girl was taken inside the butcher's by the guard who wanted to talk to her and William could not wait any longer. Escaping the scene before the hunger drove him to make a mistake in front of so many people, William ran into the other prostitutes to be killed on their way home. As daylight approached his strength was weakening and he seduced them into the side alleys with the promise of money. They died easily, and there was something satisfying about feeding on the blood of these young women. Unlike the sewer workers or the damnable rodents William felt passion inside, a sexual excitement at their weakening murmurs. It was this drive, combined with the thrill and peak of energy inside, that had led William to the brothel.

After crawling out of whatever sewer grate he had been hiding in during the day, William waited in the streets opposite the brothel, his back resting against the wall. He remembered it from his old life, having visited once before he married. He waited in the growing shadows, patiently biding his time until the last rays of the sun fell out of view. He knew he had to be fast, strong too. There would be men inside who would try to fight back, and William was sure the women would not give in to his hunger willingly. He had learned already that the beast inside was so much stronger once the light had faded, and the time outside had given him a chance to think about what Paul had said. He even spared a fleeting thought for those he'd killed, but mainly he thought of his family. Why was it that he could not even picture what they looked like anymore? It seemed to him that they were shadows, or hidden behind water, their images distorted. Every time his mind tried to focus on them the image warped and flickered away. William had forgotten how long it had been since he had last seen them. Giving up on his trail of thought the darkness swept over him like a drug and William made for the door. The longer the Rakta Ishvara lived inside him the more like a wild beast William became. He shared more traits with a lion Harold's father's ivory pipe represented, than the man he once did.

Chapter 11: SWALK

While staying home and in between reading the horrors retold in the newspapers Harold received a crumpled letter from an unexpected woman. William's widow. Harold so wanted to throw it into the fire, but he did not have the heart. Their hardships only added to his heartache. Harold had no idea how they found his address and his only guess was that they somehow had access to the guard reports. Perhaps they read about his testimony claiming that William had set the fire. Either way, the letter arrived at a time that would prove crucial for him. Harold planned to wait for his father to approach the guard, but during the night, he took a turn for the worse. By Midwek the stress of it all weighted down like the weight of so many full kegs and Harold barely spoke, apart from to read his father the news. His mother was too worried for his father's health to even notice Harold's return. Only exchanged glances letting him know she was glad he had come home.

Harold tried to convince his father to go to the doctor, but he was a strong and proud man, which also meant that he was as stubborn as a mule. When Brunwek morning came his father remained in bed and Harold had to read the news to him yet again. He was far too weak to manage the stairs or the cold of the dawn, so Harold sat at the end of the bed with the curtains pulled closed and read to him. Afterwards Harold left him to sleep and alone in the lounge Harold started to stoke a fresh fire from within the ashes of the previous night.

It was not as cold as it had been but Harold could not sit in darkness. The ashes were barely smouldering when there was a knock at the door. For a second Harold suspected it was the guard and prepared to run but there was only one way in and out of the family home and that was the front door. The knock came again and Harold had no choice but to open it. Relief flooded over him like the ocean over the beach on a stormy night when Harold saw the uniform of the postal worker. He gave him just one letter, written in a hand Harold did not recognise at the time, but has grown to know so well. It was a letter from William's wife, or rather his widow. As Harold closed the door, he knew that he had to leave the house soon. Next time a knock came rapping against the woodwork Harold might not be so lucky.

He had a few choices where to hide. The shop, the family cottage in Port Lust, but it was Muriel that Harold wanted to go and stay with. He had to see her again and anyway, Harold had promised that he would go back to see her. His hands reached for the letter opener and prized the wax seal off the browned paper. Alone and in the slowly warming room, Harold started to read. It was a long letter and Harold could see from the smudged ink that the paper had been moistened, probably by tears as it was written. Harold read the letter over and over, his tired eyes making sense of it, a little at a time. One line stood out, saying that she had seen William and she knew that he was alive. His widow had seen William in a newspaper drawing of the crowd outside the butcher's shop. Harold was relieved that someone else believed him and could confirm what Harold already suspected.

Harold dropped the letter and scrambled for the paper, left unread on his father's armchair and flicked through the pages until he found the picture. True enough William was there. His cold eyes seemed to stare right through the page into Harold's own. Harold dropped the newspaper, feeling an uncomfortable dry uneasiness and slumped into the chair. Harold closed his eyes. He had no real clue how William's wife found out his name, but she knew Harold had seen him too. Her letter begged him to explain what was happening, she wanted answers for her children. It was hard for Harold to remember William as being human and having children, as he now seemed nothing but a monster. Harold couldn't imagine what could be going through his children's minds, but prayed his wife kept them protected from the truth. Her words hurt him so much that Harold wanted to hurl the letter into the fire there and then, but he could not. Instead, Harold folded the letter and put it in his inside pocket, planning to reply one day and explain as much as he could. The letter mentioned that William's body should have rested in the catacombs of Saint Anne's but it bypassed him at the time, as it did when the inspector had mentioned it before. Harold already had too much on his mind and although educated, he was far from detective bright; he was after all is said and done, just a tailor's son.

Chapter 12: All Moved Out

Harold knew the guard would be looking for him and the letter from William's wife made him realise people knew where to find him. It surprised him that he had managed to spend a few days at home without the guard battering down the door but it should not have shocked him too much if he spared any thought on the matter, after everything was said and done the city guards were little more than rogues with a badge. Apart from a few rare and fame seeking heroes, for a pound a week they would not risk their lives and as they blamed Harold for so many bloody and brutal murders, it would be some time before they darkened his doorstep. Harold took advantage of his reprieve by thinking about his next move in the twisted game of chess he had unwillingly been dragged into by William. The board was stacked against him and all the pieces were black and Harold could feel himself getting trapped in a corner. It fell on him to prove his innocence and the only way Harold could think to do that was to find William. If Harold could somehow get William to admit to his crimes then he could go back to his normal life.

His first task was to get out of his father's home, but it was not easy saying his goodbyes with his father's poor health. Harold may seem cold and unsympathetic but he loved his family and he knew the words he said could be his last chance to say goodbyes. Harold told his mother where he was going and made her promise not to tell anyone. She agreed without question. Harold looked into her face and he could see the beauty she once had now masked behind cold eyes. Unmoving and showing no real emotions her face reminded Harold of the porcelain masks the theatre actors wore on stage. Harold heard a snivel from her as she turned away from him and her shoulders sagged but Harold knew she was a strong woman. Her mask was there for a reason, for his mother would not let him or his father find out how shattered the prospect of losing her loved ones had left her. Harold thought about going to her and holding her but if he did, her resolve might fail and she would fall into a sobbing mess in his arms. As much as he wanted to comfort her Harold knew that he had to go now or he may never be able to.

After leaving his father's room Harold made the short journey into his own room all the while fighting the tears trying to build up in his own eyes. He tossed his travel bag onto the bed and suddenly found himself filled with a renewed urgency and began gathering up what few clothes he could carry. Harold placed in two pairs of tan trousers, a couple of clean shirts, one white, one off-grey, his spare tanned tunic and his top hat made from the softest of rabbit fur. It lay uneasily on the top of the pile. Harold was almost ready to leave when he remembered that he had less than a farthing in his coin purse. Harold pulled the travel bag shut and dropped it to the floor with a thud that shook the old floorboards and for a moment, Harold half expected it to go crashing down into the lounge below. Once he realised this was not going to happen he slid the mattress aside revealing a small fluff covered satchel. Harold was relieved that his savings were still there. For the last year and a half he had been putting aside a little of money each week. Even throughout the hard times he kept quiet about his nest-egg and had managed to set aside almost thirty pounds. Harold needed the money if he had ever planned to leave home but for now he doubted he would still be free to walk the streets let alone buy land of his own. Reluctantly, and with more than a pang of guilt, he took the satchel from its resting place and with it ended his day dream of leaving the nest.

Harold sat and counted out half of the money, he was to give it to his mother before he left. The money, Harold explained to his mother who had at first refused to take it, was to maintain the house while the shop was shut. Harold knew she needed it and was relieved when she finally accepted it. He hid the rest of his savings under his hat and made for the door, out into the busy morning.

Harold decided to stick to the main roads as he figured that fighting his way through the crowds was his best way to remain hidden. It sounds a flawed plan but it is often harder to see something in plain view than it is something that is hidden. It was out of his way but Harold stopped by the shop. It looked so empty, so devoid of life, even the mice seemed to have deserted it. Since Harold locked its door on the night of the fire the only sign of movement inside a building that usually bustled with life was a spider's web. Harold found himself impressed by the speed of the little creature as the web already stretched from one of the manikin in the centre of the display to the other side of the window. The fine threads and almost perfect lacing were of a far better quality than his father or Harold could ever hope to create. Harold wondered if they could hire the little feller. It made him smile, if only for a second.

Darting inside the shop, Harold wrote out a small card which stated 'closed due to sickness in the family'. Harold left it in the shop window being careful not to damage the hard work the spider had put into making its web. The card was an explanation for the sudden disappearance. Part of him still hoped that things would go back to normal one day and that they could keep on the good side of his clients. Janet's boy would not be there for a few days and Harold hoped that the little scribbled message marked by his own hand would be enough to give him something to return to when all this was over. That done and the store locked up, Harold left it in charge of his new eight-legged friend and made for Muriel's house, hoping that she would be home.

The journey was sparingly uneventful and gave Harold time to rest his exhausted mind. He spent most of the journey dreaming about the little charcoal coloured rat he had seen giving a rat catcher the slip as it darted under one of the many bridges that crossed the canals on the Trade Road. The daydream over and Harold stood on Muriel's doorstep with a lump in his throat. Harold prayed that she would welcome him to stay. If she did not then he had no idea where he would go. The image of the summer house flashed across his mind. Port Lust was not all that far, Harold could escape there and start a new life by the sea.

It was not the first time Harold had thought of fleeing the city since all this started. He was trying to be a hero and it really didn't suit him, he should just go, he thought to himself, as he stood with his hand hovering above the knocker. Harold made up his mind, that was where he would go. If he could not even bring himself to knock on Muriel's door how could he save the city. Port Lust it was to be. He turned his back to make his way to the Neeskmouth Ridge and the road out across the plains when the door opened behind him. Muriel stood in its opening with her bright red hair caught in the wind that rattled down the alleyway. She wore the same dress as before. It was definitely a summer dress and not designed for the cold of Thresh; it was low-cut around her bosom and a thin belt was pulled tight around her slim waist. It was plain, a dull, off-white and showed signs of age. The woollen outline of the dress had begun to bubble around the edges and the once tightly knit pattern looked weathered and loose. The small lace leaves at the cuffs had stretched and looked more like misshaped palm trees.

Harold felt his nerves tingle and run rampant within his stomach as his eyes traced her outline. These observations all happened in a moment and Harold prayed she had not noticed his scrutiny. His eyes ran back over her curves and towards her eyes, but not before Harold noticed her skin had puckered into goose bumps in the seconds that had past. She smiled and greeted him.

"Harold. I'm sorry, I didn't hear you knocking. You're lucky I happened to be passing the door and saw your shadow in the glass." She shot him a warming smile and Harold was glad that she seemed happy to see him again.

"I didn't knock." Harold replied, cursing himself as soon as the words left his lips. The moment felt too awkward and Harold was not thinking straight. He was confused and focused on why it felt awkward. The last time Harold had felt like this was for Massey Jane when he was still in school shorts.

"Oh, good, then you've not been there long then." Muriel said with a playful twang to her words. She smiled again and Harold noticed for the first time she wore makeup on her lips, something most prostitutes could not afford and if they did Harold could not think of a time they would need to use it. It looked freshly put on and Harold briefly wondered if she had put it on just for him. The sarcastic tone to her voice told him that she knew Harold had stood outside for a long time. It had been at least ten minutes or so as Harold tried to pluck up the courage to knock at the door. Muriel giggled at the silence and his heart fluttered, missing a beat. The noise was so young and fresh.

"Can I come in? It's cold out here." Harold asked through quickly reddening cheeks. He felt as flustered as a child.

"Yes of course, sorry." Muriel replied, flashing him another one of her sweet little smiles. She stepped aside, though not far enough to allow him clear access to her home and Harold had to brush past her to squeeze into the door. She was teasing him, clearly able to see Harold was uncomfortable. Harold guessed it came from her line of work that she could see if a man liked her. It was part of her stock and trade. Walking in front of Muriel, Harold made his way to her lounge and took a seat by the table. Harold should have waited, really, for her to offer him a seat but he felt so at home there. A quick glance towards the fireplace confirmed his first impression. The room was as cold as ice and the fire was still bare from his last visit.

"So, you kept your word and came back then. I was not sure if I would get to see you again. Glad I have. What's new?" Muriel asked, glancing at the bag as Harold slid it under his feet.

"Have you seen the papers?" Harold asked taking her attention away from his belongings for the moment. He wanted to wait for the right time to ask if he could stay for a few nights.

"I've not left the house." Muriel replied, and Harold knew it was because she was too scared after what she had seen. She was a brave woman but Harold should have known the sight of three guard officers

being ripped apart would have done more damage than it had appeared to.

"*What about money, surely you need to work?*" Harold asked, realising it was rude but needing to know. Muriel had been so desperate for money the first time he had met her and God only knows what would happen if she did not meet the street charge imposed on her by the O'Brien's. The confident smile fell from Muriel's lips and her gaze fell down to her feet.

"*It's not safe for a working girl with that thing out there.*" She said, confirming his hunch she was as scared as he was.

"*I'll get him, I promise.*" Harold told her, meaning it with all his heart. Harold had started to develop feelings for Muriel in the few days he had known her and was already willing to throw himself at William just to make her feel safe. That combined with his overwhelming urge not to rot to death in a prison meaning he'd have to find him anyway.

"*How do you plan to do that? You have seen what he can do. Sacellum alive, he will lay a gentleman like you on his arse in seconds.*" Muriel's reply came quickly and Harold could see the concern in her eyes. It was true, Harold was not scrawny because of his job loading barrels, but he had never been a fighter. It left him with no answer to give. Harold had no idea how he would stop William.

"*I'll think of something, I promise. I want him gone as much as you do.*" Harold said half just to convince himself. "*I have a favour to ask of you though, a big one. The guard are still looking for me. My home is unsafe and I do not have anyone I can trust but you. I know we have only just met-*" Harold did not know how to finish the sentence but thankfully, Muriel interrupted him. It was not her best quality, and made him fleetingly think of his father.

"*I saw the bag as you came in. I know what you want. You can stay here, but I have only one room. You can either bunk with me upstairs or you can sleep down here. I have some spare bedding but it's still deathly cold down here at night.*" Muriel said, giving little preference for either option. For a moment, Harold saw a sparkle flash across her face again. Harold was not sure if she had really meant for him to sleep upstairs, or if it was a joke. He knew she would be forward if she had really wanted him to bed with her, being shy and a working girl did not go together. However, as much as the thought of sharing a bed with Muriel pleased him, it was not proper and most definitely not appropriate. Harold could not afford to lose himself in the madness that swirled around him.

"*I'll stay down here. I have some money for the rent, and you won't have to work until this is over. I will give you sixpence for some firewood too.*" Harold said, trying to sound sincere but it was all for his own benefit. The house was freezing and he could already feel his skin turning purple.

"You don't have to pay." She said and Harold knew she would have let him stay for free. That said a lot without the need for words. The girl was 'unfortunate' as the city called them. She was a working girl and for her to allow him to stay for nothing meant she must have seen him as a friend at the very least. Putting aside his confusing feelings Harold was happy that her friendship would be enough for now. For at that moment he needed a friend he could rely on.

"I know, but I want to pay my way." Harold replied and so it was that he moved into Muriel's house.

The place warmed up quickly with the fire roaring. Even with the price of coal being so high, his sixpence had bought a lot of fuel and Muriel had taken the initiative to use some of the money to buy some food as well. Harold sat alone in the lounge waiting for her to prepare it. If it was not for everything that was going on, Harold thought, he could feel comfortable there. The smell from the kitchen wafted through and Harold waited eagerly for the lovely mutton stew, turnips and fresh bread still warm from the baker's oven. Harold sat alone listening to the clattering from the other room. It gave him plenty of time to think.

He decided that he would have to find out what brought William back. Harold had to know what he was before he could stop him. After seeing Muriel risk starvation rather than working the streets for fear of William, Harold knew now that stopping him was more important than proving his innocence. With the strength William had demonstrated he would take weeks if not months to catch, and in that time, he would claim hundreds of victims if Harold didn't do something about him. There were only a few places Harold could think of to look for information on what William might be. The occult was not common reading in the city, with most references to magic being removed in one of the many book burnings that Malcolm Benedict had instigated. Harold personally knew nothing of it. The rumour of the devil's club that the upper classes could pay to join went through his mind, they were a cult that believed they could join the demon that threatened Valadfar and had dealings in some horrid acts hidden behind closed doors, but Harold doubted this was anything to do with William. It was a drinking club and gave bored, rich people something else to waste money on. His only other lead would be the papers, maybe they would know more. Harold doubted it though, which led him on to think of William's family again. They might have known something, but Harold could not face them, he just was not strong enough. That left but one other choice that he could think of. Harold would need to break into the guard station, find their reports on both William's death and the incidents since.

His heart sank at the thought of what the world had turned him into but fate had dealt him these cards and Harold had to play the hand out. Harold would go out and check with the Times first thing in the morning. If, as he suspected, that didn't expose William for what he was then Harold would prepare for something that seemed insane; Harold would break into the courthouse.

Chapter 13: A Meeting with Ernest and Neil

As Harold prepared for his first night at Muriel's, Reverend Paul Augustus was fighting with his own insanity. His lack of sleep over the last few days was nothing in comparison to the weeks in which Paul had suffered insomnia. His paranoia was growing and only added to his madness. He had not been home since William had attacked him for he was too scared of what would happen while he slept. The hovel of a room was not definable against the Rakta Ishvara, whereas Paul had turned the catacombs below Saint Anne's into a fortress. With the last of his dwindling strength he had scattered sprigs of the Abrus herb, which was volatile to the vampire leech, around the stairs making the decent down to the darkness painful for William if he came that way. To slow his would-be attacker down even further, Paul had upturned the table he had previously been using for his experiments and pressed it, along with two unearthed coffins he had dragged across to the foot of the stairs, their forever sleeping occupants still inside as silent guards.

Paul remained in the catacombs, feeling it was the only safe place for him. His insanity and paranoia had peaked to the point he now feared the city would learn his secrets. It had not just been his home that Paul had avoided. He had barely left his sanctuary since William's attack. He continued to carry out sermons from the church above so as not to raise suspicion, but as soon as they were over, he scurried back into the dark and clambered over his sleeping watchmen, where he sat in silence waiting and watching. So afraid of leaving the stone walled safety of the church had Paul become, that he even had to send an altar boy tasked with going to find one of O'Brien's associates. The young boy found the two brothers not far from the Greenway.

They were still busy looking for Harold after he gave them the slip at the hospital after being escorted away by the guards. When they found out that the man named William, whom Harold had sent them after, was a dead man, it had infuriated them and meant that in their eyes Harold was definitely guilty. They would have killed him and Harold should have been dead long before he made it to Muriel's but they did not know his exact address and for that Harold should have been thankful. The day the altar boy found the O'Brien's only a few doors down from Harold's home, he would have still been there. The boy had rushed back to tell Paul his achievements, sure it would buy him a coin or two but Paul had killed him off quickly, bludgeoning him to death with a copper candlestick holder. In his insanity Paul had decided that the young child had been too much of a risk to let live. He had seen the catacombs and knew who Paul was after. He was as bad as the rest, all conspiring to stop his work. Paul hadn't bothered to experiment on the boy's body. Instead he had thrown the limp cooling body into the hole beneath the sarcophagus that led down into the labyrinth below the city, all the while continuing to rant to the silence around him.

"Hush, too much crying, too much noise from the darkness. Darkness calls to me, calls for blood. It called for women, called for pets, and now for my altar boy. Given everything to darkness, just like the dark skinned ones, soon to be blessed by the dark god. The Rakta Ishvara will soon cure me. Make me well, make me a god and then you'll all stop crying. You'll all stop screaming at me. You had to die, you just had to, now, all be ushered in to the darkness. Leave me in peace." Paul whimpered. He had often talked to the darkness as he called it. The screams of his victims always rang in his ears like the tolls of the bell at the top of the tower of Saint Anne's.

The O'Brien brothers finally gave up their search for Harold and decided to accept the request that the altar boy had given them, to go and see the priest on Enwek morning, they made their way to Saint Anne's chapel where they would meet with Reverend Paul. It made even two brutes like the O'Brien's feel their skin crawl as they clambered down into that darkness and into the sight of the makeshift defences that Reverend Paul had built.

When they found him Paul was still chattering to himself in a nervous rant. He had accepted in his own mind that he had lost his grip on sanity, and in his brief lucid moments, even pondered if it was just fear of being found out for what he had done, or a sickness that drove him insane, had he perhaps caught scurvy from one of the brasses he had brought in to experiment on.

In the cold darkness the two thugs kept a close eye on the twitching vicar in front of them. His stance unnerved them and they kept their backs close to the stairs that they just clambered down. Their eyes darting back and forth wondering just what the hell was going on.

"You called for us vicar." Ernest asked nervously, the sight of the blood splattered across the floor making him nervous. Ernest wasn't squeamish around bodily fluids normally but he could sense something wasn't right here and there was the smell to. It smelt like death. It reminded him of the time he'd found the sack washed up on the side of the canals and decided to open it to find the poor helpless corpses of some unwanted kittens. The smell was the same just stronger. There

were dead things close by, he just knew it. *"I did not think you would have wanted to see us again after our little-"* He paused, taking his time to remove his hat. *"-Yes, our little chats in your confession box. You know that girl has still not shown up. If this meeting is not of any benefit to us, maybe they can have a chat about that and the money you lost us."* Ernest continued, trying to take command of the situation. Ernest was the clever one of the two brothers and no matter how scared he really was, he would not show it. With his father's death it would be him that would go on to lead the underworld of Neeskmouth's vice.

"You dare come into the Lord's sanctuary and threaten me? I know you are blasphemers and rogues, I will not permit you to foul this place." Paul ranted, not believing in the creator himself any more but still knowing the power his words commanded even through his dementia. Ernest looked back at the unearthed coffins they had clambered over.

"What do you call that over there then, priest?" He asked. *"Looks like you are doing a good job at fouling this place yourself. What is that goddamn smell? Something died down here?"* Ernest flicked his finger back towards the bulwark as he asked the questions.

"It's just a minor precaution." Paul said with a shrug. To his twisted and sleep deprived mind at that time, having a pile of coffins and leaves on the stairs was just a matter of necessity and made perfect sense.

Ernest nervously flicked a coin between his fingers in his pocket. He was a gambling man and knew it was his tell but he couldn't help it. He always fiddled with a coin when he was nervous and at that moment he was very aware he was stuck in a room with two men who were clearly insane. Neill had not even seemed fazed by the smell of dead bodies or the fact he'd had to clamber over coffins to get into the room, and busily dug at something stuck between his teeth.

"Let's just get this over with. Why have you called us here?" Ernest shot Paul a look that could have carved through stone and he half hoped it would. All the way to street level so they could get the hell out of there. They'd taken many jobs from different people in their time and had met people in all sorts of seedy places, hidden rooms, dark alleyways, even the hull of a sunken boat along the coast once, but the foreboding and devastated catacombs were a new low.

"I need you to kill someone." Paul stated unflinching. The room fell silent. Neill had never been the sharpest knife in the drawer, but even he realised this was not something a priest should be asking.

"*What is in it for us?*" Neill asked to break the silence. With the small chunk of apple finally removed from his tooth and his mind free to absorb his surroundings, even he wanted to be out of there and fast.

"*We are already short on time looking for the person that killed our old man, we's got to be picky what jobs we's be taking.*" Ernest added, wishing that he had not postponed his search for the meeting.

"*You see, this is where I can help you.*" Paul interrupted. The fear he had once felt for these thugs had disappeared. He knew his time was running short anyway. Either William or his affliction would kill him, and soon. Smiling he continued. "*I want you to kill William Bailey. He was the one responsible for the fire at your pub. Yes, William. Dark William, soulless William, and a mistake he was but soon you'll clear it up.*" Paul said without any hint of humour. Ernest's brow wrinkled with obvious confusion.

"*He's already dead, vicar. That maggot Harold already had us go looking for him. Took us a few days to realise he was a dead man. Now if you tell us where Harold is, that might buy you a few more days breathing.*" Ernest asked, realising that if the priest was sending him after the same man Harold had, then there must have been some connection between them.

"*He is not dead. He should be, but he is not. You must find him, you must kill him.*" Paul begged as he watched Ernest and Neill exchange a glance. Oblivious to the insanity of his words, he wondered what the two thugs were thinking. "*Wait, this Harold, who is he?*" Paul asked, and with that question his story was tied too irreversibly to Paul's. Ernest told the vicar everything they knew about Harold. Paul did not want anyone to know what he had done in the catacombs and although at the time Harold still knew nothing, Paul's fear of being found out flooded over his already paranoid mind, like water over a weakened dam. "*This Harold should be dealt with too. Though in any way, no need to stab the chest, mortal men die easy. Sacellum made us weak. Ashamed of us, the creator was.*" Paul rambled.

"*Just what is your involvement in all this, vicar? Why do you want them both dead?*" Ernest asked. He was accustomed to people asking him to '*remove a problem*' but a vicar wanting two people dead was definitely an unusual situation.

"*Does it really matter to the likes of you?*" Paul asked bluntly. Ernest shrugged his huge shoulders. It didn't matter really, they wanted him dead anyway, and it seems that William was at fault also. How he faked his own death they had no idea but if he had then he really would be eating worms in no time.

"*All right, let's say a wunner' and we'll do it.*" Ernest said looking towards Neill who nodded, eager to get back onto the street.

"What do you mean a wunner?" Paul asked bemused. As crazy as he had become, Paul had never been part of Neeskmouth's shadier side until very recently.

"Sacellum, you work in a church but can't even speak Neeskmouthain. I want a hundred, fifty a head." Ernest said smiling. It was an expensive charge but he could tell the vicar was crazy and hoped this would mean he was dumb too.

"I don't have that kind of money." Paul replied, furious that the goons would not do it for free. After all, so much rested on his work did they not know what they could be part of?

"Then it doesn't get done, simple. Come on Neill let's get out of this bloody place. The smell is doing my nose in." Ernest said turning his back on Paul.

"Wait." The Reverend exclaimed. *"Take the cross."* He offered, defeated. Paul needed someone to take care of William and if he had to pay, then so be it. The solid gold cross was a symbol of the Sacellum religion its four points marked the four ancient powers of the universe that the creator used to make the world and its finish represented the gold city in the skies. It was engraved with seven symbols each referring to one of the locks put in place to keep the spirit realm separate from the mortal realm and should have held value to Paul far more than it's worth in coin but he had long since lost his faith.

Ernest turned back to face Paul. He was sure he should have understood what the priest had said but it didn't make much sense as a statement on its own.

"What?" Ernest asked as he looked towards Neill to see if he had understood, it was a long shot at best and Neill just shrugged. *"What the hell are you on about now priest?"* Ernest added.

"Take the cross from upstairs, its gold. That will cover the cost and I won't tell the guard it's even missing." It would only be days before someone visited the church and noticed the cross was missing, but by the time they did and called the constables it would be too late. The O'Brien's would have already found a buyer for the relic. With the fear of the demon Rinwid sitting out by Briers Hill the nobles would pay a king's ransom for something meant to keep it at bay.

"Neill, you reckon you know anyone that would be interested in that?" Ernest asked and Neill nodded. *"Well then vicar. You better start digging two graves."* Ernest said.

Chapter 14: A Final Goodbye to Faith

Unbeknown to them, Ernest and Neill left Paul alone in the dark to face his worst fears. He knew that his time had run out. A convulsion rattled through his aged and scrawny chest forcing him to his knees as if to reinforce the conclusion. His bones clanged against the cold cobble slabs and the sharp pain that flared through his arthritis-ridden knee was nothing compared to the burn that engulfed his lungs. He pressed deeply into the stone floor with his hands, both for balance and to try to relieve some of the pressure growing inside him. Suddenly, Paul began clasping his face as the source of the pain erupted like a volcano charging for his mouth. The hacking cough that escaped sliced at his throat, adding a third agonising discomfort.

Frozen in place while he wheezed for breath, Paul thought back to a year ago when the doctors told him he had a pox on his chest. They had told him that it was just a chemical imbalance, that they could cure it. They had tried bloodletting, for which Paul still carried the scars across his wrists and lower arms. When the knives had not cured it they turned to leeches but it was useless and had not worked. The only other choice offered to Paul from his low-paid practitioner was to cut the sickness from him. Being no expert on biology, Paul still had enough savvy to know that cutting his lungs to shreds would kill him. He had begun to pray, spending almost every free hour at the chapel altar begging for salvation. When it didn't come, Paul had given up hope and in his defeat he turned to the bishop asking to travel to colonies, hoping that spreading God's word might be his final salvation. His wish granted, he had boarded a ship for The Dark Gulf. Instead of his finding a new lease of life from his God, Paul found only more heartache.

During his crusade through the colonies, his sickness began to worsen. At first phlegm had been the main problem but that was soon followed by a shortness of breath. He was so thankful that he had found the secrets of the Rakta Ishvara while in the temple, and had left the village as fast as he could, returning to the city of his birth to work on a cure before this devil's curse took his life. As Paul sat cradling himself in his arms looking at the blood splattered floor, he knew that his time was running out.

The work had been a failure to start with and was still not a total success, with William wreaking havoc on the streets. Paul had wanted to remove the need for feeding on fresh blood before he took the leech to himself but he no longer had a choice. Snapped back to the present by another minor chest murmur, Paul wiped his watering eyes, forced himself to his feet and, ignoring the agony that twisted every inch of his body, he made for the table. Because of his tests, Paul knew that by digesting enough of the Abrus herb he could take the parasite and have a few days before it took over completely. He just had to hope that it would be enough time to find the cure. It would have to be as he didn't have enough time for doubts. He grasped the porcelain jar containing the herb, and began to eat, sparing not a morsel. Once the last of the Abrus leafs were forced down his sore throat, Paul took the tongs and removed the little black Rakta which began to wriggle excitedly at the promise of a new host. Paul closed his eyes tight and let the leech sink its hooking claws into his skin. The pain was excruciating and he soon slumped to the floor again, this time falling unconscious. When he awoke a new beast would stalk the streets of Neeskmouth.

Chapter 15: Papers and Guard Reports

While Paul was becoming the second Rakta Ishvara to plague Neeskmouth, Harold awoke early. He left the house while Muriel was still asleep upstairs, his plan being to find a paperboy selling the Times before the guard had even slept off their hangovers. The wind outside was the coldest yet and the clouds threatened something worse than the downpours Harold had grown used to in the past couple of weeks. Their fluffy outer edges and the yellow colour promised snow. Hoping it would hold off until he was back at Muriel's house, Harold walked past the few other early risers and beggars, the tall stone buildings helping to shelter him from the harshest of the winds. The beggars had lit fires burning whatever rubbish they could find in the streets to stave off the cold and huddled around them like flies around a dung pile. Above him, Harold could hear the wind testing the tallest structures, nature battling against man. As Harold walked below he half prayed the wind would send them toppling down onto him, an easy escape from what Harold imagined he would soon be facing, but the huge stone buildings had survived two wars with the Dragons, and the occupation of the city, and it would take more than a strong wind to uproot them.

His daydreams occupied him and it was not long before Harold found a young boy selling papers from within the archway of a closed bakers. He did not call out as normal, no banter, and no shouts in his pre-teen voice of what news had befallen the city. It seemed to Harold that the bitter cold had managed to curb his vigour for selling the few sheets of print, even with the residual heat escaping from the cooling stoves inside. When Harold dropped the tuppence into the boy's hand, he muttered out with frozen thanks and stuck a rolled up copy of the paper into Harold's free hand. Harold left him to his statue-like vigil over Meadow Road and walked to a secluded side street close by. Shadowed and sheltered from the bitter cold, his only company a couple of pigeons roosting above him, and a rather grumpy and defiant looking rodent sat cleaning its tail on the spokes of a carts wheel, Harold began to flick through the pages taking in the details of William's latest victims.

There had been another two prostitutes found dead, the number of dead already creeping into dozens. Nothing else seemed important at first glance. There was a poorly printed picture of John Johnson, the lord mayor of Neeskmouth harbour and a puppet to Malcolm Benedict. The article beside it went on to explain how he had been proud to open Waters-edge barracks. Neeskmouth seemed to be moving so fast it had left Harold behind. His family's little summer cottage seemed like a different world and Harold pined for it so much. Disheartened, he crumpled the paper under his arm and made to return to Muriel's house. Still being no closer to finding William, Harold had but one choice left. Harold had to read the guard record of the case and for that, Harold would need Muriel's help. He'd hoped that the morning papers would have some magic solution to avoid the obvious insanity of what he was going to do next.

Chapter 16: Laying Down the Plans

Harold arrived back at Muriel's home before ten o'clock. To his surprise she was awake and answered the door quickly. It was a surprise as neither of them had been sleeping properly. Harold had hoped she would have rested in until at least noon, to make up for the restless nights, and to ease the blackening bags that had begun to hang under her eyes like aged leather saddlebags on an old donkey's back.

"Where have you been? I've been worried." She said, before sliding aside slightly, just enough to tease, forcing him to press too close than was proper in order to get in again. Harold was sure it was on purpose this time. He felt a small warm caress of breath against his neck as Harold crab-walked his way past. Once free from the confines of the entrance, Harold turned and waved his paper at her.

"I was just getting this. I thought it might give me some clue as to where William is." Harold explained. Muriel shook her head and closed the door a little harder than necessary. The aged wood creaked under the sudden pressure before falling silent. If the woodworm lurking inside the damp maple could talk, they would have told Harold that she was not at all happy with his idea of going after William.

"You're still set on that idea, then?" She said cupping her hands and blowing into them to remove the chill that opening the front door had created.

"What choice do I really have?" Harold answered. The thought of the summerhouse flashed across his mind once more. He could always take Muriel with him, and then she would not even have to work again. Harold could look after her. He wanted to be more than friends. However, if he left with her, then it would leave his father and mother at William's mercy. He could not take the risk of the violent monstrosity that had devastated the guard wagon and the Queens and now countless poor lifeless girls across the city crossing paths with them. If William was left to roam the city and Harold had turned and run like the coward he felt he was, then he would never forgive himself and besides, someone had to protect the other poor working girls. Somehow, Harold had gone from being a junior tailor to a prostitute's hero overnight. He wondered, if he did vanquish this would-be demon or renegade mage whether he'd get his own statue in Celebration Square, but it did not take long for the image of the polished marble in his imagination to warp to an old man holding a knitting needle. The stone face warping to one of sadness and then of pain as the images of the guard wagon took over and Harold could taste his own blood.

William stood triumphant in front of Harold's cold lifeless face grinning. Harold shook himself from the daydream before the fear paralyzed him.

"Honestly Muriel I would rather not have to face down a cold blooded killer. I would much rather go back to working at my father's shop but someone has to do something and it seems I am the only one who knows who is really at fault. If I run the guard will still be looking for me and while they waste their time many more girls will end up dead." Harold voiced the explanation more for his benefit than Muriel's. Harold guessed that that is what really makes a hero. It is not someone who is unduly brave. It's not someone as strong as an ox and fearless, a warrior fighting down hordes of enemies. It isn't someone who travels the world making a name that kings will remember for generations to come. It isn't even someone the bards sing of. No, Harold knew, deep down inside, right there and then at that moment, that a hero is someone who having no choice does the right thing – regardless of how bloody idiotic it is.

"You have somewhere to go, if you were to run I mean?" Muriel asked and the question stumped Harold. The girl was quick; he had to give her that.

"Yes and no, but that's not the point. I have to do this." Harold said, trying to shrug off the question. He daren't say yes, if he told her about the summer house and she wanted to go with him. As scared as Harold was for the people of the city and his family Harold knew if she said she wanted to run away with him he would have gone in an instant. Muriel's strong demeanour returned and she began walking towards him. Harold wondered if she was as robust as she looked, or if it was a front she put on enabling her to cope with her lifestyle and the slander poured onto her by her clients. Muriel sighed, but beneath the frustration on her face, Harold could see she was glad he had not taken his chance to run away and had instead chosen to help her. As Harold seemed to at almost every moment he spent with her, he thought of what her story was and if anyone had been there to help Muriel before. He wondered if he was the first to show her kindness or whether her life had been a good one until something changed. He wanted to tell her he'd give his life to making her happy but he didn't know how to find the words.

"Come on, take a seat you're making the place look untidy." She said pulling out her chair around the table. Harold joined her, keeping his chair back so things weren't too cosy. Harold wanted nothing more than to cuddle up with her, to break down and cry against her shoulder but he had to be strong, if not for his sake then for hers.

"Thanks for not running away, Harry. I need you around." Muriel admitted, and the room fell silent. Before Harold had time to reply, not that he had any words to use, she continued. *"So what have you learnt from the paper?"* She said changing the subject and looking away, her gaze staring out of the window into the world outside. Harold knew she had spoken so quickly because she was not ready to hear the words they both knew would have followed. Harold needed her too, and she could tell, but instead of taking the chance to tell her how he felt they spoke of William and the damnable newspaper.

"Nothing much at all really it was a waste of time, but I had to try." Harold said, shrugging his shoulders. *"Oh, there was one thing. The Water's edge barracks are open."* Harold jested as it was the only thing he could remember from the whole paper, purely because of the balding fat faced lord that had stared out of the paper at him.

"So you think William's there?" Muriel said, as serious as a judge in response. Harold had no choice but to actually laugh aloud, something he had not done in weeks. It felt great and when Muriel realised her mistake and joined him with a giggle the world seemed to slow down and pause. Another spark for her fluttered through his heart and Harold saw her bite her lip gently. They sat in silence for a few moments, probably only seconds but with the tension between them it may as well have been hours.

"No, no I don't" Harold said with a smile. *"But I have an idea where I might find out."* Harold said, forced to re-focus. He wished things had been different and he had time to investigate the tension further, but he did not.

"Oh?" Muriel's brow wrinkled and sent a little line down her nose no bigger than the width of a penny's edge. It was the first time Harold had seen it and he instantly adored it. He really had become smitten.

Harold understood how silly it would have sounded if he had told anyone that he had fallen for her so quickly. Even crazier was the thought that she seemed to mirror his affections. It was the stress they both were going through, each second felt like days and they both knew that the end for them may be closer than ever. It made them shake off the normality of thought and let their hearts make the orders for their bodies to follow. It was instinctual, beyond the control of thought or logic. He knew he should not have spared a thought for loving her and should have been shocked and horrified by everything that had happened, but he wasn't. It helped to think that the growing feelings for each other kept them from having nothing but horror in their lives. If he didn't have Muriel to fight for then Harold could not see how he would have kept his sanity. No, it was love that kept him going. That love, that drive was what gave him the strength to say the words that came from his mouth next.

"*I need to break into the guard station. They'll have the case notes there.*" Harold explained. Muriel's face dropped. She blinked a couple of times and her mouth fell open, as a fish starved of water.

"*Are you mad?*" She asked, leaning forward in her chair. If they had had the money for strong drink, Harold was sure she would have downed the bottle at that point.

"*It's the only way and I need your help.*" Harold said, hating himself for having to ask, but he had no idea how he could manage it alone. The same guppy-like expression mixed with one of anxiety occupied Muriel's face for a while before she relaxed into the strong woman Harold had come to know. The fire that drove her forward blazed and she spoke with a refreshed determination that still shocked him.

"*What do you need?*" She asked coolly. She really did amaze him with just how quickly she adapted to any situation and Harold almost felt embarrassed at how weak he seemed in comparison.

"*I don't know yet. We need to get inside the station somehow and read the reports.*" Harold said, feeling a little foolish that he didn't actually have a plan on how to achieve it.

"*For Sacellum sake, Harry, this is madness!*" Muriel exclaimed and she was right. Harold had never paid much attention to the guard station and had no idea of how to break in, or where to go once he succeeded.

"*Madness or not, I have to do it. Will you help?*" He said and to his relief Muriel nodded in reply. Together they spent the day sat at the table, making plans to get into the station.

Chapter 17: Thieves and Brigands

His savings wearing thin, and the trip into the market more risky than it was worth, had meant only two pots of tea and a whole day later they had come up with a plan. It was risky but they thought it would work, although it relied heavily on the incompetence of the city guard. During their discussions Harold remembered they had taken in an order by a junior constable a couple of days before everything had gone so very wrong. He had been around the same build as Harold, maybe a little fatter but with a few quick adjustments his uniform would fit him. Harold left Muriel's almost straightaway to begin work on it. While Harold hid in the back of the tailor's shop, busily amending the uniform, Muriel was, much to his disgust, out working the streets. It was risky and Harold hated the idea of it, but at least she was not in it for her normal few pence. She was after a guard officer, or his badge to be exact. They met back at hers around noon and she had been successful in getting the brass shoulder buckles from the officer's uniform. Harold did his best not to think of how she did it. Harold changed quickly, pulling the whole uniform together. The long blue coat, crisp and firm around him, its brass buttons done up to the neck. The shoulder pieces slipped under the lapels on his shoulders. Harold reached for his top hat from his bag of belongings and was ready to go. The plan was simple, Harold would pretend to be a guard officer and Muriel would play herself. They would simply walk straight in the front doors and head towards the cells. Once out of sight of the officer on the front desk, they would then begin looking for the files.

The walk to Donkey Road Courthouse did not take long. They made their way quickly from Muriel's house on the Knoll, past the candle maker's and pawnbrokers out onto Trade Road. It was still bitterly cold and Muriel shivered as they walked. How Harold wanted to put his arm around her to keep her warm but he fought his feelings. She tried to press into him a few times but Harold had to remain in character as they approached the station. They could not risk someone seeing through their disguise. His palms began to sweat with nerves. Muriel must have sensed it and turned to him taking his hand.

"It'll be all right." She whispered shooting him one of her smiles. It warmed him slightly and gave him the determination Harold needed. He nodded back to her, pulled his shoulders back, muscles tight and standing tall and determined they made their way inside. The inside of the station was bare and the floor and walls shared the same grey coat of matching plaster as half the city seemed to. They walked

quickly and all was going well. A few more steps and they would make it to the first door. Harold's hand twitched, eager to grasp the door handle and step inside the corridor that led to the cells. With barely a step remaining, Harold pushed his hand out, shakily reaching for the small latch when from behind his desk to his left a fat balding old man who seemed to be bursting from his uniform called out.

"*Hey.*" Was all he said but Harold's heart sank and his stomach leapt. Harold turned as calmly as he could and put a smile across his face. The fat officer sat down behind a rather shoddy looking desk. Its top was covered with papers, most of them having stains from teacups across their tops. A sickly plant with huge leaves sat next to the desk, adding only a little colour to the mass of grey. The room reminded Harold a little of the hospital ward in which he had woken up, but somehow this place was even more depressing, if that was possible.

"*What?*" Harold asked trying to sound calm and like he had every right to be there.

"*I haven't seen you before, what you doing here?*" The fat man said and got up from behind his desk and began to slide around it. Harold could see the wooden rattle tucked into his belt at his side ready to call for assistance. He had not bothered reaching for that though, and Harold noticed the truncheon in his hands. Harold had to think fast if he wanted to keep his teeth.

"*I'm just bringing this girl in.*" Harold said trying hard to sound like a city guard. "*I caught her trying to lift some meat from the butcher's.*" The lie sounded convincing, but Harold did not risk a mental pat on the back just yet.

"*You don't work here, what's your game?*" The old officer said, sideling up towards him. Harold saw him flexing his knuckles as he got a good grip on the truncation.

"*What? You mean this serf doesn't even work here?*" Muriel suddenly interrupted, a look full of anger flashing across her eyes. She tried to break free of his grasp with such force Harold actually had to pull back hard, the sudden jolt marking her wrists. She let out a whimper and Harold was amazed at how well she acted.

"*You better start talking lad.*" The fat man said stalking towards him. Harold knew that if the walrus-looking man brought that truncheon down on him, it would hit him hard and Harold would probably wake up in one of the cells, missing a few teeth and with a headache worse than any hangover he had ever experienced.

"All right, I don't work here but my brother does." Harold said his brain cheering at its own ingenuity. It worked. Harold confused the real officer, which bought him time to think and luckily time to remember the name of the young officer whose suit Harold was wearing. *"Frederick Swenson. You must know him."* Harold waited, trying his best to look expectant.

"Yeah, I know him" The officer replied. *"It doesn't tell me why you're here though, does it?"* He lowered the truncheon and it looked like his plan was working. Harold grinned and stepped towards him, his confidence growing.

"If you know him, it should do." Harold said, with a small chuckle. *"He was out last night and is a little unwell today. In fact, he is pig sick. You could smell him halfway down the hall this morning. He didn't want the sergeant giving him another ear-full so asked him if I would come in for him. You know, so his beat would still get walked and that, and I thought, what the hell, always good to have your brother owing you a favour right?"* Harold said, releasing his inner thespian.

"Yeah, I saw Fred leave here last night talking about going somewhere. You know, the sergeant is going to kill him if he finds out. He's already on his last warning after getting caught in the alley behind the bell with one of O'Brien's tarts." The old man's face melted and he actually looked somewhat jolly. Harold could imagine he would have many stories to tell if Harold had the time to listen.

"He won't unless you tell him, right?" Harold said, still in awe that this was working.

"You tell your brother he owes me a brew – actually make that two." The fat man said with a laugh. *"If you're anything like your brother I bet your collar here isn't coming in for stealing a bit of meat. Go on, what did she give you? Bite you when you said you weren't paying?"*

"Yeah, something like that, but don't tell him. It will please him no end. Come on you." Harold said, tugging on Muriel's wrist and leading her away.

Harold did not relax until the door closed behind them and they had walked halfway down the corridor. Harold was glad to let go of Muriel's wrist, still feeling bad that he'd had to man-handle her.

"You were great." She whispered, giving him a quick kiss him on the cheek in her excitement and Harold felt instantly proud.

"Thanks for buying me time back there. I couldn't have done it without you." Harold replied, holding his cheek.

"Come on, the files room should be just up here. If we get out of here alive and without cuffs I'll give you another kiss." She said with a giggle and Harold could tell his face must have turned a strong shade of red.

The filing room was just as Harold expected it to be, dark and filled with cobwebs and dust. A corridor between the bookshelves ran from the main door down to the far wall. Scattered about on the floor were wooden crates containing what he guessed to be the older files. There were no candles in the room and the darkness felt chokingly close and coated everything in a palette of greyscale. While Muriel held the solid door open, just enough to let in what little light there was in the main corridor; Harold pressed forward, his eyes trying their best to scan the small-carved letters under each shelf. His heart leapt, beating against his ribcage as from down the hall, Harold heard a man's voice shout out. Harold froze watching as the dust fell from the shelves. Breathing deeply, he realised the shout had come from one of the convicts in a cell and not from the guards.

"Any luck?" Muriel whispered from the open doorway and Harold shook his head, a pointless motion in the dark.

"No." He whispered back. Harold could barely see more than an inch or so in front of his nose and paranoia began to play with him. Harold could not help but feel that some unknown shadow, something lurking in the dark, was watching him. It was a stupid idea but one that all humans shared. A sudden squeak as his foot hit something small and fluffy followed by the sound of tiny feet running for cover exposed his stalker. A rat scrambled under one of the nearby bookcases. Harold had no idea why he followed the rat's path, maybe out of frustration for the shock it gave him. Harold wanted to kick the little blighter, so he followed it. Harold stopped once he reached the bookshelf where the rat had made its escape. Harold could see two shiny orbs glowing back out from under it, watching him. His eyes squinted upon the plaque at eye level. It was either the letter 'r' to 'u' or 's' to 'v', Harold really could not tell in the darkness but either way this was the rack Harold needed. Harold couldn't help but feel like somehow the rat had meant for him to find this shelf.

Harold used his finger to run across the bound files feeling for dust, until he came to one that felt crisp and new. Harold pulled it free, being careful not to knock any of the other files to the floor. They were not far from the main reception, and any noise could bring that aged, but well built, officer running from behind his desk to investigate. Harold carefully made his way back towards Muriel, doing his best to avoid the litter of crates on the floor and leaving the rat to its solitude.

"You got it?" Muriel asked, obviously eager to get out of the place.

"*I think so.*" Harold said glancing down at the file in his hands. In the slit of light from the door Harold could make out the word 'Spinks'. This was indeed his file. "*Yeah this is it.*" He added. With the file now in his hands it then occurred to him that in their rush to get in and acquire the file, neither Muriel nor Harold had actually thought about how they would get out of the station unchallenged.

Chapter 18: Some Strength Never Dies

While Muriel and Harold were trying to think of a way to escape Donkey Road guard station the O'Brien boys had begun closing the noose around the neck of everything he held dear, or so they thought. The two thugs stood on his family's doorstep. They had already knocked and no one had answered. His mother was upstairs writing in her journal and peaking through the upstairs window; careful not to let the light from her candle escape the gap between the curtains as she peered out. She did not dare open the door with his father in such a weakened state. It is quite funny that even with the sheltered life his mother led; the harshness of the streets of the common district had seeped its way into her heart and worried her terribly. She was right not to open the door though, and if only his father had fitted a new lock as he had planned, things may have been so different. A second knock yielded no answer so Ernest pulled a river trader knife, the ones with the curly maple handles and thick blade almost like a butcher's cleaver, from his pocket and rammed it in to the split between the door and frame. He knew just how to pop it open from his years of brutal debt collection and enforcement for his deceased father. The old lock gave way within seconds under the thugs' strength and the door fell open.

Harold's father was asleep in his chair, slippers on and smoking jacket wrapped around him tightly. He was unaware as the two thugs stampeded into their home. Ernest made straight for the stairs while barking an order for Neill to check downstairs. Ernest checked the upper rooms finding Harold's mother and grabbing her quickly he bound her hands, gagged her, and tied her to the bed. She couldn't put up much of a fight, she was well into her fifties and not able to even dent Ernest's assault. She screamed out for help through the poorly tied gag but with the degradation of the city, a women screaming for help during the cold of night had become all too common and anyone who heard it allowed her screams to fall on deaf ears.

Ernest went back downstairs to join Neill, leaving Harold's mother tied to the bed panic ridden, listening to what evolved on the ground floor below. His father awoke to see Neill standing in the lounge, knife in his hand. The house was old and echoed like the acoustics from one of the theatres as the aged and dampened beams readied for what was about to happen.

"Where is he?" Neill demanded, not taking his eyes of the old man in front of him. There had been a little bit of doubt in his heart if

they had the right house when they first arrived but the old man looked so much like Harold, it had to be his father. Harold's father ignored the question as he had a fair few of his own that he wanted answered first.

"Who are you, what are you doing in my home?" He challenged, trying to push himself up out of his chair. Adrenaline surged through his body making his vision blur and his heart race.

"Look, old man, just tells us where Harold is." Ernest said from the doorway. Harold's father was a strong and stubborn man and the mention of his son's name seemed to infuriate him even further. He reached for the iron fire poker, which he kept close to his chair during the colder parts of the year. Grasping it like a Polearm his father swung it with the strength Harold always imagined he wielded during the battle for Neeskmouth some twenty eight years before. It struck Neill, who had been standing just in front of what used to be Harold's chair. For a big set man Neill's sharp scream sounded more like that of a wounded child at the first successful blow. The iron poker cut through flesh sending a spray of blood across the fabric of Harold's chair and splattering up the wall. It followed the sound of metal clattering against the ground as the knife fell away from Neill's fractured wrist to the floor. As resilient a thug as Neill was, this bone breaking blow made him recoil in agony and Harold's father swung again not missing his chance to get the upper hand in battle. It had been years since he disregarded his title as one of the Pole, but he had not forgotten the art of battle. Rage filled his body as Harold's father pushed the brutes back out into the corridor.

"Ernest." Neill called out, ducking under another swing of the poker. Harold's father swung repeatedly even through flu-ridden limbs. The table was sent flying with a kick from his aged foot and smashed against Neill's leg, closely followed by his father's stripy escaped slipper.

"What the hell?" Ernest exclaimed, finding himself forced back up two or three stairs before he fell onto his back as the deranged old man with the iron weapon swung it madly in his direction. It sliced at his cheek, digging in deep and sending a spray of Drow blood against the wooden railing that crawled up the stairway. The power of his swing sent his father stumbling forward, and with a push from Ernest as he stepped aside, Harold's father ended up face first on the stairs above the injured Drow. Ernest took his chance and scrambled on all fours like a dog towards the open front door and fled into the street leaving a trail of dripping blood from the wound on his cheek all the way.

Neill had been left alone to face the aged Pole. It was then his father made his mistake. He turned to the open doorway to face the fleeing Ernest while struggling to stifle a cough as he got up from his knees. The temptation to chase him would have been strong, but the sickness rapidly drained the surge of adrenaline that had brought his father to his feet. Neill seized his chance and leapt from the lounge elbowing Harold's father hard in the chest with his good arm. His father fell, crashing to the floor once more and he could only watch as Neill escaped in pursuit of Ernest. It was not like the old days when a blow like that would have taken moments to recover from. Harold's father did not know how long he lay there before he managed to get to his feet and close the door but it seemed like an age. The sickness left him fragile and the blow to his chest would have loosened the phlegm that clogged his lungs. After whatever wait his father needed to regain his composure he got up and closed the door, noticing that the lock was broken. It would remain so until Harold visited again. His father, weak as he was and coughing terribly, struggled up the stairs gasping for air as he went to free his wife. Together they sat on the bed in each other's arms, his mother shaking and sobbing heavily, the trauma of the attack had broken the mask she had worn to hide the sorrow of his father's sickness. She had been crying so hard that she had not even noticed when his father fell asleep. In his weakened state, it had taken everything he had to put up a fight against the intruders.

Chapter 19: Jailbreak

While his mother and father lay in bed recovering from the attack, Harold had sat in the dark confines of the storeroom for too long. The officer on the front desk must have been growing more and more suspicious of his delay in the station. After all, how long did it take to put a woman in a cell? The only reason they'd been left alone is that he suspected him to be bedding Muriel. However, the officer whose brother Harold was pretending to be, could come back at any time, so they needed to think of a way out, and quickly. The way they came in was out of the question. Harold could have easily walked out alone, but that would leave Muriel stuck inside and if they went out together then the guard would know something was up. Although Harold could probably overpower the guard if he needed to, it was not a guarantee. They had to think of another way. There was no back door for them to use, and the few windows on the floor all belonged to holding cells and had large bars across them. If Harold could get outside on his own somehow then he could get a cart from somewhere and pull the bars from a window, like he had read in the story books at school. But that was unlikely to work – the noise would alert every officer in the building and Harold was still trying to prove his innocence, not confirm his guilt. That left only one choice. The second floor windows did not have bars. Harold would have to walk outside leaving Muriel with the documents and catch her as she jumped out.

"Muriel, I've thought of a way to get you out." Harold whispered in the darkness of the storeroom door, hoping not to horrify her with his suggestion.

"How's that then?" Muriel asked. Harold could sense an edge of doubt in her voice. Her resolve was weakening and he hoped she would not break when he told her his idea.

"The windows on the next floor are not barred. You could jump out and I'll catch you from outside." He said, but could tell from the look on her face she did not like his idea. They were not given time to discuss it, as from the reception room they heard the voice of the guard.

"Hey Fred, you finally got over your hangover, then?" The old guard said and Harold did not wait for the other officer to reply. He grabbed hold of Muriel's arm and made for the stairs. They heard the sound of the wooden rattle coming from the main entrance, as the officer called for reinforcements to subdue the would-be infiltrators. Its click clack sound was so loud it could be heard over the sound of the pair's shoes

clattering on the hard stone floor. The sound of their footsteps would give them away but they did not have time to creep.

Harold cleared the steps two at a time dragging Muriel behind him. He thought afterwards that they seemed to have gone full circle. She had saved him when she had dragged him down the side alley and away from danger. Now Harold was returning the favour, the only difference was that he had brought her into danger in the first place. She should not be involved in any of this. At the top of the stairs Harold heard a door fly open below them and the sound of footsteps moving swiftly in pursuit. They had to hide and fast. Harold darted into the first room on the right, shutting the door as quietly as he could. The room they ran into was well-decorated with deep blue wallpaper and a thick carpet covering the floor. There was a well-crafted desk in its centre facing the door and a bookshelf built of solid oak close by. It looked aged and must have been a relic from before the war. Thankfully, the room was void of life. Harold did not waste the sudden luck they'd been granted and let go of Muriel and darted for the desk, leaping over it and scattering papers in his wake. It was heavy but Harold begun pushing it towards the door. Muriel caught on fast and came around to help him, her tiny arms shaking with the effort of sliding it across the deep carpet that began to bundle in waves. The bookcase came next. Harold could move that alone. He dropped it on top of the desk scattering guard records across the floor like leaves in autumn. The doorway was now completely blocked. Muriel had brought across the chair and was jamming it against the handle of the door, arching it across the top of the desk. It would buy them time, but not long with the gathering number of officers the rattle had called. Panting Harold made his way to the window, the glass would not open and Harold had to break it. He brought his foot up into the corner of the window and it shattered instantly, sending down an array of sharp fragments to the ground below. Harold turned, pulling the documents from his pocket. With his back to the window, Harold gave them to Muriel.

"*Here, hold these.*" Harold said, passing them over his hands shaking with fright.

"*What are you doing?*" She asked as she took the documents from him.

"*I'm going to have to climb down.*" Harold said. "*Once I'm out then you jump down to me.*" Harold did not give her time to argue. It was another occasion where if she had said 'no' to him, Harold would have lost his nerve. He was scared enough, and as he started to climb out of the window, learnt quickly he wasn't a fan of heights either. Harold did not need much talking out of it, but he knew they had no other choice. He stepped out on to the small seal around the window, slowly lowering himself down until he was hanging by his fingertips, his toes desperately seeking a crevice within the brickwork to balance him. It took only a few seconds for his fingers to feel tired and start to ache as he began to edge down the wall.

As he slid lower, the upper ledge of the barred window below became his podium. Harold could not climb down any further and envied the spider in his father's shop, not for the first time. It would have made the descent look easy. Harold kicked off from the wall and dropped towards the floor, hoping to catch the ledge below as he fell. A crowd had already gathered outside the station, watching the entertainment of one of the Rinwidian cultists many rants about the end of days. Harold was thankful that the spectacle drew enough attention that no one noticed him clambering down the building like a wounded fly.

The Rinwidian cultists had sprung up not long after the shadow demons had first been seen in Briers Hill. They spent their time bellowing at the top of their lungs how the end was coming and to repent their lives back to the rightful ruler of Valadfar, the demon Rinwid. As their numbers seemed to have grown they had taken to organizing and were now almost famed for their blackened robes and the god-awful smell that followed them around. For some reason, which Harold did not have time to think on as his fingers were growing ever more tired; the cultists had taken to wearing the rotten heads of Smooth-hounds around their necks. The dead fish symbolized to them the power and rancidness of their demon god. The practice of the cultists was illegal and so the guards turned a blind eye when the peasant folk stoned them or beat them mercilessly in the streets, so whenever one started preaching it always gathered a crowd eager to either join in on the assault or watch it. The cultist drawing everyone's attention stopped the calls that would have come otherwise and alerted the guards of Harold's escape.

His legs hit the ground and his knees buckled, casting him down on his rump. His backside bruised instantly but, other than that, Harold was not injured. He pulled himself to his feet ignoring the chorus of accusations from the crowd who still hadn't noticed him, and readied himself to catch Muriel. She was already hanging over the ledge and dropped quickly. Harold held his breath as she sailed through the cold air and did not breathe again until he closed his arms tightly around her. It is a strange thing that can happen to you even in the turmoil of the worst of moments. With Muriel pressed tightly against him, time seemed to stand still. Harold could feel her heart beating rapidly. The warmth of her body returned blood to his chilled fingers, and Harold held her, savouring the moment. Their eyes met and Harold knew Muriel could read his thoughts. He knew that he had been falling for her, and now she had literally fallen into his arms. Harold did not want the moment to end but the world snapped back at the sound of the guard calling out from the window above them. Two tiny heads poked out glaring down, before disappearing back inside. The pair knew they would be coming down for them so they began running again, pushing past the crowd and disappearing off into the streets of Neeskmouth. As they ran, Muriel reached for Harold's hand once more.

Interlude 3: Of all the luck

Dante couldn't believe his misfortune. In the last few days he had escaped a fire with only a few scorched hairs. Dodged rat catchers, dogs, cats and the creator only knows what else as he made his way back and forth across the city. He'd scrambled across the cobbled streets, in and out of houses, explored the sewers and the rooftops as he tried to make his way to the harbour. He'd come close to getting there a few times, even hitching rides on the underside of horse and carts, but somehow something kept getting in his way. It was like fate didn't want him to make it back to the ship he so desperately sought and now to top it all off; he sat in a damp cell trapped under a tin bedpan.

He'd been happily sitting in the dark chewing the edges of a rather tasty paper folder when some big footed moron had stumbled in and kicked him. Dante really couldn't understand why humans had so much paper neatly pressed into files when they could just as easily tear it up and make a nice comfy bed out of it. Regardless, Dante had taken off on his toes again and hidden under a bookcase until all hell had let loose and the noise of the wooden rattle had sent him scrambling through a hole in the wall, which had led him into the predicament he was now in. The bedpan had come down so fast Dante didn't have time to avoid it, and to make it worse, it had trapped his tail outside of it.

Dante didn't know it, but the strong smell of ammonia that burnt his tiny nose hairs belonged to that of William Boatswain, who was the once famous pirate king and governor of Neeskmouth after the last war. William had lead the city during its gold age and should have retired gracefully back to the White Isle when his governorship failed, and that is what most people thought happened to him. The truth was much darker than that, and showed just how far Malcolm Benedict would go to ensure he remained in power. It had been years since William had seen the outside world and he had readied himself, not for the first time in his life, to die in prison. The reason he'd trapped the little rat was a simple one. William had torn off a corner of his sheet and written a letter using the charred edge of a fragment of wick from a candle in the hall, and the rat Dante would be his unwilling postman. William knew it was a one in a billion shot that anyone would see the letter tied to the rat's tail, and even more desperately crazy was the idea that it might even end up getting to, the person it was meant to but he had to try. He'd never managed to tell her.

The letter was to his daughter, Erin. The string tied tight, William pulled the bedpan up and, just like that Dante was gone scooting back out through the hole he'd entered the cell through, leaving William to his unjustified fate. Back inside the dark storage room, Dante sniffed at the letter attached to his tail. He'd chew the strings and get that off just as soon as he was somewhere safe, for now he had to get back out of that place and into the streets.

Chapter 20: A Safe House

Harold and Muriel ran most of the way from the guard station back to Muriel's and by the time they got there they were both exhausted. They stopped only to have a hushed conversation on the corner of Trade Road amidst the potent smell of candle wax.

"Muriel." He gasped. *"You get back to yours. Wait for me until the sun sets. Give me the files and I'll take them somewhere safe."*

"Where is safer than mine? No one would connect the two of us, Harry. No one even knows we've spoken." Muriel said, afraid to be alone on the way home.

"The guards might have followed us. If they have they'll be after me. I don't want to lead them back to yours. Please trust me." Harold said and reluctantly Muriel handed over the bundled file. Muriel would go home and Harold would return after dark. Muriel grabbed Harold and pulled him in close, closing her arms around him. The embrace only lasted a second, and then she was gone, heading off into the distance leaving Harold to watch her walk away.

He had to store the documents somewhere safe and have time to read them. Harold didn't want to take them to Muriel's. Giving him only a minute or two to gather his breath Harold began running again towards the shop. It would be a perfect hideaway and Harold was confident that it would take some time before the guard even realised what was taken and connected it with him. The run there did not take that long, but the temperature had plummeted and snow had begun to fall, only a flutter for now but it threatened to get heavier before the day was through. By the time Harold made it to East Street, his lungs burned with an icy chill and his legs felt as if someone had coated them in molten bronze that was rapidly solidifying.

To his surprise the shop was open, and it was only then Harold remembered that Janet's boy was watching the store. Charles had dusted down the shop and evicted the spider. The distinctive smell of bleach filled the air and mixed with that of fresh cotton. Charles had made a start on the late order of uniforms and from the potent smells; Harold knew he was in the process of bleaching them. Harold went towards the back of the shop and through a small-bricked arch into the private working area and found Charles in the back workshop. It was not large being only big enough to house one loom, the bleaching bucket and the racks of different cloths and spools.

"Good evening, Charles." Harold said trying to sound as normal as he could. Charles jumped slightly, dropping the needle he was

holding into his lap. He was obviously not aware Harold had walked in. That was one aspect of his trade Harold enjoyed. The time you had to spend working alone and uninterrupted in dull light always gave him plenty of time to daydream.

"All right boss, I'm about mid way through this order for you. Won't be done on time, but it'll be done." Charles said. Harold knew the young lad was hoping to earn a few extra coins and maybe even an apprenticeship with them. His work was of good quality and he was fast too. Had things been different Harold might well have offered him the work, but things were far too confused now to involve the poor boy.

"Actually Charles I'll be taking over now so you can go home. That is some great work though. If you ever fancy yourself some extra coin feel free to pop in, but not for a few weeks. I have a lot to sort out." Harold hoped he could get him away from the shop without the need to explain what was going on. Charles was a poorly educated boy and Harold doubted he had read the paper any time this week. If he had, then he might have run off to the guard and told them where to find him.

"Are you sure? I was told I would be working at least a week and to be honest Harry, I could use the money." Charles replied putting down the garment he had been working on. Feeling sorry for him, Harold rummaged in his pocket and found two small pound coins. That should cover his week's wages and maybe a little on top.

"Here, take this. Do us a favour, though, on your way home. Go see if my mother needs any help around the house. My father's not well as you know." Harold said with a smile. Some people did not like Charles as he had the kind of eyes that never seemed to blink and his slurred and slow speech made him seem very simple, but he was a good lad really, it was just that his mother and father knew each other a little too well.

"Yeah, right you are boss. Should I finish this lot I've started first?" He asked with genuine concern.

"No need, go on now, get." Harold flicked his thumb towards the door and Charles seemed to take note nodding his head.

Harold followed him to the front door and slid the bolt, sealing himself from the outside world. With one final glance up the street Harold made sure he was alone. No one appeared to have followed him and with the snow now falling in a blizzard, the guard would, Harold hoped, be heading either to the warmth of the station or the local taverns. Harold had snuffed the candles in the front of the shop and in the quickly darkening day, it looked deserted, achieving his aim. Harold pulled the guard reports open on his lap and started to read:

On the night of 16th Thresh, an arson attack upon the Queens tavern razed it to the ground, in which a currently untold number of people lost their lives. Officer Bradley was first on the scene and confirmed it to be an arson attack and possibly a counter attack to a gang war between the lower classes. Witnesses confirm that a male they now know to be Harold Spinks had been loading something into the cellar moments before the fire started-

Harold flicked on through the section with the interviews at the hospital as it would not tell him anything he didn't already know. That is something you have to love about the guard force, some drunkard pointed his finger at him lying in the road unconscious, and instantly Harold was the criminal.

On the evening of 19th during transit to Paddington guard station, suspect Spinks along with, as witnesses confirmed, an accomplice as yet unknown, escaped from custody. The attack upon the guard transit was both brutal and fatal. Early reports from the mortuary confirm that the three officers were killed in a bestial way with bite marks being a primary cause of death -

The report went on to describe the bloody way in which the officers died mentioning how the attacker had somehow drained a large amount of their blood. It gave him no clues as to where William might be, but at least Harold knew they were looking for him too. Taking a deep breath to settle his rapidly twisting stomach, Harold continued reading:

On Dumon 22nd, Harold Spinks remains at large -

Harold was beginning to think the files would not give him any clues and reading the last extract from Dumon morning confirmed his suspicions. It told little more than the papers did about the killings of the prostitutes, containing little detail on how they died. It only served to confirm the images his mind had already conjured. There was no mention of anything happening since Dumon but Harold was sure there would have been more victims. At that moment, his only choice was to wait for William to strike again and hope he could track him down from there. Harold was still not sure if he could kill William. Harold had already decided at that point that he must be some kind of vampire, but he was real, not just a story written to scare people. Harold wondered if he should take heed from the stories and have to use a stake on William, carry garlic or wear a Brilanka cross. Harold hoped that he was human enough to die by some means, at least. He was a normal father and husband not so long ago, after all. Harold shook the confusion from his head, snuffed the last candle and made for the door.

It was dark outside and the snow had already settled to around an inch thick. The walk back to Muriel's would not be a pleasant one but at least it should be an uninterrupted one.

Chapter 21: Winter Wonderland

Leaving the documents stolen from the guard, along with the articles Harold had gathered from several newspapers, at his father's store he arrived back at Muriel's house late Mindmon night. Harold had already decided they would just have to wait for William to make the first move and had not enjoyed telling Muriel of his lack of success at finding anything new in the guard reports. She seemed to relax a little as if she had been hoping they wouldn't find anything. She hugged Harold again overjoyed that he had not been caught, and any doubt Harold had that Muriel was starting to feel for him too, faded. Harold still did not know if it was love or friendship though, so he had to wait. Even the solid stone floor with just a blanket to warm him could not stop him reminiscing of the closeness they shared. The night provided a well-needed break after the fatigue of the previous day and Harold fell into the limbo of sleep as soon as his head hit the pillow. However, he did not sleep well. Visions of William and his victims rolled over his slumbering mind and dragged him back to the waking world several times during the night. When morning finally came, the sight of settled snow filled him with some joy, as Harold knew the guard would calm their search while the weather was this bad. They would not want to leave the warmth of the taverns and that meant Harold could actually relax a little.

He was disturbed from his window-gazing by Muriel as she walked down the stairs behind him. She still wore that same summer dress and Harold then realised it must be the only clothing she possessed. Harold made a promise to himself that he would sort her out with some new garments once this was all over. It was not uncommon for the poorest to make do with rags and hand-me-downs but the weather in Neeska was far too bitter to get by with just one summer dress.

"*Good morning. What you looking at?*" She asked, rubbing the sleep from her eyes with a yawn. Her hair all entangled made her look like she'd been pulled through a hedge backwards but Harold couldn't help but find it cute.

"*The snow's settled.*" Harold said. "*I was thinking of going for a walk.*" He added and Muriel's eyes lit up and a childish glow ran across her young face that Harold had not seen before.

"*I love the snow, can I come with you?*" She asked playfully. Harold liked the thought that it was because he was with her that she was able to enjoy the turn in the weather rather than having to work the streets in its blistering cold. She had only had to service one man since he had met her. Even before his feelings for her had flourished Harold had wanted to keep her from prostitution and he'd done it. So why not enjoy a little time with her and have some playful fun in the gift of winter.

"Of course you can. We should be safe while the weather is like this, and we have to wait for William to make the news again, anyway. Do you have something a bit warmer to wear?" Harold asked not wanting her to freeze the moment they opened the door. The question seemed to pull hard on an emotion strong within Muriel and her happy expression flickered, just for a second, but Harold was beginning to notice the little cracks in her reserve.

"I'll be fine in this." She answered refusing to admit that it was her only frock. It was another thing that had seemed out of place for a working girl. Most would not have cared in the slightest about admitting something like that and again it made him wonder what her story was. Harold was sure she was no ordinary streetwalker. There was definitely more to Muriel than even his longing eyes could see.

"You want to borrow my coat? I have a spare in my case." Harold did not give her time to answer before he was reaching into his case pulling it free. Harold passed it to her and she put it on. He chuckled. She looked funny, her long red hair floating down over the collar of his jacket and the jacket itself almost reaching to her knees. Its width was almost twice that of her own and she pulled the belt tight, causing the tanned material to bulge.

"Thanks." She said struggling to get the wooden button through an eyehole with the sleeves trailing down over her hands.

"You look good." Harold jested pulling his own coat from the stand and fastening it up to the neck. Together they made their way out into the perfect winter wonderland.

The streets outside amazed him. They actually looked clean. A pure white blanket hid the filth and kept the beggars within the shop doorways. It made a pleasant change not to have them pestering them for spare change. Children playing in the snow replaced the normal streets that always seemed to be filled with sin of some kind. A snowman smiled at them from the centre of the road. It had stones for its eyes and one of the children's scarves around its neck. Muriel walked close to him and they wandered aimlessly around. They passed the giggles of happiness and for a moment Harold felt human again – not quite so washed out. The pigeons roosted up on the windows of the buildings and every now and again they would send down another flurry of loose snow. As they turned a corner, some children had upturned a cart onto its side and were using it as a fort for their snowball fight. A stray ball skimmed his shoulder and Muriel began giggling next to Harold. He bent down grabbing a clump of the white powder and tossed it back lightly at the kids, who scurried for cover behind their fortress. Meanwhile, Muriel had wandered away from him and scooped up a ball herself. She threw it and hit him in the chest. They joined in the game. Harold cannot remember how long they played but, by the end, his hands were frozen and he found himself coated in snow, Muriel was a good shot. The pale sun had grown high in the sky and Harold guessed it to be just after midday. It saddened him to know that within a few hours the streets would be bare again, but Harold had enjoyed himself enough. His time playing with Muriel will be something he would never forget. They laughed and joked all the way back to her home. She slipped her hand into his and ran her thumb against the inside of his palm. It was magic.

"*Harold, isn't it?*" A voice enquired, breaking the spell. Taking his hand from Muriel's, Harold turned, relieved to find it was just Janet, his mother's friend.

"*Yes, Janet what can I do for you?*" Harold thought she would be mad about him sending her son home, and readied himself for a sharp rebuke. Many a time as a child Janet had dragged him home by his ears to get a good hiding off his mother. Instead, she seemed to want the latest of the gossip and started to interrogate him.

"*I saw the guard at your parents earlier today, what's happening?*" She asked bluntly as her eyes took in Muriel. It would be more gossip for her to spread around the church group next Dumon.

"*I don't know.*" Harold answered truthfully, knowing that he would have to sneak back and check on his parents. It was a shame to cut short a perfect day, but Harold had to make sure they were alright. He had managed to fool himself for a few hours that things could be better than they were but the dream had to end and he had to go to them.

Chapter 22: Death and Love

Excusing himself from Janet's company as swiftly as he could, Harold made his way to his father's house alone. His mind fighting hard to try and ignore the foreboding he felt. The beauty of the streets had melted into a black sludge that washed through the gutters turning his mood worse. As Harold approached the house he noticed the door was open and the doctor's horse-drawn cart sat outside. The fear for his family over powered his caution and not caring if the guard were there or not, Harold quickened his step and forced his way past the crowd. The ground floor was empty and Harold made his way up the stairs, taking them two at a time. By the time that Harold reached the top step, he could already hear his mother weeping. His heart sank and his eyes begun to burn, but Harold fought the tears off. He already knew what he was about to face.

Harold entered his parent's room for the first time in his life without knocking. As soon as he stepped inside, his mother fell into his arms squeezing him so tightly that Harold found it hard to breathe. Looking over her shaking shoulder Harold could see the lifeless body of his father lying on the bed. The doctor turned and gave him a half-hearted saddened smile while pulling a sheet over his father's emotionless face. Harold knew he meant well and was trying to tell him that he understood the pain, but it brought him no solace. His father was the last pin that held the family together.

Inside Harold wanted to wail, he wanted to fall to his knees and sob until it brought him back, until the creator himself heard his anguish and gave back that which he took but for his mother's sake, Harold did not. Instead he held her silently, the two of them unmoving in a trance as the industrious throng of people swarmed around the room. Harold had to hold his mother forcefully within his arms as they took his father's body away. She wanted to go with him. To hell with it, Harold wanted to go with him, to whatever lay in the realms outside this world, but he knew he could not and neither could she, and so, ignoring her screams as she struggled to free herself from his arms, Harold held her tightly. Once the front door clicked shut, her struggle ended and she sagged in his arms softly sobbing once more. Harold and his mother sat alone in the lounge for most of the evening, both of them glazed and distant. Harold had always relied on his father's strength and now he was alone. He did not know how he would cope. He remembered all the times with his father, those good and bad, his mind flickering through memories like pages of a falling book. The silence was choking but Harold could not think of any words to comfort his mother. For forty years, this man had been part of her life and now he was gone. The lump returned to his throat and Harold had to bite down hard to stop his eyes filling. In the end his steadfastness abandoned him and Harold too cried.

"*Mother what happened?*" Harold called out to the ghost of a woman sitting close to him. There was no reply, no change to her porcelain face. Her tears had dried on her cheeks and she stared lifelessly at the wall. Harold knew she had turned off and was not in that body any more. "*Janet said that the guard were here earlier. What happened?*" Harold continued. He had to know who was to blame or if it was just the flu that took him.

"*Don't worry about it dear.*" His mother said. She did not look at him as she spoke but instead her eyes stayed fixated on the wall as if trying to look through it.

"*Mother, what happened?*" Harold repeated. He did not like forcing her but he could not let it be until he knew.

"*Someone tried to rob us, but your father saw them off.*" She said before letting her head drop to face the floor.

"*Who - What did they look like?*" Harold asked, worried it could have been William or the O'Brien's.

"*I don't know it happened so fast.*" She said faintly, as her memory replayed the horrid events that had happened. "*I was upstairs, they tied me up but I heard them downstairs. I heard it all.*"

"*What did they sound like?*" Harold asked, hating himself as he did. He could tell his mother didn't want to relive the events but the anger inside him made Harold want to find the people responsible. His mother gave him a puzzled look, but she was too tired and too sad to care why he wanted to know. She removed her stare from the blood stain on the wall for just a second before she answered.

"*They were Drow. Your father took the fire poker to them and they ran off.*" Harold knew her heart must have broken. His anger peaked as the image of the two bastards from the hospital came to him, but he knew he had to keep calm for his mother's sake.

"*You're not safe here, Mother, you should leave.*" Harold said. She nodded and Harold could tell she did not want to be alone and wanted him to stay with her but Harold could not. He could not give up on William. If he did, even more people would suffer and it would not be long before the guard or the O'Brien gang got to them again.

"*Why don't you go stay with Aunt Elizabeth?*" Harold asked, knowing his mother had not seen her sister since her wedding day.

They had always been close before that, but both married shortly after each other and had been busy raising their families.

"*Oh no, dear, I couldn't. I wouldn't want to impose on them.*" She said and Harold saw the frozen mask fall from her as a small flicker of herself returned. He could still see the redness to her eyes and she looked exhausted but it was his mother again, at least for the moment. Harold did not reply, his look said enough and his mother knew that she had no real choice. It was Aunt Elizabeth or the summerhouse alone, and at least Aunt Elizabeth lived in Neeskmouth so his mother would be close for the funeral.

Chapter 23: Dealing with Grief

Harold left his mother at around 3 in morning of the 24th. She had finally fallen asleep in his father's chair and Harold could not handle the horror of sitting and watching her any longer. His emotions were ready to break free and Harold had to go before she saw that. He walked through the streets alone and in the dark. He knew that it was William's most active time, but Harold did not have the determination to try to find him. He couldn't face going back to Muriel's either. No matter how much Harold wanted to hold her, tell her his woes and have her make them better, it wasn't right.

He wandered aimlessly down the familiar cobbles replaying memories of time spent with his father. Good times like when they fished at the cottage. He had switched the rods so Harold caught the fish he had baited and he thought Harold had not noticed. He had often done little things like that and Harold was never stupid enough not to notice, but he played along to make him feel better. The image flicked onto the next. They were climbing the trees outside in the orchard. Harold must have been young at the time, as his father had a good head of hair. Harold had been stuck close to the top of a tree after reaching for a juicy red apple. His father sat at its base telling him how easy it would be to climb down. When he realised Harold was too scared to move, he climbed up to carry him down, but before he even got half way he fell from the tree crashing into the ground. Oh, how he'd cursed. For a second the sadness subdued and through tear sodden eyes, Harold smiled at the image of his father sitting on his backside looking up at him, it was not as easy as he had thought.

Harold had not planned his path but he found himself outside the shop – his shop now, Harold guessed. He unlocked the door and made his way inside, swiftly locking the door behind him. Alone in the darkness, Harold was sure, just for a moment, that he got a whiff of his father's tobacco in the air, but the smell faded fast and Harold put it down to imagination. He had to focus his sorrow. He could not let it consume him, not yet. There would be time for tears later, but now was not it. Harold reached for a bolt of thick cotton and made his way out to the back. Muriel needed a new dress and Harold knew that would give him the focus that he needed. Harold laboured through the night, pouring every part of himself into his work and by daybreak Harold had completed the dress. It was perfect, the best piece of work he had ever done. Harold had dyed it brown, an almost shiny copper coloured brown that glinted in the candlelight like sequins. It layered over itself in three tiers from waist to ankle. Flowers of pure white grew up it, each connecting to the fold above. There was no slit for cleavage, instead a thicker layer enclosed up to the neck where lace netting ran around and then down. The sleeves would hang to her wrist and flare out like trumpets. This gown was fit for royalty and would have fetched a fortune for the store but, instead, Harold would give it freely to Muriel. He managed a smile as he folded the dress up and readied himself to go and collect her.

Harold had decided during the night that they would leave her house and stay at his parent's home. Harold hoped she would be willing, and that way if O'Brien's boys returned Harold would be waiting for them. He would not back down this time. The sickness may have been the thing that finally took his father from him, but the O'Brien bastards had been the ones to cause it, and they would pay.

It was still early when Harold arrived at Muriel's, even though he had arrived as late as he could, even stopping en route at the library to borrow as many books as they had on the occult. This turned out to be five and even they looked like they had been pulled back out from one of the many Benedict book burnings. Harold was not sure, but it might just help. Surely they would have some reference to whatever it was that William had become. Harold sat in the lounge flicking through the pages of one of the thick books filled with tiny scrawl but, before he could find anything interesting, the sound of a door opening hinted that Muriel had woken. She had not bothered to dress but instead stood on the stairs in her under garments. Harold's heart fluttered a beat and he forced his eyes to remain on hers.

"Sorry I woke you." Harold said lamely through rapidly drying lips.

"That's okay. Is everything all right? You rushed off so fast yesterday." Muriel said with a yawn, she came and sat close to him at the table. Harold was glad that there was no hint of anger or annoyance in her voice, but just the normal caring tone she seemed to carry. Harold wondered how it was that a woman who had lived such a harsh life as hers could have learned to be so caring. He would ask her about her past one day, but as always, it was not the right time.

"It's my father, he was attacked." Harold said with his voice failing to hide the sadness, and he felt that same lump return to his throat that he had been fighting since seeing the wagon outside his parents' home. Harold wondered just how many more bloody times he would have to swallow it down.

"Was it William that done it? Is your father okay?" Muriel's took his shoulder in her hand, her palm closed tighter, and Harold felt his perseverance break. He could not keep up his defence under her caring embrace. No more could Harold swallow the lump down. His eyes began to fill with water as he looked into her concerned face and that sad little smile on her thin lips that told him she knew what Harold felt. It was the same look the doctor had given him but with her, it felt more real. She pulled him close, pressing him tightly in the strongest of embraces he had ever felt. It was as if she was trying to squeeze the sadness out of him. Harold had not needed to say the words for Muriel to know his father was no more. Harold sobbed in her arms. He did not ever want to let her go.

"I'm sorry." Harold said finally, pulling back and wiping his eyes when his heartbreak subsided enough to feel embarrassment for his outburst.

"You don't need to be." She said and went to pull him close again. Harold gently shrugged away knowing if he felt her warmth again, he would break down once more and Harold had few tears left inside to shed.

"My father was a great man and I'm going to miss him, but now isn't the time to mourn for him." Harold said trying hard to convince himself. If he stopped his pursuit of William and the truth now, then he would have died for no reason. Harold just wished he had had the time to say one last goodbye and explain why all this happened.

"I never met him but he raised you, so he's got to be a true saint." Muriel smiled, her playful banter helping him more than she could know. Harold really did love her, and his sadness just added further confirmation to this. With the loss of his father Harold began to rely on her even more.

"I've got something to ask you, Muriel." Harold said before he lost his nerve.

"Go on." She replied expectantly.

"My father's home is to be empty now as my mother is going to stay with family. It has more space than here and seems a shame to let it go to waste. I was wondering if you wished to come and stay there with me, just until all this is over. I'd feel much safer with you there." Harold asked. He had only left the house a few days before for fear of the guard finding him but the weather should keep them at bay and Harold just wanted to be close to his father.

"I don't know what to say. Sure, I guess. I'll just get my things and we can go." Muriel said trying, unsuccessfully to hide her disappointment that

Harold had not asked something else. Without doubt now Harold could tell she wanted to be with him. She paused midway up the stairs to give him a smile. "*It'll be okay you know, Harry. We'll get through this.*" She said continuing up the stairs and out of view.

When Muriel finally came back down without a bag and in that same, low cut and soiled dress, Harold smiled, knowing that she would soon have a new gown. The gift Harold had made himself was waiting already hidden at home and Harold planned to give it to her that night.

"*Ready?*" Harold asked, trying his best to seem happier than when she left him. Inside Harold still ached but he had to be strong. He was his father's son, and Harold knew he would not have cried, even at the end. Harold would do his best to be like him.

"*I'm ready. You sure you want me there?*" Muriel asked wanting more confirmation on how Harold truly felt.

"*I wouldn't have asked if I didn't now, would I?*" Harold shot her a smile and continued. "*Anyway it will make me feel safer with you there. Plus, if you haven't noticed, I kind of like having you around.*" Harold offered up, hoping that his feelings were right and that Muriel would not reject him.

"*I had noticed. You are an easy man to read, Mr Spinks, not that I mind your attention. Did you sleep at all? You look exhausted.*" Muriel moved across the room close to him. His heart turned into a swarm of butterflies that rattled around inside him.

"*A little, I can sleep when all this is over.*" Harold replied. The surge of energy from the excitement of the admittance of affection between them would no doubt lead to another sleepless night.

"*You still plan to track down William, even after all this?*" Muriel asked. Harold knew she still disapproved but he had not picked this path for himself. Harold felt like a penned in goat at the slaughterhouse just rattling along until the end, He just hoped their ends were different.

"*I don't have any choice. The guard still think it is me, and the O'Brien's boys obviously want to find me, too. If I don't find William, I'm as good as dead.*" Harold said giving the same excuse. He didn't know at what point that had become a lie. He wanted to find William now to kill him. To make the streets safe for Muriel and to get vengeance for what he had put him through. It was no longer about proving his innocence. That didn't seem to matter anymore as much as making the city a bit safer for Muriel and taking vengeance for the death of his beloved father.

"*You don't need to be the hero you know.*" Muriel said running her soft hands down his cheek. "*There is no shame in running away. It's not your job to make the streets safe."* Muriel said, seemingly reading the truth behind what Harold said. He could tell Muriel realised the same as Harold did, the chances of taking down William alive were next to none, but he had to try.

"I was there when this all started. Somehow I feel like I have to try and do something." Harold said and Muriel looked at him, trying to think of something to talk him out of it, but she gave in.

"Fine, you bloody fool. Let's go then." She said and with that Harold grabbed his suitcase from its resting place and made for the door. It would feel good to be home again, and even better to share it with Muriel. They left her house and made their way to his home. As they walked the streets of Neeskmouth, hoping the guard would not notice them and praying they did not bump into O'Brien's gang or, worse, William, Muriel helped to keep things light hearted.

"So have you always been a Neeskmouthain then? It's just your accent don't fit?" She asked.

"I've lived up here since I was about five or six. Before that we were down in Port Lust." Harold said, thinking fondly of the summerhouse.

"Oh, I've always wanted to visit the country. I saw this picture book when I was younger of a cow. I'd love to see one." She said so honestly that Harold laughed. *"Hey, be nice."* Muriel said, punching him in the arm for laughing at her. She knew she knew little of the world beyond the Neeskmouth ridge. *"So, why did you move down here anyway?"*

"My father came here during the war I think. He moved down to the coast before William took the throne. That's where he met my mother. She was the daughter of the owner of the tailors he worked in. I don't know how he managed to woo her, but he did." Harold said smiling at the thought of his father being young and cock sure. *"It was my mother's father that paid for our house up here. You see my father wanted to move back to the city. He always missed it and her father wouldn't have her moving back in a working class condition, so he sold half the company to buy our family home."* Harold explained.

"So, she came from money?" Muriel asked, seeming shocked.

"A little but not much, it was more from the spoils of the war. When my grandfather died they moved up here, they ended up with their house as a holiday home. My mother was an only child so was the only person in my grandfather's will. They used this to open our shop over on East Street. They did not come from money as such. They just got lucky enough to make ends meet." Harold concluded. He didn't know for sure if his father had come to the city as an invading Pole but Harold left that bit out regardless.

"I thought when I saw you that first day heading to the docks there was something different about you." Muriel said, smiling at him.

"You mean I didn't treat you like cattle?" Harold said as Muriel laughed. Now would have been a perfect time to ask about her life story, but Harold was too shy and the moment soon passed as they walked on in silence.

"Would you ever move to the country?" Muriel said, choosing not to answer his question but asking one of her own.

"Yeah, I would. I've wanted to for a long time, but there is not much call for a tailor down there – at least not one that does the style of work my father taught me." Harold said. There was also the fear of the demons at Briers Hill. At least within the city wall the guards kept watch for movement of the shadow demons. Harold dodged the contents of a slop bucket, which someone threw from the upper window close by snapping back from another daydream.

"What is it you make, then?" She asked and actually seemed interested. Most people grew bored and the mere mention of a tailor's work.

"We mainly make suits for businessmen and bankers, some uniforms for the bigger factories too. Sometimes we make evening dresses for the ladies of the city and make the odd repair, but not many." Harold said, trying to make needlework sound less boring than it was.

"You mean them dolled up scarlet's?" Muriel's brow wrinkled and Harold could not help but chuckle. That was the reason he had never found the right type of girl, the noble and middle classes were more like dolls than people and Harold would never have been allowed to date below his standing.

"Yeah, I mean those types. Well there it is." Harold said pointing at the house. Harold was thankful to see that there was no guard wagon anywhere in sight. Surely only a lunatic would come home when the guard were looking for them. That was his genius. At least Harold hoped the guard wouldn't think it was his stupidity.

Chapter 24: A Plan for Love

As soon as they went inside Harold showed Muriel to his parent's old room. It was hard for him to walk into the room and be surrounded by the memories of his father, but the lavish blue carpet and thick mattress would seem like a palace to Muriel. It helped to ease his pain a little to think of her enjoying that which his father had worked so hard to provide for his mother. The house felt chilled and empty and Harold wanted to inject life and love back into it before it became a mausoleum to the memories of the horror that had unfolded there. Muriel had no luggage to stash away and no need to unpack so they spent the rest of the day trying to plan what to do next. They sat around the coffee table in the lounge not far from the chair that had not long before been Harold's father's favourite resting spot. The sunken imprint of his years of sitting in the fabric still showed and Harold had to fight the sadness to think that even that would in time fade. The memories would always be there but they would come up less. Only the odd smell or thought would jog a memory of a time spent together and the pain of the loss, but it would become less often. Time would heal all wounds but for now Harold sat fighting his thoughts with a pile of books from the library scattered around the ornate top like playing cards in some strange game.

"Harold." Muriel said looking from behind one of the books. *"This seems to be describing the way that William has been acting."* It had surprised Harold that Muriel could actually read. He had not had many dealings with working girls other than seeing them go in and out of the Queens, but he doubted the ability to read the written language was a needed skill for their line of work. Some of them could barely speak Neeskmouthain let alone read it. It felt like another missed opportunity to find out more about her but he had other things to focus on. She slid the book across the table to him and pointed to a faded article inside. *"There, that page."* Muriel said pointing to a sun stained page that had been read by countless eyes over the centuries. Harold took the book from Muriel and begun to read. *In eastern parts of the Green Stone Isles during the early parts of the fourteenth century of the old calendar there were reports of men and women who seemed to move in packs, much like that of wolves. These humans slaughtered countless victims and consumed their blood in the most hideous of cannibalistic ways. This led to stories that these people had been consumed by the spirits of wolves in the local area. The wolf people of the jungles would later spark stories of vampires in traders and sailors that encountered them during the early exploration of the known world. The wolf men seemed to share a single intelligence,*

a pack mentality which allowed for their blood lust to drive them on to pillage and ravaged the small villages of the Isles but they seemed almost protective of each other. When Maria Theresa of Stratholme, the leading power in the world at the time, ordered the complete annihilation of them, the general office kept several specimens found inside the temples for observation. Defiling the temples and slaughtering many of the so called wolf people dispelled the false belief that they had been in cohorts with demons or wolf spirits. The specimens kept for testing within Stratholme led to other theories. Such as, these unknown substances secreted by the leach-like creatures that filled the spawning pits at the hearts of the temples, changed people.

Harold rubbed his tired eyes focusing on the old text as he continued reading. *These vampire-like or blood-sucking people seemed to possess extreme strength and a reaction to sunlight. It seemed that the sun actually weakened them. The reports from the brave knights who valiantly battled the wolf men reported that the only way to kill them was to sever the head from the body or to drive something deep into the chest cavity where a large crab like structure was almost always present. However, there have been no reports found in the ransacked libraries after the Orcish invasion of Stratholme to confirm they even existed and the wolf men of the isles have subsequently vanished into myth with no temples remaining since the great crusades, unless they are hidden so deep within the jungle the scholars and bards have yet to find them.'* Harold let the book fall closed. At least they had some idea what they were after now. It wasn't some magic abomination or raised zombie. It was a creature of a kind that had somehow existed since the old times. It may have even dated back to the time of the titans. Harold would later learn the wolf men, or in their own tongue the blood god, Rakta Ishvara and the battle with the Stratholme knights had not been the first time their kind faced being wiped out. Their kind had clung on since the fall of the titans and the sealing of the demons from the world. They predated Sacellum and held secrets most mortal races and even the long living Elves had long since forgotten.

"This certainly seems like him." Harold said, wondering how they suddenly reappeared after so long absent from the chronicles of the world.

"Maybe he's a survivor of that." Muriel said sliding the book back away from Harold so she could read more.

"No, he can't be. He had family here, remember? The guard found his body some time ago. Someone must have done this to him." Harold said, feeling the letter from his wife turning into a lead weight within his chest pocket.

"You mean there might be more of them?" Muriel said, letting the book slip from her hands back to the table.

"There could be, but I don't think so. We would have heard about them but that's not to say there won't be if we don't do something soon." Harold said trying hard to convince himself.

"At least it says how to kill him." Muriel said relaxing slightly. Harold nodded doubtfully. Inside Harold was filled with uncertainty. After finding out how to kill the Rakta Ishvara he should have been filled with hope. After all, it was what they had been seeking for many days but despite all Harold had achieved since the explosion, he did not know if he was capable of slicing a man's head off. It would be a step further than Harold had ever thought to go. He worried if he really had it in him to do that to a man even one as evil as William seemed.

"Are you okay, you look pale?" Muriel asked looking at him with her deep and beautiful eyes.

"I'm all right, just in a little bit of shock. How are you taking this so calmly?" Harold asked. The shock and horror had faded from Muriel so fast Harold was worried she was bottling it all up and would pop like an overheated cask of wine.

"I'm a whore remember, I've seen the evil side of humanity. I know there is a hell and I know that there are demons. Most of them walk the streets of the harbour at night. There's little that can scare or shock me any more Harry. I've serviced mages, I've lain with thugs. William is nothing compared to some of the sick and strange things I have seen. That I have had to do." Muriel said with a heavy heart. Harold had no words that could follow a statement like that and noticed Muriel was uncomfortable with the silence so he broke it the only way Harold could think of.

"It is getting late. If you want a bath, feel free. The bathroom is next to your room. Shall I start heating the water for you?" He said. It was all Harold could think of to say. He didn't even realise it himself but on some deep level inside himself Harold had asked it as he wanted nothing more than to wash the soiled memories from the women he had started to love. To cleanse her from all the hardships she had before he found her.

"Yeah, I might if that's all right." Muriel had replied, it would make a change to bath in warm water and she had noticed the coconut milk on the side on her way in. It would be a luxury to take her mind away from the memories trying to force their way to the surface.

"Yes of course. I'll start the fire now." Harold paused. The next question was one he'd wanted to ask since he had found out how quickly it was going to happen, but as with everything Harold often tried saying, he couldn't find the words. *"Say Muriel, my father is going to be*

buried tomorrow, will you come with me?" He asked not wanting to face it alone.

"Harold. I'm so sorry but I don't think it would be proper." Muriel replied and Harold knew it was just because the only dress she had would not be proper for mourning.

"Could you at least sleep on it and give me an answer in the dawn?" He added. *"Enjoy your bath."* Harold said, but the truth was he needed the support of her being there. The funeral should not be this quick but with his father's sickness they wanted to get him in the ground quickly to stop the chance of any infections. The stories of the plagues from Stratholme in the south still fresh in everyone's collective minds.

Harold waited until he heard the last bucket of water poured and then made his way upstairs. Harold had taken the dress he had made for her from under his mother's chair and cradled it under his arms. Muriel's soiled dress lay crumpled on the bed. Harold moved it into the wicker basket that sat on the floor and in its place laid her gift in pride of place, waiting for her return. Smiling to himself, he made his way downstairs to finish cooking the turnip soup, the excitement of Muriel's surprise pushing the sadness from his mind. With perfect timing, Harold heard Muriel come out of the bathroom just as he was dishing the soup up into little bowls on the table. The last of the candles lay between in brass holders giving a dim light to the room. The fire flickered slowly on the damp logs to keep them warm. Hearing steps on the stairs, Harold held his breath and turned, expecting to see Muriel in her new dress, but Harold was mistaken. Instead, she stopped on the stairs, wrapped in a towel with her still wet hair hanging in red clumpy locks around her shoulders. There was no makeup or powder on her young face, yet she was beautiful to him. She held the dress Harold had made in her arms loosely as if she may break it.

"Harold, this dress-" Was all that she said as she stood there holding it in the dim light from the flickering candles. Muriel had never held such a wonderfully made dress and no one in her life had ever given her something so beautiful without expecting something in return. Harold really was different to anyone else, she decided that then.

"It's for you. I made it for you. Don't you like it?" Harold asked worried he had made a mistake in her taste of got the sizes wrong. Harold had after all only gone from his memory of her figure to make it.

"It's beautiful, but I couldn't take it. It's too fine for me." She replied. Harold could see in the reflection of the dim light that her eyes had

glazed. Her hard exterior breached, she was so close to tears. Now was his chance and, as scared as Harold was he had to take it.

"*Nothing is too beautiful or fine for you.*" Harold said standing up from the table.

"*Please stop.*" Muriel said, but the look in her eyes told him she did not mean it.

"*Muriel. I have to tell you. I might not get another chance. Ever since I first saw you, my feelings for you have been growing. I have never felt this way about anyone.*" Harold said through dry lips. His throat was so parched but he could not stop. He could not waste this chance. For once he would find the words he needed, for he could not let the only women he had ever loved get away. So Harold pressed on. "*You are the most perfect woman I've ever met.*" Harold said feeling his hands shaking.

"*Harold I don't know what to say.*" She said with small silver tears staining her cheeks. The smile she gave him then would stay with him to the end of his days.

"*Then don't say anything. Go and get dressed. Our soup will soon go cold.*" Harold said smiling back and sitting back down.

"*Harold-*" Muriel said. "*Well, thank you.*" Discreetly as she could she trotted back up the stairs. She never actually said anything but from that moment on Harold knew he was not alone in the world. It was true what Harold had told her of all the women he had known in his life Harold had loved none as much as he had grown to love her. It could have been because everything else had been stripped away and she shone out like a beacon in the night of something good, he did not know or care for the reasons. All Harold knew was how much he loved her. Muriel did come back down in the dress Harold had made and an angel could not have looked more beautiful. As they sat down to eat a rather plain soup, the meal seemed to taste better than any before in his life, his taste empowered with a new zest for life even with the loss of his father never far from his thoughts. Seeing her in the candle light Harold felt his father would approve.

Chapter 25: Goodbye Father

Harold found it so hard to rest that night, knowing his love was asleep in the next room and knowing that he had finally told her of how he felt. But the exhaustion finally won and he awoke with a warm feeling in his belly and his heart feeling fuller than ever before. This should have been a perfect day to start the rest of his life but as fate would have it, it was not. Today was the day Harold had to bury his father, but at least he would have Muriel by his side. That would give him the strength he needed to make it through the day. She had told him as they washed the pots the previous night that she would come with him, and had held his hand later that evening while they sat in the lounge watching the fire. They had not spoken much. They did not seem to need to. They just sat watching the flames dance until Muriel grew tired and started to nod off in the chair next to him. Harold woke her by gently shaking her shoulder and she awoke with a smile staring back up at him with tired eyes. Harold helped her up to her room before saying goodnight. Muriel lent in and kissed him on the cheek before closing the door to her chambers, Harold retired to his all the while holding his cheek.

Those moments seemed like an almost distant dream as the morning of Duwek started. Harold couldn't believe how quickly the month of Wastelar had come around. The early snow hinting that it would be yet another hard winter. Harold took out his suit from the wardrobe and put it on. Black silk and a white shirt both pressed to perfection, a nice change to the life living out of a bag that he had recently become used to. Harold pulled his top hat on so it pressed down tightly, completing the sombre look and Harold made his way across the corridor to see if Muriel had awoken.

The funeral was not for a while yet but Harold did not wish to be late – his father could not abide lateness. Harold dared not give himself the time to mourn. With the lack of time to prepare since his father's passing, neither Muriel nor Harold had the funeral clothing they should. This would have saddened him if Harold did not know his father would not have wanted that anyway. Harold knocked on Muriel's bedroom door and waited for her to answer. She opened the door dressed in the frock Harold had made for her and she looked wonderful. Although Harold had guessed her size, the dress fitted her well and confirmed to him how much his eyes must have traced her form in their time together.

"What time will the carriage be here?" Muriel inquired in her soft and caring tone.

"Around an hour, maybe just before." Harold said reaching for a packet of cigars his father had left on the side of the chair. He never seemed to smoke them as they were *'to be saved for a special occasion'.* Harold could not think of a more appropriate time, so he opened the dusty packet to find just one cigar and a match. It was as if he had known. Perhaps he had known the sickness would take him. If he had, then it would not have surprised Harold that his father kept it to himself; it was his way of staying strong. Lighting the cigar Harold took a deep breath in fighting the urge to cough. His lungs hadn't hurt as much since the fire. Harold could barely believe it was almost eleven days since the fire at the Queens.

"Are you okay, Harold?" Muriel asked from the other side of the lounge. Perhaps he looked tired or worn down, or it could have just been the green colour filling his face. Harold had not smoked in a long time but for some reason felt obliged to today. Looking back, Harold guessed it was his way of grieving. The foul smell reminded him of his father and all he wanted to do was feel him in his arms once more. To say goodbye to the man that had raised him. *"You should have your family around you now."* Muriel continued and Harold nodded. It was true. If this had been a normal funeral then the family would have been there all morning. They would have gathered and sent off his father in style, but Harold had not been prepared for this.

"Yes, I'm okay. I'm just glad you're here with me. I don't think I could do this alone." Harold said. Muriel crossed the lounge and wrapped her arms around him tightly. It happened so fast Harold almost caught her with the hot tip of the cigar and only a swift flick of his wrist saved the dress that he had worked so hard on. Harold did cry again, but this time he did not care. He trusted Muriel enough to show her the pain inside and she was right, he should have had his family there. It was usual to have a feast held at the home of the deceased before the funeral. The body of his father should have been present but he was not there, instead he waited in the morgue of the hospital.

Harold's heart sank, and as much as he didn't want to, Harold seemed to be forced to think of what they would have had, if only they had been given the time to prepare the goodbye as they should have. There would have been ham, cider, ale, pies and cakes freshly baked by neighbours or aunts. Not only would the immediate family have been present, but all the distant relatives too. Harold wondered how his family would take to Muriel, but he did not really care. She was his and that's how it would stay. Harold managed to get control again but did not pull away. Although his father did not have the send off he should have done, Harold guessed he would have known Harold did the best he could. The morning was a little blurry for him but Harold stayed clasped between Muriel's arms until the knock at the door marked that the hearse had arrived. It was time for one last goodbye.

Chapter 26: The Funeral

A funeral procession is always a sight to behold, and this one was no exception. It was led by various foot attendants as they made their way through Neeskmouth. A pall bearer carrying batons at the forefront was followed closely behind by the feather man, and scattered behind them walked the pages and mutes dressed in gowns and carrying wands wrapped in blackened bows. Harold did not know the reasons for why things were done this way but whatever the reason it was a beautiful sight and well worth the six pounds his mother had paid. The weather was as cold as ever but at least the snow had melted and it was not raining. The cold weather made him think of the one sure thing Harold knew about the mutes and that was because these men often had to stand out in the cold, they were given lots of gin to drink. Harold whispered a silent prayer that they would behave themselves today and not ruin the last walk of his father.

The first coach in the procession was the hearse pulled by six black horses with ostrich feather plumes on their heads. The hearse was also black, with glass sides and lots of silver and gold decoration. Inside laid the coffin, an inscribed plate running along its side in his father's name. A purple cloth showing the crest of their family covered it and Harold recognised it as the same cloth used at his Uncle Alfred's funeral, which explained how things had been put together in just a couple of days. Flowers were in abundance, his mother having picked the water-lilies that shone in a brilliant white comparison to the darkness. Harold carried on looking out through the slim slit behind the curtain of his carriage. His mother, Muriel and he were in the first of the coaches to follow the hearse. His mother was still in shock and had withdrawn into herself, seemingly unaware of Muriel's presence. The two coaches behind their own contained more mourners, no doubt distant family members.

The procession made its way at walking pace from his father's house along the main roads to the cemetery of Saint Anne's. Their family had been buried in a tomb bought in its depths since it was built. Not only did his father share the same hearse and plate as his uncle, he would rest alongside him too. Harold found it almost nice to see the busy streets stop and give respect to his father. Most of them would not have even known of him, yet still, as the coach passed, men dropped their top hats and women looked down at the ground. A kind of silence followed them through the city. After a while everyone on foot climbed on to the coaches, and the procession was led at a brisk trot. It would not be long until they got there.

Harold could feel the sadness growing in him, making it real – there was no way his father was coming back. Muriel must have sensed his sudden sorrow and slipped her hand into his. Harold looked up into her beautiful hazel eyes and could see they were moist. This was saddening for her yet she still found the power from somewhere to support him. On arrival at the cemetery gates, the foot attendants climbed down from the coaches, and the procession once again continued at walking pace. This was the first time Harold had been to Saint Anne's in a long time, but it was not to be the last. The procession stopped at the chapel. The mourners, many faces Harold did not know, remained dignified and calm as they entered the chapel. The coffin was carried in and laid on a bier and Harold was thankful to put it down. There were four of them carrying it but it still felt heavy. All those sad faces turned, looking at him as they carried it onto the bier. The sad little whispers and covered sobs from the ladies were hard to bear. Once his father rested at the front of the church Harold returned to Muriel's side and sat down next to her and his mother. While waiting for the priest to start, Harold glanced around at his family. The men wore full mourning suits with crape bands around their top hats. The women wore black gowns also made of crape, with black veils and black gloves. They held black-edged handkerchiefs to their eyes. Mourning fans made of dark ostrich feathers were carried by their tortoiseshell handles and there was him and Muriel the only two without them. Harold did not care. He knew if his father was watching he would not have minded. Harold could even imagine him chuckling to himself at the odd sight they made at his funeral. His attention was snapped back to the front as the priest started the reading.

"Dearly beloved, we are gathered here today to celebrate the life of James Spinks and mourn his loss as he passed to Sacellum." Harold could not help but notice the priest's eyes shifting across the crowd so swiftly, from one side to the other, never seeming to stop. There was a strange hollow and laboured sound to his voice which seemed out of place, but Harold didn't know why. It sounded like he was out of breath, as if his chest was hollow. At the time, Harold thought maybe he had been crying himself. Surely a man of the cloth would feel sorrow before every funeral he had to conduct. All the while the priest rattled on, Harold drifted aimlessly for what felt like forever. His mind once again flashed back to past times spent with his father. While the priest spoke Harold remembered back to the first day his father took him to work with him.

He could have only been eleven or twelve. He had rattled on for hours about different types of cloth and ways to cut or dye them. The smell from the bleaches had made Harold's head spin even more than listening to what he had to say. Then he had given him a needle and taught him how to stitch. It was that first pricked-thumb-filled day that had led him to the life Harold had known. It was his father's patience with his unskilled hands that had allowed him to make Muriel the dress she now wore so proudly. The world would be a sadder place without him. A while later a press against his arm awoke Harold to what was happening around him. Muriel got his attention and passed him an open hymn book. The song had been picked by his aunt. Although she was from the lower classes she liked to think she was better than the rest of the family, so she had always kept a step ahead of the rest of them in the arts. It was a sign of her determination to avoid her true place in life. Harold focused and sung with all his heart hoping that his father could hear him from his golden seat in Sacellum. As a chorus of one the church was full of voices.

'Oh Father, thou that dwellest in the high and glorious place, When shall I regain thy presence and again behold thy face. You reply thus came, not until thy holy habitation, thy spirit once reside but now will I be nurtured near thy side?'

'For a wise and glorious-purpose thou hast placed him there and withheld the re-collection of his former friends and birth. Yet oft times a secret something whispered, a breeze of thought, a memory shared, but alas for a time you're a stranger there, and now he wanders a more exalted sphere. Sacellum'

'Alone my father walks in heaven, this falsehood, called out for what it is, for we ask the skies are parents single, no, the thought makes reason stare. Truth is reason and truth eternal tells me. I've a mother there. When I leave this frail existence, when I lay this mortal by, Father, Mother, may I meet you in your royal courts on high. Then, at length, when I've completed all you sent me forth to do, with your mutual approbation let me come and dwell with you in the golden kingdom. I will see you again one day in Sacellum.'

The song ended, and as one they all put the prayer book down. Hushed sniffling filled the room and the whispered voices of condolences. Harold returned to his memories. He knew he was crying but all strength to hide it was gone. Harold could see his father's face, he could smell his tobacco pipe and all he wanted to do was reach out and hold him. Harold felt Muriel's arm around his shoulder in a comforting embrace but barely had the energy to lean into it. Reverend Paul rattled on again but Harold's ears were numb to the words he said by the pounding inside his own skull. The organ burst into life, startling him from his daydream and Harold saw the coffin being lowered into the catacombs by the mutes, each holding one of the heavy ropes. The trap door pulled shut and people prepared to leave the church. Harold hadn't been to many funerals but he was sure this was something normally done at the pace of those mourning but the priest seemed so eager for them all to leave and something about his stance seemed odd. It may have been because of his heightened paranoia from the last few days but Harold couldn't ignore his strange behaviour. He linked his arm through Muriel's and dragged her towards Paul as he tried to retire behind the dark red silken curtains hanging at the rear of the church.

"*Father, please wait, Can I have a moment?*" Harold said, his throat still filled with sorrow that made his voice weak. Harold didn't know at the time what made him call out, nor did he know why he felt the need to speak with the priest at all but when Paul didn't stop Harold became more determined. He called out again, quickening his step. "*Father, please wait. I need to speak to you.*"

"*Harold, what are you doing?*" Muriel whispered next to him, her bemusement clear on her face. Reluctantly, the vicar stopped and turned to look at him. His stone cold eyes glazed staring past Harold and Harold could sense his frustration at his interruption during his escape.

"*What is it my child?*" Was what Paul actually said, but Harold could tell it was not what he wanted to say. He wanted to tell them to get lost and leave his church. The words might not have been said but it was clear from the way he looked towards them.

"*I just wanted to say thank you for the service, my father would have loved it.*" Harold lied, not that his father would have not been satisfied with his send off for he would have been.

"*Why, thank you my child.*" Paul said, but again, his words didn't match his attitude and his eyes hungrily fell on Muriel. She noticed it too and stepped behind Harold for comfort.

"*Harold, I think we should get going.*" Muriel said, turning away from the priest's ravenous stare. "*The coach is waiting.*" She added, and begun pulling away from Harold but not letting go of his hand so he would be forced to go with her.

"*Harold?*" The Reverend Paul questioned and Harold nodded, before being forced to turn around by Muriel's quickening retreat towards the open door. Her hand still in his was clasped down tighter giving him no choice but to follow, trotting behind Muriel. They quickly made their way outside. Whatever it was that had been so urgent to the Reverend behind that curtain seemed to have slipped his mind as he stood staring at them as they left. At the time Harold wondered if he was still eyeing up Muriel but Paul was looking at him. Paul had thought he recognised the name from when the O'Brien's had mentioned it. Harold Spinks should be a dead man. Paul realised Harold was the one he had hired the O'Brien's to kill.

Chapter 27: Good Little Sacellum Boys

It is strange how things turn out and Harold sometimes wondered if everything was pre-ordained. After they left the intrusive stare of Paul behind they slowed down to a more normal walking pace. The main chapel behind them, they had walked through the solemn crowds, the coaches already filling fast by the time they got there. Harold glanced around for his mother but she was nowhere to be seen. She had been led away by some well-meaning relative. The burial over and the family all made their way back to Harold's house. They drank far too much and ate the food brought in by distant relatives whose faces Harold had long ago forgotten. It was the night to begin the mourning of his late father but also for Harold it would turn out to be one graced by hidden blessings. Ernest and Neill had been searching for him since they had retreated from Harold's father's rather surprising turn of strength. Their interest in seeing him dead had doubled by the embarrassment of the defeat by an old man. The O'Brien gang had been losing face ever since the *Queens* burnt down, and having a tailor's son eluding them just added to their problems. The harbour had already started battling for control over vice. Several would-be gang lords had appeared and brawls had become even more common in the sea salt coated streets. If the O'Brien's clung to any chance of holding onto the dominance their father had built up, then they had to show they still had might enough to be reckoned with. They had to step up their hunt for Harold and in doing so it was only a matter of time until they came back to the site of their defeat looking for him.

While Harold and his family sat drinking and reminiscing, his father's body still cooling in Saint Anne's catacombs, Ernest and Neill closed in on them. Word had got back to them about the old man's funeral passing through the streets earlier that day and they could only hope that Harold would be at the wake. The plan was a simple one. Block the front door, the only way in or out of the Spinks household and, with a fistful of Fire Sticks and pound and a half of gunpowder, they would turn the inside into an inferno. Ernest stomped in front of Neill who kept rubbing his arm that had swollen in size and looked like he was smuggling golf balls under his skin the bones obviously broken. Ernest swigged down the last of some unknown alcohol before he pushed the dirty brown bottle back into its resting place inside his jacket. Life seemed a little easier after a tipple.

The city streets were dark because of the heavy rain dowsing the candle lit street lamps making it hard to see. The wet cobbles were slippery and already half-drunk, the two muddled on through the wettest night of the year with difficulty. A sharp crash and clatter followed by a sharp outburst from behind made Ernest stop.

"*Sacellum-n-dam*" Neill called out; kicking the small tin soldier figure he had tripped over into the road. "*Bloody brats 'ere are rich enough to leave their toys out to rust in the rain then, kids, I bloody hate kids.*" He continued rubbing his sore shin that had been stabbed by the tiny tin warriors' sword.

"*You hate everyone you báltaí.*" Ernest chuckled as they turned another blind corner in the dark. They were greeted by an empty road, and the lights here had been snuffed too. Only the faint glow from house windows shone off the surface water along the road marking the edge of the footpath that ran either side of the gutter.

"*Téigh trasna ort féin*" Neill replied in native Drow. His ankle was still throbbing as he hobbled close behind. "*You even know where we are going?*"

"*Of course I know where we are going. You think I'm daft or something?*" Ernest stopped abruptly. He couldn't help but feel unnerved by the lack of people on the streets around them. They were both unaware that something had tracked them down. They'd made their way lurking in shadows in the foulest of nights and they'd thought they were completely alone but something had been following the odour of tobacco and spirits trailing behind them. That something was William. They had paved a clear and colourful path through the night and now he watched from the darkness like a mountain lion waiting to pounce.

"*Come on you half wit try to keep up and leave the kids toys alone.*" Ernest said, fighting the nagging feeling he was being watched. He turned his back on Neill and made his way onwards, now only two roads from Harold's house.

William had tracked the two since they left the pub. The cold and rain really did not bother him but it kept the working girls inside and his hunger never seemed to fade. Male flesh was not his preferred meal but beggars could not be choosers and it was better than the rats or dogs he snacked on normally. By now, any trace of William, the husband and father, had died to the Rakta Ishvara. He was the blood god of the small tanned skinned people from the beautiful Green Stone Isles. It was amazing the knowledge and history he had thrust upon him. He knew everything that the Rakta did, from the first days when the tribe of man encountered the Rakta lava, the leech. The glory years when the Rakta had hunted in packs ripping through the weak humans, taking some to make their numbers greater. He knew how those golden years had ended with the fall of the titans. Tribes of men fell on the encampments killing every last Rakta Ishvara and burning the bodies. William felt their pain just as every single host had. The Rakta had gone into hiding, until only one survived. It had learnt of the humankind's stupid need for a god and used this to control them. William felt the burn of the spearhead that had pressed into the chest from the chieftain as if it was his own. The face of Reverend Paul burned into his mind like a jack lantern. The priest that had brought Rakta Ishvara to this place was the same man who killed the last blood god and now William was experiencing a new feeling. The shared conscious knew that the weak and frail creature named Paul had forced itself inside. They could not allow this. The Rakta could not risk a weak link. For so long they had remained hidden from man they had been able to survive. Now this fool would ruin it. All this information sloshed around William's mind as he skulked in the shadows. The two thugs walked past the Cheapside school only moments away from Harold's home. As they turned onto the Greenway the sound of the hard rain crashing against the windows hid their footsteps. They were close now and William could sense this, fearing he would lose his prey. He had to take his chance to strike now and he wasted no time.

His turn of speed would have left a stallion standing as he literally pounced towards them. He went for Ernest first. The smell of testosterone oozing from his pores signalled that he would be the harder prey to bring down. Ernest spun on his heels as he heard footsteps splashing through the puddles aligning the pavement. He pressed his hand down into his jacket trying to grab for his knife but his reaction was too slow. William closed in like a bull and knocked him to the floor. The impact hurt but Ernest was tough and he would not go down without a fight. With William on top of him Ernest threw a punch at his attacker, but his hand was stopped in mid air, being clamped by Williams own. Ernest yelped as his bones shattered like a broken window. William's unmatched strength crushed Ernest's hand flat as if it was nothing more than a grape. Ernest was sure he would die right there and then but Neill moved quickly and sunk his blade into William's lower back puncturing a kidney. This would not kill William, not now, not much could. The only true living part of him was the parasite deep within his ribcage, but he still felt the pain. His concentration lapsed for just a second but that was long enough for Ernest who seized his chance and kicked out with both legs. This sent

William staggering back a few paces before he regained his balance. He glared at Ernest and watched as the little Drow gasped for breath and scrambled backwards, away from his attacker. Ernest, his right hand hanging lifelessly from his wrist watched William pull the knife from his back with a roar of agony. Neill had managed to push it in so deep that removing it sent a spray of blood into the rain from the torn artery. As William stood holding the blade Ernest noticed his eyes. Those pure black pits that made it feel like looking into a gateway to hell. William seemed to grow bored of his prey and was more interested in what was going on behind him. He dropped the blade to the floor inches in front of Ernest before spinning, his injury seemingly not disabling him in the slightest, and closed the same crushing strength that had ruined Ernest's hand around Neill's throat. What happened next would scare and sicken Ernest more than anything he had seen before in his life. William opened his mouth with his jaw parting wide like a snake swallowing a rat and he bit down into Neill's neck. Neill opened his mouth to scream but nothing came out. He tried to fight off William bashing him with both his good and fractured arm, but without success. Soon his body began shaking violently with uncontrollable spasms as William drank from him. A steady trickle of blood escaped Williams' mouth and ran down his chin mixing with the rain it dripped onto the ground. The colour drained from Neill and his eyes rolled back leaving him looking like a waxwork. By the time William dropped Neil to the ground he was dead.

William turned his attention to Ernest who was still where he had left him, paralysed in shock watching his brother's last moments literally sucked into nothingness. A mix between pain and panic blended inside Ernest's stomach as he sobbed, trying to roll himself onto his knees. As the shock faded into realisation Ernest tried to crawl away but he was unable to stand. His legs had turned to jelly. William laughed and slowly walked around until he blocked Ernest's escape.

"*No please, please don't.*" Ernest begged. William ignored the plea and pressed his foot onto Ernest's back kicking him to the floor hard enough to sever Ernest's spine from his pelvis with a crack. William reached down and grasped Ernest's short cut hair and wrenched his neck back until he heard a snap and saw as the skin pulled taught over sinew and bone. He felt it free from the rest of the body. The fight over, William knelt down to finish his meal. When sated, William stood and walked away without looking back. The night was growing late and dawn was not far away. He knew he would feel weak then. It was time to return to the sewers, time to rest. William did not know at the time but he had saved Harold that night. Saved Harold but doomed the harbour to a bloody war to stake claim to the whores of the docks. The remaining Drow would have to fight hard if they wanted to keep their place in the city and there was many an Iron Giant and White Flag that would happily kill to take the money to be made that the last O'Brien would no longer collect, but this bloody story is one for another time.

Chapter 28: Realisation

On Midwek morning, Harold was still unaware of how lucky he was to be alive. The first of his family left just before daybreak to head home. Once the sun had risen the day was not much brighter with the rain still pelting down outside. Only his mother, aunt and a cousin remained. He was so glad to see his mother when he had arrived home. Part of him had worried needlessly that she may have done something stupid after they left the church, but Harold would not have admitted that to her. The room was uncomfortably silent and Harold tried to warm the atmosphere with small talk.

"Will you be going to church today Auntie?" Harold asked. She was renowned for her talking and Harold hoped getting her going would lighten the mood. His father used to say she never shut up and that was what had sent Uncle Peter to his grave, just so he could get a rest.

"No not today. Are you still fine with the idea of your mother coming to stay with me?" She asked, stuffing another pastry into her mouth. She was a larger woman and it seemed the loss of his beloved father and her distraught sister did little to dampen her appetite.

"Yes, I think it will do her good." Harold said, thankful at the thought of his mother being away from the house.

"What about you?" His aunt asked, meaning no doubt for him to go with his mother and stay with her. It allowed her to feel important in the family but Harold had no interest in going. He had to finish what he had started with William.

"I have Muriel, I'll be alright here." He said, hoping she wouldn't ask any more questions. Harold could tell she wanted to pry by the glint that flashed across her eyes as she looked over at Muriel, who was warming her hands by the fire, but Harold was thankful of her reserve that his aunt managed to refrain from asking.

"We better get going soon. I want to get us home before the city wakes." She said reaching for the dregs of wine in her glass. The liquor cupboard had been drunk bare overnight. It had been stocked rather well and Harold couldn't help but feel that people hadn't just used the wines and spirits to soften the pain, but instead had taken the liberty to use the excuse to drink to excess.

"Let me grab your coats." Harold replied, keen to see the last of his guests leave so he could think about heading up to bed. The goodbye was swift, his mother, still in shock, said nothing to him as he kissed her on the cheek. He waited and watched as they climbed into the black carriage and waved them off before stepping back inside and

closing the door. Harold rested his back against it and closed his eyes, far too tired to even make the trek upstairs. Harold sat down on the floor and listened as his aunt's coach rattled off southwards out of Greenway. Harold would later be so glad that they left that way instead of heading north. Moments after the last clip clop sound of their departure, his eyes were snapped open as the sound of a woman screaming somewhere just north of his door echoed into the night. His body found an energy pocket from somewhere, and Harold stood and threw the door open. With no shoes on, Harold ran through the puddles, striding as wide as he could and covered the few hundred yards to where the scream had come from in seconds. The noise had actually come from a young girl who now sat cuddled up against a neighbour's front door, sobbing. She did not look up as Harold approached and he soon saw why. Ernest and Neill lay dead in the street. The pavement was stained red and a morbid trail led into the centre of the road, making it look as if it had rusted.

Harold did not know who to go to first, the crying child or the thugs. Self-preservation drove him to examine them first. He had not forgotten their faces from his hospital bed and it didn't take much to realise they were there for him. Harold went to Neill who was slumped against the front wall of the Briers, an elderly couple who had lived down the street from them for a few years. Neills's neck had been ripped open and Harold did not need to check his pulse to know that he was dead. Stepping over him, trying not to think too hard about what had happened, Harold checked on Ernest and noticed not only the same gaping neck wound but also that his neck had been snapped in two. His hand was a mess, bone poking through the skin and blood congealed over it making it look like sliced bacon left too long in a stewing pan. Again, Harold did not need to check his pulse but for some reason he went closer. His tiredness having drained any emotions Harold may have had left, he pulled Ernest onto his side, and began to search him. Harold almost cut himself as his hand pressed into his chest pocket where a broken bottle of absinth rested. There was something made of paper in there and Harold pulled it free quickly, putting it in his own pocket. Harold would read it later when he didn't have the eyes of the neighbours' all over him. His hand was about to move lower to check the rest of Ernest's pockets when a door opened and Mr. Briers came out holding an old worn rapier, probably his weapon of choice in his younger days. He looked at Harold expecting some kind of explanation.

"They are dead." Harold said lamely as he hovered only inches over Ernest. Yet again, Harold was the first on the scene of a crime but thankfully he had the best of alibis this time and they would not be able to pin this on him even if they were still looking for him for the other murders.

"I can damn well see that. Do you know what happened?" Mr Briers demanded as his wife led the young girl inside.

Harold never did find out why such a young girl was on the streets so early in the morning. That was a secret between her and the women she called Granny.

"I don't know." Harold lied. He didn't know for sure but he had a good idea who was to blame, William. Harold began to walk away, only now realising his bare feet were soaked and frozen.

"Hey wait." Harold heard Mr. Brier shout from behind him but Harold did not stop until he was home. He went straight to the kitchen, washed the blood from his hands before settling by the fire to warm his feet. Harold chose to sit in his father's old chair. Muriel was sitting in his chair; the concern was clear on her face.

"What's going on out there?" She asked him. Harold had been surprised she didn't follow him into the kitchen when he first came back in. Surely the sight of his blood soaked hands should have raised some questions, but then again, maybe a man coming in covered in blood was not as much of a shock to a woman of Muriel's profession as it would have been to him.

"There's been another murder, two in fact. I doubt it'll be long before the guard are called. It's early so many of them will still be sleeping their hangovers off but there's the odd one who still remembers what being a city guard is all about and they'll come to investigate." Harold said, closing his eyes. He had known he wouldn't have long to mourn his father but he had barely been in the catacombs of the church a mere twelve hours and once again, fate had thrown Harold into the scene of another gruesome act of the horror that was becoming his everyday life.

"So are we going to have to run? We can always go back to mine again." Muriel offered up. Harold didn't say anything in reply; he didn't know what to do. They had only just moved out from Muriel's back to his father's home, in the hopes that Harold would get a chance to take revenge on the O'Brien's, and now they laid dead outside in the street; the house once again became a mausoleum to his father. Harold pulled the piece of paper from his pocket that he had found in the dead thugs pocket. It was damp and stunk of alcohol, but it was still readable.

'To the O'Brien family, I have tasked my altar boy with finding you in the hopes that you can do me a service, a service that will benefit us both. Reverend Paul Augustus.'

Harold read and almost dropped the paper in shock and his mouth hung open. Harold read the name repeatedly. Reverend Paul Augustus. The man who had buried his father, the priest that Harold had been standing next to yesterday with the acid in his stomach churning like soar milk telling him something was wrong. Harold had been face to face with someone who had dealings with the O'Brien's. It all fell into place for him at that moment; it was like looking at the box while doing a puzzle. All the little things that Harold had missed fell into place. The fact the William had been buried at Saint Anne's and that his body must have been dug up there. The way the priest looked at Muriel, the blackness to his eyes, there was something unsettling about him. The letter connecting the O'Brien's to him made as irrefutable evidence that Paul had dealings with the underworld. A priest should have no need to contact criminals. He had something to do with it all. He was either involved in it all in some way or he knew who was. Harold had to go back to the church to find him. Harold could rest later.

"*Muriel. I have to go somewhere. Wait here for me. If the guard come, light a candle in the front bedroom upstairs and I'll know not to come back. I won't be long.*" Harold said trying to hide the fear from his voice.

"*What's on that bit of paper? Tell me what's going on?*" She begged, not missing the change in his demeanour after reading the note.

"*I think the priest has something to do with all this. The two murders outside were the thugs that attacked my father. With them dead I only have to watch out for the guard but they'll no doubt be here soon so I have to go to Saint Anne's now. I have to find out what the priest knows, if he knows about William or what's behind all this. It might help prove my innocence or, if nothing else, help me find out who started this.*"

"*Just come back safe Harold.*" Muriel said, before turning away from him and walking towards the stairs. Harold slipped on his shoes with his feet still damp, but he did not care as he headed out, leaving Muriel to try and sleep. It was too risky to take her with him, for all Harold knew William could be at Saint Anne's waiting for him.

Harold left in such a hurry he forgot his coat and was soaked through before he got to the end of the road. He briefly thought of going back to change, but the chance of the guard being on their way was too great, and he couldn't get caught now that they finally had a lead that might start answering some questions. Harold battled onwards, twitching as the ice-cold droplets dripped from his sodden hair down his spine. As he turned out of Greenway heading towards Saint Anne's a guard wagon rolled past him, steam rising from the lead horse's nose in the biting cold. Harold hoped they did not see him. They did not stop and as soon as the coach rattled past, Harold quickened his step almost breaking into a run.

The cobblestones slid past underfoot like waves on the ocean. The city was just starting to wake up and Harold jogged past families dressed in their best as they headed off to morning mass. It did not dawn on him until he was halfway to Saint Anne's with his legs ready to buckle under him that there would be a sermon on when he got there. Harold would not be able to rush in and confront Paul. He would have to wait at the back or he would risk being lynched by devout Sacellumists. The cold was starting to sting and Harold felt the goose-bumps spreading up and down his arms so he quickened his pace to a sprint. His legs complained even more and his chest started to wheeze but it kept him warm or less cold at least.

A strong wind blew across Celebration Square as Harold turned the corner into the Common Road. The granite statues that had been put back up during William's lordship looked black, and the pigeons that normally defaced them, hid below the legs of the sculptures trying to keep out of the worst of the weather. The rain was starting to ease, but it was so damnably cold Harold was worried his shirt would actually freeze to his back. Harold did not want to go the same way as his father and just hoped that with all the bad luck he had been having, he was due some good and would avoid the flu. By the time he got to the fence that he Harold had consumed had burnt from his system but his legs were still wobbly and he leant against a metal fence to hold himself up while he caught his breath.

Harold could hear the sound of singing from inside and could tell the service was underway. He had not had the chance to take in the beauty of the church on his last visit, his mind being preoccupied by the weight of his father's casket resting on his shoulder. Panting for breath, Harold spared himself a moment to take in the splendour. Three distinct sections made up the church itself. The left section was a tall pointed building with a large square base and contained a grand, stained glass window showing pictures of religious idols. Below the window, a pure white plastered arch that masked the doorway inside. The central section was a smaller version of the last with a white arch and two small stained windows. It looked, to his mind, like a child stood next to its father and Harold wondered if the architect had planned it like that. The huge spire on the right climbed skywards and Harold could just make out the cross on its top. The church was huge and had taken years to complete. They had started building Saint Anne's in the year 107ab and construction was still ongoing periodically as the numbers of the faithful Sacellum seemed to grow in the city. It was a massive structure and had taken hundreds of people to construct the huge stone towers even with the strange machines borrowed from the Dwarves. It was the biggest building erected since the Dragon overlords were pushed from the city, and rivalled the Handson castle. It should have taken centuries for the cathedral sized church to be built, but had been done in only decades. This made Harold wonder just what splendour the Dwarves had hidden in the deep roads of the under dark away from the eyes of humans if their machines could create things like this so swiftly.

Sliding open the gate, which creaked with the effort, Harold made his way to the large arch and slipped through the door, scuttling like a scared crab as he made his way across the chequered floor to the back pew. It was empty as were many of the other seats in the nave of the church. Harold guessed the foul weather had kept all but the most devout at home. Reverend Paul Augustus led the sermon from the front of the church, backed by another collection of four stained glass windows. The light shining behind him gave him a glowing halo even in the grim weather. Harold sat and listened all the way through the sermon, listening to how wonderful this creator god was. It annoyed him. It's not that Harold didn't believe in the golden city in the sky or disagree with the monks; after all, it was them who would, if anyone did, push the demons back from the world. What annoyed Harold was that with everything that had been happening to him, how could he be so wonderful, this creator god who steered their fates? As angry with the creator as Harold was at the end of the sermon, when it was time to pray, he found himself down on one knee. Harold prayed that he would make it through the day. He prayed that his mother would find the strength to deal with her loss, and, mostly, Harold prayed for Muriel.

"*Atone thee creator.*" Harold said in chorus with everyone else to end the prayer and he hoped that if there really was an all powerful being he heard his wishes. Harold watched as Reverend Paul made his escape behind the curtain that led down into the catacombs with the same haste as he had tried during his father's funeral. Harold waited as the crowds left slowly one by one, keeping his head bent as if he was still praying and not wanting to draw attention. For someone who, only a week before, had been a tailor's son and someone no one would have recognised, Harold was learning fast about what it took to survive in this new world of infamy that had opened up to him.

When the last straggler was gone and the door shut behind them, Harold began tiptoeing towards the curtain, pressing his feet down as softly as he could against the stone floor. Harold tried to stay on the deep red carpet to deaden the sound. He wanted to catch Paul unaware, so he could see what he was doing down there. Pushing past the curtains Harold was thankful to see that the wooden door at the head of the stairs was ajar and he knelt beside it gazing down into the darkness. At the foot of the stairs Harold could see two coffins against which was propped a table. Harold wondered how the old man was able to hop over them each time he came down there. Surely his old bones should have disintegrated under the effort. Then Harold saw something which sickened him. Sitting deep in the shadows was Paul Augustus and one of the residents of the catacombs. It was his father's body and that bastard was biting it. Harold had seen William do the same to the guard officers the night he had escaped. Harold gave up his hiding place and tossed the door aside, making a rapid descent and almost losing his footing more than once on the herbs that were scattered on the steps. Reverend Paul dropped Harold's father to the floor and turned to face him.

"Harold! How wonderful of you to join us. We were just having lunch." Paul said smiling with blood soaked teeth.

"Screw you, priest." Harold bellowed as he clambered over the coffins, kicking the table aside. It was out of character for him but his anger turned to fury, and Harold wanted to kill him there and then. Harold forgot that he came for answers, to find out what William was. None of that mattered in the light of his father being desecrated like that. Harold wanted to see the priest dead. He slammed his foot down on the leg of the table, breaking it free from the frame. He was tired and it took a lot of effort but, with his blood boiling, his muscles pulled tight with the surge of power felt only in the purest moments of rage. The broken leg in his hand, Harold made his way towards Paul. His mouth was dry and his heart beat faster than it ever had before in his life.

"Now, my child, let's not do anything hasty." Paul said. Harold was too enraged to argue back. He could not shake the image of his father's lifeless corpse sullied in such a way, when they had lowered his father's body down the day before it was to rest forever with his lost kin, not to

feed some crazed old priest. *"Harold. I think I owe you some answers."* Paul continued, wiping his mouth on a handkerchief he pulled from his robes.

"Too right you do old man and once I have them I intend to kill you." Harold said, tightening his grip on the table leg. The whole time Muriel and he had been planning to kill William, Harold had no idea if he had it in him to kill someone, but standing there in front of Paul, Harold had no doubt in his intentions.

"I've come to know a lot about you, Harold. I know about the Queens. I know how you got blamed."

"Is that why you called O'Brien's boys here, to tell them of my innocence?" Harold said, hoping to surprise Paul that he knew the priest had involvement with the O'Brien's and now, after seeing him feed on the blood of his father, Harold knew Paul was no different to the beast William.

Paul answered quickly and calmly. *"No, course not, I didn't even know about you until they came here. I called them here to kill William. You see, he was a mistake of mine. The O'Brien's made me aware of your involvement and I could not risk you ruining all of this. So I ordered them to kill you too."* The priest's honesty shocked Harold and he found himself looking around the room while trying to think of what he wanted to say back. Harold noticed an opening in the wall where a coffin would once have rested. There was a pillow just inside of it and huge amounts of the herbs that coated the stairs. Harold guessed that Paul had been sleeping there and using what knowledge he had gained from reading the occult books of mages and how they had used garlic and other plants in protective wards Harold guessed that hideaway would have been to protect the priest before his change.

"He was a mistake? What do you mean a mistake?" Harold asked holding the table leg out in front of him more for protection than in anger now.

"It's a long story, you sure you and your lady friend have the time? I mean while you're here she is all alone." Paul said trying to anger him. He wanted him to make a move, to lunge at him.

"Don't you dare threaten Muriel, priest." Harold said.

"I'm not, but William is still out there. He knows about you, too. You see, we share the same memories. All of us do. We are more than you could imagine." Paul said and this was the first time Harold heard about the shared, hive mind of the Rakta Ishvara.

"What are you on about, old man?" Harold said, taking another look around the cold damp room. The brickwork changed halfway

down the wall and even with his limited knowledge of the lore of Neeskmouth, Harold could tell the catacombs had broken into the old labyrinth below the city.

"*You're really not the brightest of young men, are you?*" Paul said. "*You look at me as evil. I can see that in your eyes, but you are wrong. You do not realise the power the Rakta Ishvara, the blood god, can give you. I've learnt how to control it. The leaves you see around here stop it taking total control.*" Paul said, turning to point around the catacombs. It was at that moment Harold took his chance, swinging the table leg as hard as he could at Paul's head. It never made it. Paul's movement was lightening fast and he splintered the leg with a sideward swipe.

"*You fool of a boy. Don't let my looks deceive you. You cannot win. It is only by my restraint that you still breathe.*" Paul spat at Harold with venom. The lunge had taken him past Paul and Paul was now blocking his escape back up the stairs. Harold could see the mass on Paul's chest starting to pulsate. It was almost instinctive on his part, like the jack rabbit to dart into its burrow at the sight of a hawk's shadow. Harold dropped the shattered stick to the floor and darted into the wall opening. Harold hoped that if Paul really had been using it to sleep safely without fear from William then the herbs would keep Paul at bay now too. It worked as Paul skulked back and forth keeping off the mass of leaves. Harold was lucky.

"*It seems you are not as stupid as you look. You have an understanding of the old magic's it seems. It matters little though for you sadly Harold. I might not be able to risk touching so many Abrus leaves but I am not going anywhere. Let us see how long you can stay in there, shall we? Maybe me and your father could get back to dinner while you watch?*" Paul disappeared from Harold's line of sight. He was right though, Harold could not stay in there forever. Harold closed his eyes and pressed his hands over his ears trying to block out the sucking sound as Paul returned to feeding on his father's corpse. The mention of the old magic's made Harold wonder if these beasts were the demons the Sacellum warned the people of. Had the time of the last seal finally come?

Chapter 29: Blood Lust and Protection

Harold hid in the rocky crevice for almost an hour listening to the priest pottering around just as if Harold was not there. He couldn't see what he was doing but maybe that was for the best. Thankfully, he left his father's body alone after a time. Harold was more worried about Muriel than himself. She would have woken by now and Harold had left so quickly. He hoped she wouldn't come for him. If she did, then Harold did not think he could save her from the demon creature that Paul had become. Harold had little to do but sit and worry as he grew colder and damper. It was then that Harold noticed Paul's journal which must have been knocked into the crevice when he upturned his table. Harold had the time, stuck with the shadows and spiders to read through it and learn what he could from it. It was hard to see it in the dim light given off by the wall mounted candles outside of his hideaway but Harold had to do something to keep his mind off what he had just seen and heard. Even while reading, the image of his father's body slumped against the wall flashed in front of his eyes, sometimes followed by one of Muriel laid out the same.

Harold had to keep reading, maybe there was something in the diary that would help him. It turned out there was. The pages were written by a mad man but between the rants of insanity was a wealth of knowledge inside the book. It explained everything Paul knew about the Rakta Ishvara. How the race of the Rakta Ishvara was around since long before man and they survived in the muddy swamps of The Dark Gulf. Harold did not know much about the colonies but he knew they had their own religions that dated back to the time of the Titans, but how many people worshipped the Rakta Ishvara there, and how many were treated like cattle because of it? Harold wondered how many followed these false gods and for how long people had their loved ones slaughtered to feed these beasts. It was then Harold realised, if he was killed and failed to stop Paul and his creation William, then that was what would happen to the city. The creatures could gain a strong foothold before people realised and they would all fall to them. The city was so afraid of the demons in the fields they would not notice the darkness spreading in the streets around them. It would be worse than being under the ruthless rule of the Dragons again.

His mind was sucked away from its gruesome daydream by the sound of creaking upstairs. The large wooden door at the entrance to Saint Anne's had opened and Harold could hear the clatter of shoes against the stonework. They stopped somewhere above on the ground floor. There was a click as the latch sprung open on the door to the catacombs. Whomever it was had started descending the stairs. Harold's heart skipped a beat.

"No, not Muriel, please not Muriel." Harold prayed to himself and waited to hear the priest move. Harold's muscles had gone to sleep in the cold dampness but he forced them tense, determined that if Paul made one move at her, he would leap from his hiding place. Harold would probably be dead before he even wounded the demon priest but it would give Muriel time to escape.

"William?" Paul called out and Harold's heart jumped over with happiness before realisation dawned. William being there did not bode well for him.

"Why do you use that name for me priest. You know nothing of this host remains." William said as he continued to creep down the stairs. Harold risked sliding forward and peaking around the edge of the shaped igneous rock. William had stopped only a few feet in front of Paul and Harold waited, watching as events unfolded much to his surprise.

"I will call you by your spawn name then brother השני את אחד. *I hadn't thought I would see you again."* Paul said. Even through his death rattle Harold could sense his nerves. William remained silent. Harold wondered if he had spoken in another way. Paul had said they shared one memory. It seemed only reasonable that they could communicate the same way without the need for words.

"Stay still एक कमजोर *and I will make this painless."* William hissed after whatever silent conversation may have taken place beyond his hearing. Harold risked leaning out further as William had not noticed him and Harold studied him. His clothes were torn and grubby and he looked like a beggar, with his mottled brown trousers ripped and threaded. Even from a distance, Harold could see the dried blood matted within his hair. Harold could relate to why they had once been called wolf men with his bestial appearance.

"But השני את אחד *I am one of you now, soon to be your brother, your kin."* Paul pleaded, interrupting Harold's study of William.

"No, old man you are not. You may have one of my brothers living inside you, but you are too weak. Your sickness and weak mind make you a risk to us. Your foolish antics have already disgraced us and we will not let your pride risk ending our kind. You studied our ways but you are not of us, you have shamed us. Three million years we have existed behind the eyes of man and you risk it all." The moment the last word slid between William's tight lips he attacked. The fight between them both shook the very foundations of the church.

The first blow that William sent crashing into Paul's chest, should have killed the frail old man, but it did not.

Harold watched from his hiding place assessing just how strong the Rakta Ishvara made each of them. Harold had seen William kill the guard but that was back outside the hospital just after the *Queens* fire and they were just normal people. Paul would give him a true match of strength and Harold wanted to see just what he was up against. A hit sent Paul flailing backwards, crashing into the rear wall of the catacombs and bringing down an array of rubble and loose mortar from above. The coffins within the wall rattled as if their occupants were banging on the wall annoyed by the ruckus of their neighbours. William did not give Paul any time to recover and lunged at him again. He covered the distance between them in no more than three bounds. He sideswiped Paul with his iron-like hands across the face, sending him to the ground. Even from his relatively safe haven, Harold could hear as the bones in Paul's face crumbled. To his sheer amazement the priest rolled as he hit the floor and was back on his feet facing William. The blood on his face seemed old, like that which you would get from a pheasant that had hung for some time before you slit its throat. It was Paul's turn to attack and he did so quickly, swiping one of the small brass candelabras from the side wall, ripping the bricks away with it. He made for William, the burning candle held out at arm's reach like the point of a sword. It collided with William's neck, sending wax flying until the cold hard metal connected, tearing through the flesh. Harold closed his eyes not wanting to see the fountain of life fluid squirt free. After not hearing the splatter that Harold had been waiting for he slowly opened his eyes just in time to see William go back at Paul, the wound seemingly not affecting him as it was barely bleeding at all. It was then Harold realised the body did not matter much to the Rakta Ishvara – it was just a shell. Much like the hermit crabs Harold had played with at the beach as a boy – if the shell broke, the crab would find another, only the parasite had to survive. As if to back up his presumptions, William sank his teeth into Paul's neck, tearing at it. Chunks of flesh fell to the ground before Paul managed to push William back. The final blow came shortly after – William pressed his fist into Paul's chest. Harold heard his ribs crack and Harold watched as Paul's black eyes faded to white. Paul fell forwards into William's grasp, his legs falling out from under him. Harold knew he was dead.

William pulled a small black sphere from Paul and Harold guessed it was the parasite itself. He moved towards a jar that rested in an alcove not too far from him and placed the little ball inside. Harold saw the creature inside squirm and uncoil, it was still alive.

Chapter 30: Peace for Saint Paul

Harold waited for what seemed like forever after William had finished dressing his wounds before Harold even thought of leaving the chapel. After William had finished feeding on Paul, he wrapped the rags that he had ripped from Paul's clothing around his wounds, yelping as he pulled them tight. Although his wounds would not kill him, they still seemed to have hurt William. Even in his weakened state, Harold did not want to face William now. Harold knew he would not stand a chance. Harold would be killed before he could get close enough to kill the creature in his chest. Harold would have to leave it for someone else. He would have to rely on the city building an army to face William. Harold had the letter from Paul to the O'Brien's and his diary now. He could actually prove his innocence.

He made his way out of the catacombs into the main church. Harold was thankful William had left. There were no clues as to where he had gone or how long ago. With no sun to tell the time it looked the same as when Harold had arrived, the only difference being the morning rain had moved off and the afternoon downpour was washing in from the front arch. Harold was not sure of the time but it could not be any later than three or four o'clock. He had spent most of the day squashed into a small corner of damp stone and his tired body yelled at him with aches and pains. Harold stood flicking through the church records and finally found what he was looking for, Paul Augustus' address. Harold left the church of Saint Anne's and made his way back across the city, heading to Paul's home in the hopes he could find something more to prove his innocence. Paul's journal would go a long way to proving it, but Harold had to be sure the guards couldn't dispute his innocence.

The alley outside Paul's residence was busy, bustling with traders and patrons who made their way to market. Harold knew he would have to be quick, Muriel would be worried sick and Harold was beginning to feel nauseous from fatigue. He was thankful Paul lived in such a slum area where people would be used to the sound of the collection of unpaid dues. Harold called on all the strength he had and kicked the lock just below the handle, the old wood gave way much easier then Harold had expected. A ragged old mutt who had been sniffing through a pile of rubbish close by raised his head and barked, warning him against disturbing him again before returning to his foraging but that was the only creature that seemed to take notice to Harold breaking an entry.

Inside Paul's hovel it was black. Harold kept the door ajar while he fumbled across a shadow he presumed to be a table. Finally, his fingers rested against the matches he had been looking for and Harold slid them into his hand, careful not to drop any. Lighting them gave off a gentle glow across the room. In the centre Harold could make out a coffee table and what looked like a candle, so he made his way towards it, almost falling over a pile of books left in his path. With the candle lit, the room slowly started to light but Harold did not have to look far for what he was after. A diary, which predated the one Harold had read, was the only book not piled on the floor or hidden away in the spider-infested bookshelf. Harold was tempted to sit there and read it but he worried that, although no one looked up at him when he entered, someone may well have alerted the guard.

The sound of the rattle from outside told him Harold was right, and he bolted for the door, crashing out into the street with the diary held under his arm more protectively than most would hold a baby, and Harold ran. Ran with all the decorum of a shot fox, but Harold ran all the same. He took the side roads most of the way home, never stopping. The streets were busy, it was not easy and his chest burned with ice in the cold air. It had begun raining again, not surprisingly, the short break in the clouds fading back to darkness. Harold knew if he stopped he would not have the energy to start again and he had no idea if the guard were tracking him down or not. The last thing he wanted to do was get thrown into a cell for breaking an entry now he was so close to clearing his name. After what seemed like forever Harold fell against his front door panting, waiting for his breath to return before knocking. His legs as weak as a rotten beam, Harold waited until he felt safe before slipping the book into his left hand and rapping against the woodwork with his right. The door slid open slightly

"Harold, is that you? I was worried sick. The guard were here earlier." Muriel said and his stomach churned over like a mason's drill.

"Are you okay, did they hurt you?" Harold asked, taking Muriel's face in his hand looking deep into her eyes. She pressed into his palm and Harold felt his fear melt away, if only his exhaustion had gone with it.

"I'm fine. They only came about the men down the street. Someone said they saw you there."

"What did you tell them?" Harold asked looking out through the sodden windows to see if anyone was watching the house.

"Nothing much, I told them I was watching the place for your mother and as far as I knew you had gone with her down to Port Lust." Muriel said.

"My mother hasn't gone to Port Lust." Harold replied somewhat puzzled.

"I know that. Didn't think you'd want them going snooping where she is though." Muriel said, smiling at him again. She always smiled, no matter what and Harold loved that about her. Muriel's street life had given her a wisdom Harold was still trying to learn fast. Her simple lie was believed, and why wouldn't they believe it. The guard were looking for a murderer and a prostitute, not a woman who could afford the kind of dress Muriel was wearing. Harold knew they would not return. The house was safe at last. He would still have to watch out on the streets but he could sleep safely within his own bed for the time being. The guard would send word to Port Lust and the village constables could look for him there until he had time to organise his defence. Harold sat to rest in his father's chair and began telling Muriel what had happened. He drifted off to sleep before reaching the end of his story.

It was still dark when Harold awoke covered in a blanket Muriel must have lain over him as he slept. Harold could hear the bell towers in the distance ring out five times. Muriel must have left him in the night and gone to her room upstairs. He crept up, making sure the old stairs did not creak under his feet. Harold remembered the times he had snuck out when he was younger, and knew exactly where to put his feet so the old beams remained silent. Harold listened at Muriel's door, her gentle breathing letting him know she was safely asleep, before making his way downstairs again where he returned to his father's chair with Paul's diary in his hands once more. Harold flicked through the pages reading as quickly as he could. Paul had written everything right up to the moment he hid himself away in the catacombs. Harold now had the two books he needed. One filled with the mad scribbling of a dying man, the other containing the full story of what he had done since his return from The Dark Gulf. Harold closed the book and laid it to rest above the fireplace.

Harold had been reading for hours. The sound of the bells chiming ten must have woken Muriel as Harold heard the bed springs shift and the door creaking open shortly after. Today was the first day of the rest of his life – or so Harold thought at the time. Muriel came downstairs, her hair still entangled from her sleep and already dressed in her new gown – it seemed that she now had two dresses but Harold was not sure she would ever want to wear her old one again, he would have to find the time to make her more. She sat down beside him and

Harold began to talk, trying to find some answers from the night before, his memory still blank.

"*So what happens now then, Harold?*" She asked, fiddling with the embroidering at the edge of her sleeves. "*Harold?*" She repeated with such urgency Harold felt confused.

"*We try to enjoy ourselves a bit.*" Harold said throwing her a smile, hoping to lighten the mood. She returned it but only half-heartedly. Harold could tell Muriel was unsure if things would last between them now that normality was on the brink of returning.

"*What do you mean?*" She asked nervously, rubbing the sleep from her eyes.

"*How about we go visit the palace, go watch the guards change with the rest of the toffs?*" Harold hated to admit it but he enjoyed walking through the noble parts of town, the cobbled roads and statues. The noble's houses themselves had been restored under William's wise leadership. The irony of the best and worst person to enter the city sharing the same name was not lost on him. Although nearly all of his saving had gone, he could not reopen the shop yet so had the time to spare.

"*I don't think it's wise to. We should get your evidence before a noble so they can represent you in a court hearing. Just showing it to a guard won't necessarily mean you'll be free.*" Muriel said. She was happy it might all be ending but she could tell Harold really had no idea what to do with the books he had gathered or how to use them to prove he wasn't behind it all. She could see him handing them over to some guard who would lose them and cash in on the bounty no doubt now on his head.

"*I know a noble, I used to do work for him; He's something to do with the newspaper presses. I'll get a courier to take word to him later today I promise.*" Harold said not questioning how Muriel knew so much about the legal workings of the noble houses.

"*So it's finally over for us?*" Muriel asked.

"*Yes, the guard will have to find and stop William now. We know what he is and how to kill him and once the court pardon me I can reopen the shop and we can plan what we'll do next.*"

"*So you still plan for it to be 'us' then?*" Muriel asked bluntly.

"*Of course Muriel, you mean more to me than I think you know. Tell me, how did you come to be on that street the day this all started? I want to know it all.*"

"*If I tell you Harry, will you still want to be with me?*" Muriel asked and Harold nodded. He called her over with a gesture of his arms and they sat together in the armchair. For so long he had wanted to know everything about Muriel and that morning might have been his last chance.

Harold listened intently as the strong woman that he had fallen in love with melted as she started her story and told him everything.

Her mother had run away from her drunkard of a father back in Bracetire Harbour when Muriel was just five years old. They had taken a ship straight to Neeskmouth docks. Her mother changed her name shortly after arriving, wanting a new start in a new kingdom. She took her name from the current lord at that time, William's wife, and her surname from one that seemed so common within the city, thus becoming Adelaide Smith and her daughter Muriel Smith. Neither of them could speak Neeskmouthain when they first arrived and the first few weeks were hard until Adelaide managed to get a job as a dancer at the *Plucked Eagle*. Things were going well until Adelaide was viciously attacked one night coming back to the board lodgings they had been staying at. She was raped and severely beaten. Her legs had been so badly damaged by the three men that had soiled her she was unable to walk properly again, let alone dance. Once her wounds healed enough to walk the harbour Adelaide took to being a sailor's woman, having three or four 'husbands' that helped pay the rent and came back to visit her while they were on land instead of dancing for coin she turned to the only other trade that seemed plentiful for a women of poor birth.

When Muriel turned around ten she remembered finally moving out of the boarding lodges and having a permanent home in the public harbour. There were a lot of other working girls in that street that became like sisters to Muriel. While her mother was entertaining her 'husbands' Muriel would go out, sometimes until late at night and spend time with these women. This lasted until around Muriel's twelfth birthday when one of her mother's sailors brought an unfortunate gift back for her mother. Not a fine necklace or spices, but instead cholera, brought back from another of his wives in The Dark Gulf. Muriel took to looking after her mother as her symptoms worsened. At first it was just internal disturbances, nausea and dizziness that led to violent vomiting and diarrhoea. Muriel cried as she told him of how at such a young age it worried her so, but when her mother's stools started turning to a gray liquid and the muscular cramps followed, she could not cope alone anymore.

Muriel's street sisters started caring for her mother, sparing what money and time they could for the little girl they had got to know, but they couldn't keep it up forever. It took almost a full year for Adelaide to die. Muriel told Harold how the image of her mother's puckered blue lips in a cadaverous face stayed with Muriel forever, it was how when she had seen what William could do she was not scared for she had seen something worse and did every time she closed her eyes. Alone and scared, Muriel relied more and more on her street sisters who took to showing her their trade. Muriel's first client had been when she was just thirteen. She would never be able to forget that time, the feelings as the man's hands roughly probed her. The rawness she felt and his sharp thrusts as he ignored her yelps of pain. She told Harold that sometimes before she met him she would awake screaming at night, still able to smell the foulness of spirits on his breath and feel the blood that stained her legs after he had finished. Muriel had worked as a bunter, a helper for the older girls for the next few years, just trying to make enough money to pay the rent on the house and keep fed. She had learnt the language well and you would never have known she had not been born to this life. Things had been hard for her and she had seen and done things no child should have to, but she had been lucky in some aspects to work for herself. That was until one night she took on a Drow client. He was over from Portse on work, or so he said. It turned out that he had been staying for a long time. Her 'still tight cunny' as he put it would be worth more than she was getting and he offered her a home in return for a share of money each week. That was how she came by her current home and had been working for O'Brien's gang down by the docks that night. O'Brien had been good for her, when he was sober, even helping her to learn to read in return for a little action now and again. Muriel had planned to learn to read and get away from the docks. She wanted to get a job as a scribe for a noble or even as a house maid but it hadn't worked out that way.

When O'Brien was drunk, the night she had met Harold, he had beaten Muriel for not getting a client, demanding double the money by the end of the evening. Muriel's voice trailed off and with her story over, Harold did not know what to say to her. Harold longed to make her happy, to take her away from all this but the horrors she had been through came as such a shock to him that all words failed in its wake. It was no wonder Muriel had been so strong for him; she had always had to be. She didn't know any other life than of pain and fear.

"*Muriel, I don't know what to say. I wish I could take all that away. Give you the life you deserved. Stop all those things happening.*" Harold paused. "*I want you to have the keys to Thistlebrook Cottage. It was our summer home when I was a boy. It's the place I told you of in Port Lust. It needs work but you will be safe there. I want you to have it.*" Harold said. Muriel cradled his face and smiled before shifting around so she sat in his lap. His heart began racing and she kissed him. Harold knew she felt it as his excitement rose beneath her. With the same caring grin Harold had loved since he'd first saw it, Muriel smiled at him.

"*But only if you come with me.*" She said kissing him again. Muriel had never told anyone the story of her life. It was too shocking for her to cope with most of the time and she expected people to run away after hearing it. People tended not to be able to see past what she'd done. They saw her as soiled but Harold wasn't like that. Not anymore. Her hands reached down to his fastening and gently she took him and caressed him as he grew hard they begun to move as one. Their beings entwined as their bodies combined and their lips met repeatedly. Panting and glowing deep red, she laid abreast him. She moaned and Harold's body replied. He could see the sadness in her eyes still but it was fading, being replaced with warmth.

Chapter 31: Green Mile

Harold didn't know how he got from the saddest story he had ever heard to lying with Muriel. It had all happened so fast. Harold guessed they had both been feeling that way for days and the prospect of finally being free spurred it to happen. They crawled from bed around four in the evening it was still calm and mostly dry outside with only a few clouds threatening to change that and bring the rain back. They both dressed and prepared to make their way to find a courier to take a letter to the Times noble. It is strange really how pleasant the walk was. The long lie-in had fully re-energised them and any doubt they had of being together had been washed away in the moment of ecstasy. Harold thought to hell with what was proper for a middle-class-gentleman and he held Muriel close to him, their steps perfectly in time. The sun's golden rays cascading down over the water reflected a beautiful contrast to the city, even with the water as soiled as it was. The moment in time was perfect. They stopped at the jetty just outside the fishmonger's guild and there, below the setting sun, Harold kissed Muriel for the last time. As Harold pulled away still feeling her warmth on his lips he watched as Muriel's eyes grew wide. Harold moved too slowly as he saw her gaze turn to fear. The impact hit his ribs like a war hammer and Harold fell into the water. The world spun out of control as Harold went under sinking deep into the icy waters. With barely a moment to think he struggled and crashed back into the open air gasping for breath. His eyes found Muriel grasped tightly in William's embrace.

"You did not think we had forgotten about you did you, Harold? You know where to find me if you're brave enough. It might even be in time to save your little sweetheart if you're quick." William said, and then forcefully kissed Muriel and began to drag her away. She struggled and tried to scream but his hand was clasped tightly over her mouth. Harold began swimming frantically for the jetty but by the time he pulled himself to the shore, she was gone. The crowd of people that had stopped and gathered in the street did nothing but stare at him. It angered him that the typical city dweller would not raise a hand to help a women being dragged off like that, a sad fact of the time it had become all too common. Not one of them had moved to save her. Harold knew they would not have stood a chance but at least it might have given him the time he needed to have got to her. Harold had no choice now but to go and face William after all. It seemed that what the priest said had been true. The Rakta Ishvara would not leave anyone that knew about it,

alive. Harold left the canals and headed home to prepare. He would risk death for a chance to save Muriel.

Nightfall came and Harold had taken to hiding in the attic. The guard came more than once to search the lower floors but they didn't come up into the small hatch that was all but hidden above the wardrobe in what had been Muriel's room. Alone in the dark with a few candles burning Harold read through the priests diaries looking for some clue as to how to beat William. The silence drove him to insanity by the time the bells called out midnight and this is where this story goes full circle. When this tale started, we joined Harold alone and scared of shadows flicking from his candles, scared for the beast that is the Rakta Ishvara and now it is time to tell of what happens after. When morning came, Harold finished writing in his diary and slammed it shut; sealing it with twine along with the books he had kept from Paul before sending it to his mother. Harold knew it was unlikely he would return and proving his innocence was now second to explaining to his mother why she would lose both men in her life so close together. Harold hoped she would understand. He had lived in fear for weeks, but he realised he could not run anymore. He attached a note to the books in which he instructed his mother to sell the shop. After all, he was not coming back and Harold was no longer a tailor. He could see no way of returning to that life now. There was only one way he could see him beating William. Even if he could save Muriel, his life would be changed forever. He ended the letter by telling his mother how he loved her but that he could never come back. Harold planned to go back to Saint Anne's. He would arm himself with the herbs the priest had so stupidly told him were toxic to the Rakta Ishvara. Grabbing the iron fire poker his father had used so well as a weapon, Harold slipped it under his trench coat and made for the door.

The morning outside was still as dark as night and in the distance the wind howled through the valley of buildings. Harold had been on edge as he made his way to Saint Anne's. When he arrived he was worried the guard had been there, although there was no sign of it other than a shuffling of the leaves upon the floor. Harold was beginning to get a sense for their presence. He found the door to Saint Anne's locked. The fire poker wedged into the side of the frame made light work of the latch and the door flew open after the second or third tug. Inside, the smell of flash powder from detectives confirmed Harold's suspicion. The church was all but empty, only the bats fluttering above in the wooden arches of the roof and the odd moth unlucky enough to become lunch as it followed Harold inside, kept him company. Thick clouds of mist from the river blocked any light from entering the chapel's windows. Harold strained his eyes in the darkness, looking for the prayer candles he'd seen on his last visit. He found them atop a table not far from the font and lit one of the small wicks. The gentle glow it gave off was fairly useless, but it was better than nothing. He cradled its tiny flame from the breeze created as he walked, and made for the catacombs. Creeping as quietly as he could Harold made his way down into the darkness. There was a swift darkening shadow below that almost made him drop the candle as the breeze caught the flame. A second dark shadow raced across the wall much closer. There was a crash from below and the sound of something soft hitting the floor before scurrying off. Harold sucked in his breath ready to face William.

"*Muriel?*" He called out. The scratching stopped but no one answered. "*Muriel, are you there?*" Suddenly a shadow caught the corner of his eye. Harold dropped the candle and swinging the poker with all his might, he struck something soft. Harold heard a squeak and watched as the mouse's beaten body fell down behind the candle towards the foot of the stairs. His heart pounding, he gazed into the room below. William was not there and neither was Muriel. Harold was glad to see that the bodies of Paul and his father had been removed. At least it had not been left to be feasted on by rats. It was just a shame the smell of rotting flesh hadn't left with them. He gasped for breath as he held onto the handrail running down into the depths. The coffins had been slid aside and most of the leaves gathered up into piles. He scooped up a good handful of the leaves and couldn't believe what he was actually going to do next.

The *Queens that* was where it had really all started, the first time he had seen William. Using three of his last five shillings, Harold took a cart to the building site that had already formed around the tavern's old ashes. Just as he hoped, the hatch was still accessible. As Harold waved the cart off and paid his dues, he approached the hatch. Even better, the lock had recently been broken. Harold scattered a few Abrus leaves around the entrance of the hatch his skin burning as he did so. He hoped it would persuade William to stay in the darkness below. He crushed the rest of the leaves against the iron fire poker, the oil coating the bladed edge. Harold gripped the handle and he remembered the description of the spears in the temple from Paul's diary. Now wasn't the time to daydream though, he needed to focus. Keeping an image of Muriel in his mind, he made his way down, dropping into the darkness below. The cellar was dull, but the holes in the roof where the tavern supports had once been, let a shallow light slither through. The dusty beam of light seemed afraid to enter the cellar fully. There were no cockroaches scuttling around down there and Harold knew it was because William was there, somewhere out of sight. It was too quiet, far too calm. Even the noise from the busy dockyard above did not seem to be able to breach the walls and cascade down. There was no sound of loose rubble falling, no sound as stones heated up from the freezing night. Even the noise of continual dripping sounded wrong. It was as though the droplets fell reluctantly. Standing there mesmerised, Harold gazed around trying to take in every shadow that might be a threat. To his immediate left, a pile of rubble had fallen from the ceiling. A scorched oak beam had collapsed with it and jutted out like a tree growing in the forest. The western wall that was once filled with kegs from floor to ceiling was now empty, the brickwork battered and flaking. The plaster was crisp and hanging off in weak strands, if the wind could find its way in from above the wall would have fallen easily, bringing in the moist soil that lay just beyond it and the sound of rushing water hinted that an underground river passed close by or a flooded part of the labyrinth at least. To Harold's right lay a small doorway leading to the second room of the cellar. It was the entrance to the larder. Harold remembered how it used to smell of fine herbs, strong meats and fresh vegetables. As he approached the doorway, the door itself blown through and burnt, all he could smell was smoke and ashes. Pausing with his back against the lime bricks making up the arch, Harold listened through into the next room. Somewhere inside was a faint breathing sound carried on the breeze.

"*Muriel.*" He called out, unable to help himself. The sound of a muffled voice was heard in response.

"*You surprise me Harold. I really wasn't sure if you would be foolish enough to come.*" William said from out of the darkness of the small room. Harold needed to get him talking, to pinpoint where he was, before leaping through into the pitch black.

"*You better not have hurt her.*" Harold shouted. He listened for a reply so hard his eardrums ached with the effort.

"*Not yet, you are lucky. I found a steady supply of whores to feed on while I waited. I wanted you to watch this one die.*" William took a step, the ash below his feet parting softly, but not silently. This let Harold know he was to the right of the doorway, somewhere close. Harold felt a light dusting fall down the back of his neck and knew that William was directly opposite on the other side of the wall, less than a foot of brickwork separating them.

"Let her go and I will be yours without a fight." Harold said trying to buy some time.

"What would I have to gain from that? You won't win against me and I would lose a snack." William's confidence annoyed Harold but he knew he must not get angry. He needed to keep a clear head that was the answer.

"This is your last warning השני את אזה." Harold said keeping William behind him on the wall. William laughed giving Harold the chance he needed to move himself along slightly his fingertips tracing the edge of the doorway.

"Well you surprise me with the length you would go to. I hope you are ready to deal with the consequences'." William said. Harold knew exactly where William was and the revelation that Harold had taken one of the Rakta onto himself shocked William for just long enough. Harold had hoped William wouldn't be able to sense it as it was too soon but it would still give him a fighting chance. Harold gripped the wall's edge with his free hand and spun himself around the wall, swinging the iron poker in front of him as he went. It clashed against William faster than even he could dodge and pinned William against the wall. William growled and pushed back hard, gripping Harold's neck like a vice. Harold choked on his own blood but he would not give up that easily. Harold, with his hand still stinging from the impact against the brickwork, wasted no time in lunging again in Williams's direction. The poker pierced flesh and Harold kept pushing, William's resistance, at first strong as an ox, seemed to be failing as Harold used all his might pressing into the unseen. The Abrus oil seemed to be working as William's grip weakened. Harold had no idea where he had punctured but he didn't care. Charging forward the two interlocked and crashed into the central wall, bringing down a landslide from above as the roof fell in as they broke through the dividing wall. Daylight flooded in and for the first time Harold saw William clearly. His dark black eyes stared, fixed squarely on him. Both William's hands clasped the sharp end of the poker which was rammed into his gut. Harold so much wanted to spare a glance towards Muriel, just to make sure she was safe. To check that the roof hadn't hurt her as it had fallen but with William waiting for his chance, and the room rapidly filling with freezing water from the adjacent tunnel, Harold knew he couldn't afford the luxury and had to be fast. He let go of the poker just long enough to cup his hands together into a fist and he smacked down onto the poker handle, forcing the pivot in the poker to rise upwards. Harold's hands were sliced open like soft cheese but he hit it again. The sound of breaking bone and a screech from William was followed by a spray of congealed

blood as the poker wedged itself between Williams's ribs and the callus of the Rakta Ishvara. William's body fell limply to the floor. Harold hit the handle repeatedly wanting to be sure that William was really dead. Eventually the poker ripped free and sank to the bottom of the water. William's ribs had been cracked open, exposing the weak larva inside for what it was. Clasped around William's heart the small creature pulsated for a few seconds, and then finally stopped. It let go of the heart and went to swim away. Harold bent down and picked the small leach-like creature up. Holding it in his lacerated hands the creature was no bigger than a halfpenny. He dropped it to the floor and with his heel put an end to it all, only then able to look for Muriel. She lay close by coated in filth and her mouth barely above water level but she was alive. She'd been lucky and avoided the heaviest of the cave-in. Harold fell to his knees and quickly pulled the rag from Muriel's mouth.

"*Is he dead?*" She asked glancing over at the body that had fallen to the ground behind Harold.

"*Yes, it's over. It's finally over.*" Harold said as he kissed Muriel. Her lips were still as soft as he remembered. Her smile afterwards still as sweet, and the feeling still as perfect. "*I can't wait to show you the coast.*" Harold said helping Muriel to her feet.

Epilogue: The Sun Sets on the 16th

The sun set over the canals that night and Neeskmouth continued under its deep red rays. The evening newspapers filled with the story of the killer priest denting the faith people had in Sacellum but it would not be hindered for long as soon farmers would come in from the fields with more stories of the shadow demon Rinwid and people would flock back into the pews of Saint Anne's. The catacombs would be sealed shut to bury the sins of this mad man forever in the bowels of Saint Anne's. The flooding below the Queens would wash Williams's body into the canals and eventually out to sea. It would not be long before people forgot about the poor dead prostitutes as more flocked in to take their place. A city is a fickle beast and Neeskmouth had always seen more than its share of death and pain.

Neeskmouth ridge fell behind Harold and Muriel a mile at a time as they headed west. The cart rolled onwards with its windows pulled shut to the setting sun shining through the lush blue material. There was silence, apart from the clatter of horseshoes on the uneven road and the gentle sound of Muriel's snoring as she slept in Harold's arms. Harold would propose once they reached the beaches. He didn't know what would become of him. If Paul was right he would be able to control his hunger. If not then the lands of the north would have another monster to fight. Somehow though, Harold felt that with Muriel on his arm he'd battle his demons and win. The horrors of the last few weeks fell into oblivion in his dreams as he wondered if the beaches would look as wonderful as he remembered. Harold slid his eyes open slightly, just enough so that he could see her. She was sleeping still. Harold pulled her closer, a slight murmur signalling Muriel's ease in his embrace. He knew he would one day have to face the choice he made but until then he would be with her.

Dante's journeys led him to the Cassandra and climbing up the wet chain of the anchor marked a new journey for him. One that would take him all the way to the Green Stone Isles, oddly this little creature's journey would play a part in the events of Neeska long after his death that would one day be legendary. The letter from William still tied to his tail was also a story for another time, much like that of the match girl and Granny, for we have not seen the last of the haggard old woman of the north.

* * * * *

In the abandoned tailors shop on East Street, a couple of mice played happily around a dusty ball of string. A strange odour filled the air. A memory of fresh tobacco smoke sailed through and went as quickly as it came. It was gone. *Spinks and Son's* had shut for the last time.